P9-DNH-793

Triangles

Also by Ellen Hopkins

Crank

Burned

Impulse

Glass

Identical

Tricks

Fallout

Perfect

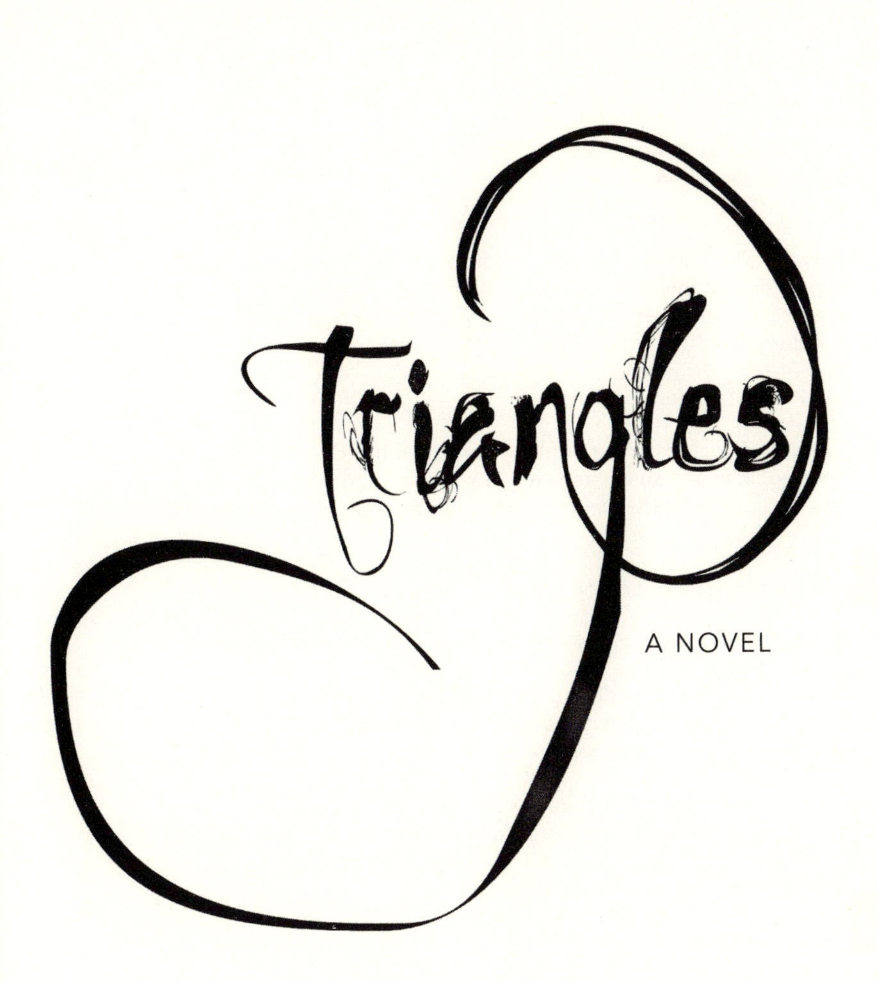

Triangles

A NOVEL

ellen hopkins

ATRIA BOOKS

New York London Toronto Sydney New Delhi

A Division of Simon & Schuster, Inc.
1230 Avenue of the Americas
New York, NY 10020

This book is a work of fiction. Names, characters, places, and incidents either are products of the author's imagination or are used fictitiously. Any resemblance to actual events or locales or persons, living or dead, is entirely coincidental.

First Atria Books hardcover edition October 2011

ATRIA BOOKS and colophon are trademarks of Simon & Schuster, Inc.

For information about special discounts for bulk purchases, please contact Simon & Schuster Special Sales at 1-866-506-1949 or business@simonandschuster.com.

The Simon & Schuster Speakers Bureau can bring authors to your live event. For more information or to book an event contact the Simon & Schuster Speakers Bureau at 1-866-248-3049 or visit our website at www.simonspeakers.com.

Designed by Jill Putorti

Manufactured in the United States of America

10 9 8 7 6 5 4 3 2 1

Library of Congress Cataloging-in-Publication Data

Hopkins, Ellen.
Triangles / Ellen Hopkins.—1st Atria Books hardcover ed.
p. cm.
1. Self-realization in women—Fiction. 2. Female friendship—Fiction.
I. Title.
PS3608.O647T75 2011
813'.6—dc22 2011009537

ISBN 978-1-4516-2633-9
ISBN 978-1-4516-2636-0 (ebook)

This book is dedicated to some very special friends,
who shall remain nameless here.
But you know who you are.

ACKNOWLEDGMENTS

Immense thanks to my husband, John, whose faith in me remains steadfast. And to my family, which grew by one this year, and serves as a never-ending source of inspiration. Also to my Simon & Schuster family, which grew by an entire imprint this year. Thank you, McElderry Books, for your continued support. With a big shout-out to Jon Anderson, who encouraged this new writing venture. And thank you, Atria Books, for your warm welcome. With special nods to my editor, Sarah Branham; publisher, Judith Curr; the design department, which has to work extra hard to make this book look right; and to marketing, which now has to work hard to make it a success. And, of course, to Carolyn Reidy, an amazing woman who took more than one chance on me.

TRIANGLES

Scientists say every action
initiates an equal and opposite
reaction. I say that's just the start.

I say

every action initiates a most
unequal and unpredictable
chain reaction, that

every

filament of living becomes
part of a larger weave, while
remaining identifiable. That each

line

of latitude requires several
stripes of longitude to obtain
meaning. That every universe

is part

of a bigger heaven, a heaven
of rhythm and geometry,
where a heartbeat is the apex

of a triangle.

Holly

NOT BIG

On perimeters and diameters.
Math was never my best
thing, not even when school
was a "thing." I was an English
freak. Lit classes and creative

writing, yeah, I could go for
those. Escape. That's what
books were. Are. I should
have finished college. Given
myself some choices. But no.

Instead, I let someone build
me a box. Cube me in. Okay,
it's safe inside, and safe is
not a bad thing to be. Except
after twenty years, stuffed

inside my secure, little box,
I'm in need of a good stretch.
Pushing against the sides. All
it will take is one good shove
for the walls to tumble down.

And every day
I wonder, will
this be the day?

AS ALWAYS

I wake to anorexic rays of morning,
prodding gently through cracks in the blinds.

The breathing beside me is even. Familiar.
Safe. Once upon a time, I might have slid

a leg up over Jace, reveled in the way he
stirred, hot and hard before the rest of him

surfaced from dreams. But not today. Not
in many, many days. I ease out from under

the sheets, slip into shorts and a sports bra,
grab my running shoes, gentle my way

out the bedroom door and into the silence
of my house, asleep. Even after school starts

up again, I won't see the kids until after six a.m.
But early June, the mad dash to cereal rarely begins

until nine. Which gives me almost four hours
to myself. I take three bites of a PowerBar,

wash it down with Smartwater. Outside,
the sun has yet to crawl over the eastern hills,

yet warm waves temper the night-cooled air.
It's going to be a hot one today. A quick stretch

and I start my daily run downhill. Can't do it
any other way, since we live on top of a sage-

crusted knoll. A series of hills rims the lake-lush
valley where Jace and I bought our home, fifteen

years ago. Down. Along. Up. Along. I run, flushing
rabbits. Quail. Squirrels. Hopefully, no coyotes,

hunting for the rest. I see them every now and then,
eager-eyed and scruffy-coated. Sometimes they trot

straight up the roadways, unconcerned about
human intrusion. In fact, they relish it, and

the opportunities it brings. Trash on Fridays.
Cats on their own evening prowls. Small dogs,

let out to wander. But they don't bother me
and almost seem to enjoy my company. No

coyote escort today, however. I fall into my well-
practiced rhythm, draw deeply of the dawning

morning. Here, in the zone where every breath
takes on such meaning, I find the best part of my day.

Today, I discern some subtle shift. Perhaps it is
the earth's lean toward summer, but there is motion.

Unexpected. Disorienting, as if I'm running
somewhere new. But am I running from? Or to?

I USED TO HATE RUNNING

In high school, I always trailed
the pack, running laps in P.E.

After graduation and into my one
year of college, I avoided most

forms of exercise, except skiing
and the occasional bike ride.

Three pregnancies, two years in
between each, didn't do much

except breast-feed and eat. By the time
all three kids were finally in school,

I was a big sack of blubber, afraid
to even start an exercise program.

It took staring down probable
diabetes to make me consider

how much I wanted to stay alive.
I cut carbs. Started walking. One

mile a day, then two. After a while
I ran downhill. Later, uphill too.

Now, less than a year later, I run
more than five miles every day. My legs

are amazing, my body is tight, and
I love how that feels. How that looks.

Certain neighbors have made it a habit
to come outside and watch me run by

every day, despite the early hour.
There is power in that, in the ability to

manipulate the intent behind the smiles
and hellos. And while I would never

take up with someone this close
to home, knowing I could makes me

happy. I run to be happy. Run to
be strong. Run to be successful

at something besides being
a mom. And when I run, I can think.

AND TODAY

I'm thinking again about geometry.

About cubes. Squares. Triangles.
How they're all made up of lines.

A line is a collection of points

along a straight path that goes on
and on forever in opposite directions.

Two lines that never intersect

are parallel. Two lines that intersect,
forming ninety-degree angles,

are perpendicular. Perpendicular lines

cross each other. Crossing lines.
Today I'm thinking about how easy

it is to be perpendicular. And about

how, while parallel lines may not
intersect, parallel lives too often do.

WHEN I GET BACK

All out of breath and sheathed in a shimmer
of perspiration, Jace is up and heading
toward the shower. "Coffee?" I ask.

He takes one look at me, smiles. *In a few.*
But first, come here. Did I ever tell
you that sweaty women turn me on?

"Thus, your addiction to beach
volleyball?" I go over for a morning
kiss, sex the farthest thing from my mind.

Jace, however, is totally in the mood,
as advertised by the twitch of his hard-on.
Come on. We haven't had a morning

go in a while, and I don't have to be
in the office until nine. He coaxes me
toward the unmade bed. *Pretty please?*

I start to protest, to say something
about having to change the sheets,
but it's simpler just to give in for the ten

whole minutes it will take to make
him a satisfied man. And me a dutiful
wife. He leans me, stomach against

the rumpled spread, over the bed,
tugs down my shorts. I close my eyes
as he slips two fingers inside me.

See, now? You're ready for me.
Strangely, I am, and when he pushes
more than his fingers inside, the sex

is comfortable. Easy. No work at all.
It doesn't even take ten minutes
until I feel the familiar tightening

of his thighs. Jace comes. I don't.
He punctuates his final thrust with
a soft *Oomph.* Pulls away, sticky,

starts again for the shower. Dues paid,
I'm a little less guilty about reminding him,
"Don't forget I'm going out with Andrea

tonight. Mikayla's spending the night
at Emily's. But Trace and Brianna
will be here. Get home on time, okay?"

HE'S ALWAYS HOME ON TIME

Unless he's on a really big case,
but lately even his litigations
are slam-dunk average. Some
would call that lucky, I guess.

I find it ho-hum, but it pays
the bills, and pays them well.
I watch Jace towel off. At forty-
five, his hairline is sliding back

a bit, and shallow lines have
webbed his eyes. But he stays
fit enough and women, I'm
sure, find him attractive.

Attractive. Reliable. Good
provider. Always home on
time. Even-tempered. Caring
father. Adoring husband.

(Sounds like an obituary.)
What more could any sane
woman ask for, right? Which
says a whole lot about me.

OBITUARY

She decides to write her own,
rather than leave it to strangers;
studies the paper, develops
an obituary template:

In loving memory of
[complete name goes here],
who passed away
[say when, but not

how]

after [number of] years
on this earth. [He/she]
is survived by [spouse, children,
parents, siblings, if applicable].

She considers her life,
how it will end. What

do

you write, she wonders, if
none of those things applies?
What do you say about
someone who realized no

dreams,

who never found love, never
wanted commitment? What
do you say about someone
who clearly wanted to

die?

Marissa

FUCK HER

I swear that must be what God said
when he agreed to implant me in Good
Old Mom's uterus. I can see it now:

The angel of making men horny meets
up with the angel of making women
stupid. "Let's create a problem for some
lame earthly couple," he says.

(Making Men Horny Angel has to be
a guy. Why would a woman angel
bother with making men horny?)

Uh, you mean, like rip a condom and SNAP . . .
baby? Sounds like a rainy afternoon,
agrees Making Women Stupid Angel.
But we should prob'ly ask the Big Dude

in Charge what kind of baby to surprise
the lucky couple with, and which lucky
couple, out of all the worthy people
on earth, most deserves the surprise.

So off they go to see God, who's kicking
back with a bottle of brilliant red wine
and a couple of cute Waiting on God
in Short Togas and Crooked Haloes Angels.

God, who is so not amused, booms:
IT'S BEEN A CRAP CENTURY AND I'M
REALLY NOT IN THE MOOD FOR GAMES.
PICK A RANDOM PAIR OF COLLEGE

BEER PONGERS AND GIVE THEM A GIRL.
AND JUST FOR KICKS, MAKE HER LIFE
A CLUSTER SCREW. LOUSY CHILDHOOD.
MISERABLE MARRIAGE. AND HEY, WHY

NOT TOSS IN A SMART-ASS GAY KID AND
ANOTHER ONE WHO CAN NEVER WALK—
IN FACT, ONE WHO WILL NEVER GROW UP?
MARISSA JOY SNYDER TRASK? FUCK HER!

All I can say is, he must be turning
cartwheels up there. Sipping champagne.
Smoking cigars. Distracting himself

from the looming destruction of Planet
Earth, listening to Broadway music while
watching megascreen clips of natural

disaster shows, extreme sports outtakes,
and human melodramas, more than
a few of them starring yours truly.

ONE OF MY COSTARS

Grabs center stage right now.
Her coughing rattles the intercom,
and I run, as I must, to her room.
"Mommy's here, Shelby."

I adjust the face mask of the cough-
assist machine, a mechanical miracle
worker that keeps my little girl
from aspirating. The miracle happens

one more time. The cough quiets.
Shelby tries to smile. The noise
she makes is part hum, part
melody, and means, *I love you, Mommy.*

"I love you too, Shelbykins."
Adore her, my baby. Hate her,
for what she is, and that makes
me a monster mommy.

My manicured claws smooth her hair.
Check the tube that sends necessary
sustenance directly into her tummy.
The tummy that, like the rest of her,

is much too small for a four-year-old.
But she is still here at four. Another
miracle, this one straight from God.
I swear I can hear him laughing.

A COSMIC JOKE

That's what Shelby is. I wanted
a daughter for more than eleven years,
from the very day I gave birth to Shane.
It took that long for the proper sperm-

egg connection, and I was forty years
old before it happened. I'd pretty
much given up hope by then, and
had I known that my beautiful baby

girl would be born with a "condition,"
I might have considered abortion.
Had I known a thing at all about spinal
muscular atrophy, I would have run,

full speed, to the nearest gated clinic.
The joke part comes into play when
you consider the fact that both parents
have to carry the recessive gene to make

SMA occur. Shane was born perfectly
fine, despite the same genetic pairing.
One in four. That's what their odds were.
God gave Shelby SMA. Shane just got "gay."

BREATHING STABILIZED

I turn Shelby onto her right side.
          "Just like a pancake," I soothe.
          "We don't want that left side to
get too done, do we?" Old joke,

one she can't know the meaning of.
          Shelby will never eat pancakes.
          "Once it cools off, Mommy will
take you for a walk in your stander."

          The promise elicits a giant smile,
                    and a soft *Ooh.* I see a flicker
                    of what my child might have
          been, but I have no tears left

to cry. "Oh, look. It's time for
          Barney." The big purple dinosaur
          is a daily staple. "You watch. Mommy
will be back soon, okay?" Her eyes

are already locked on the big-
          screen TV, the only one we have
          in the house. I figure Shelby
deserves it more than the rest of us.

HER BROTHER

Is way too plugged in as it is.
His computer is his life,
at least his life here at home.

When he was younger, we used
to play board games. He kicked
my butt at chess, but I always beat

him at Scrabble. In the evenings,
we watched sitcoms and horror flicks.
But that was all before Shelby.

Now, what his interests are outside
these walls, I really
can't say, though I'm more than

a little sure they revolve around
marijuana. I can smell
the barely masked scent of it now,

leaking out from under his bedroom
door. Little shit knows
how much I hate confrontation.

Summer vacation sucks. Guess I'd
better play concerned
parent, even though I know Shane

will do exactly as he pleases. Not
like I'm going to call
the cops. Who needs more drama?

I SHOULD GO IN

Like I might, though. I give the door
handle a vicious twist. Locked. Duh.

"Shane!" My fist flails the old wood.
"Open up right this minute!" No response.

"I'm not leaving until you open the door."
Nothing. "I know how to unlock it, you know."

Finally, I hear his chair scoot back across
the oak floor. Footsteps thump toward me.

The lock clicks. The door jerks open.
Yes, Mother? What can I do for you?

I push past him, stomp over to his desk,
where the evidence smolders on one

of my good china saucers—a treasured
wedding gift that has long languished

in the hutch in the dining room we no
longer use. "What, exactly, do you think

you're doing?" I must look stupid, hands
gripping my hips, because he bursts

into percussive snorts of laughter.
I would think that's obvious, Mom.

I'm smoking weed and checking
out a little guy-on-guy action.

"Wha . . . ?" For the first time, I look
beyond the smoke, resin, and incense-

stained saucer to the computer screen,
where one very buff and obviously

very gay guy is doing unmentionable
things to another very buff and obviously

even gayer guy's oily backside. I've
never seen anything quite so vile,

not that I've ever gone looking. "God,
Shane!" Two clicks of the mouse and

the disgusting video disappears. "How
are you paying for that? And how are you

paying for that?" I point toward
the not-an-ashtray. "Do you have any

idea how much that china is worth? Your
grandmother must be cartwheeling in her

grave. What in the *hell* do you think
you're doing?" I repeat. With emphasis.

He ignores the first two questions.
You never use the china anyway, Mom.

And hey, summer vacation is all about
stress relief, something you need more

of yourself. That's top-quality weed. Want
me to turn you on to my connection?

I think he's serious. "No. I. Do. Not.
And I don't want you smoking anything

in the house. You know what smoke can
do to your sister. Do you want to kill her?"

The grin falls from his face. *Shh,* he says.
She can hear you, you know. He lowers

his voice to one notch above a whisper. *No,*
Mom. I don't want to kill her. He slices me

with blue quartz eyes, pierces me through
with his words. *But I wish God would.*

GOD IS ON A WALKABOUT

Won't say where. The Outback,
perhaps, or an uncharted tropical
isle. Someplace where peace drifts
like smoke in the silence.

God

doesn't want to hear complaints
for a while. No grievances, desires,
or entreaties. He is in serious need
of a seventh-day kind of rest. It

isn't

that he's angry. Disappointed, yes,
to a degree. Sick of the bickering
going on in his name. And anxious.
Homo sapiens, his favored, are

taking

such a long time finding their humanity.
His First Noel should have been the key.
But people still haven't grasped
the light. So, until further notice, all

requests

may be directed to him, care of
the celestial switchboard. No follow-
up calls, please. He'll get back
to you. Sooner or later.

Andrea

BEST FRIEND MELTDOWN

Is a hard thing to watch. Especially when
you've been there, done that, and you're certain

fulfillment is not on the far end. Holly and I
have known each other for over a decade,

since our girls did toddler playgroup together.
I've always secretly envied what she has—

a McMansion on the hill overlooking the wide
lake-fed valley that divides the south reaches of

Reno from the northern grasp of Carson City.
Three great kids. An adoring husband who, while

not exactly movie star material, is precisely
the kind of man I dream of. But Holly glimpsed

her fortieth birthday, fast approaching. Panicked.
Dropped sixty pounds, thinks she needs to lose

more, though size four is starting to look baggy
on her. She runs miles every day, lifts like a man,

all, she says, so she can enjoy her nightly libations
and keep turning heads. Like now. They swivel

in our direction as we come through the big glass
door. Reno is an enigmatic city, and its bars are

representative. Tucked away with the weekly
motels are cheap booze dives. Near the university,

campus hot spots and sports bars draw young
crowds. Downtown, casino neon and noise deny

easy conversation. But here, on the Riverwalk near
the business district, this bar is polished brass,

oiled oak, and low-lit crystal. Not the type I used to
frequent before I quit looking for Mr. Amazing

in every wrong kind of place. This is the right
kind of place. Unfortunately, all these spit-shined

Versace guys are checking out my married friend.
I'm getting used to it. Sort of. I guess. Good thing

I've given up on men. Focused on my career
and daughter, who is thirteen and starting to ask

those difficult questions a mom should be available
to answer. Tonight, however, Harley's on a rare

visit to her who-wants-to-be-a-dad-anyway
father. Which is why I'm here, watching

my best friend flirt like *she's* the single
mom. And I'm mostly along for the ride.

IT'S A SMOOTH ASPHALT CRUISE

At the moment. I follow
Holly's metered hip sway
to a tall table, unoccupied,
midroom. *Check it out,* she
says. *It's our lucky day.* One

can only hope. She shimmies
up onto a suede stool, tough to
do in a skirt that short. I join
her, and before our butts are
firmly planted, a guy at the bar

begins the ol' eyeball prowl.
I could save him some time,
tell him now he doesn't stand
a chance. Too medium height.
Too average build. Too Jace.

And why is it the guys who
least stand a chance are the
most determined? He checks
her out like she is merchandise.
Maybe he thinks she's for sale.

A waitress meanders over,
takes our order. Mojito
for Holly. Fat Tire for me.
Holly crinkles her nose.
Not only beer. Chewy beer.

I smile. "Carbs, and I need
them. I didn't have dinner."
I expect an admonition—
don't drink on an empty
stomach or something. But

no. She nods approvingly.
*I had a salad. Didn't want
to get too messed up. Then
again, it's been a while since
you and I tied one on. Too*

long. Her eyes relentlessly
scan the room. Finally, they
touch down on me. *So what
have you been up to? How's
work? Still a love-hate thing?*

"Pretty much. The state of
Nevada is worse off than
California. Furloughs. Budget
cuts. I still have my job, and
that's a good thing. But no

cost-of-living raises for DMV
employees this year. In fact,
that promotion I got? The title
'supervisor' means nothing,
moneywise, and won't for

the foreseeable future. It's a
pisser." Holly keeps nodding
like she has a clue what it means
to cling to a day-after-day, same
ol' thing job. Okay, with benefits.

She doesn't have to work at all.
Jace Martin Carlisle, Esq., sees
to that. Holly should count
her blessings and give her
husband credit where it's due.

If he were mine, I'd spoil him
rotten. Neck rubs. Gourmet
dinners. Breakfasts in bed,
followed by protracted
post–French toast lovemaking.

> Our drinks arrive and Holly
> lifts her glass. *Here's to girls'*
> *nights out. Cheers!* She takes
> a long pull as the average guy
> initiates an obvious approach.

"Don't look now, or do look
if you want to. You're about
to get some company." This
could be fun. You can't pay
for entertainment like Holly.

AVERAGE GUY

Saunters up to the table, or at least
does his best saunter imitation.

Good evening, ladies, he says.
May I buy you a drink? He aims

the invite at Holly, who says, *"I'm good,*
thanks. But you could get my friend

something that doesn't smell so much
like beer. How about a mojito, Andrea?"

She just told the guy my name! "Uh,
no thanks. And, HOLLY, I like beer

just fine. Even if it is chewable."
We both laugh, leaving Average Guy

knowing our names but completely
confused. *Well then, may I join you?*

Holly lifts her left hand. *"Don't think*
my husband would appreciate that."

She says it, straight-faced, while lasering
a come-hither smile at a striking guy

who is sitting with a cute-but-not-
gorgeous friend at a nearby table.

Average Guy turns to see what Holly
is staring at. His ear tips immediately

blister red and he starts to pant. *Are
you saying I'm not good enough?*

*"Not even close, sweetie. Now, if you
don't mind, we were in the middle*

of a private conversation." She picks
up her drink, disconnects completely

from Average Guy, whose entire
face is now tinted cranberry-crimson.

Whatever, he hisses. *But so you know,
you're not so special either, bitch.*

Holly shuts him up with a single filthy
look. *"Darling, I am the kind of special*

*a guy like you can only dream about.
Now go away before I yell 'pervert.'"*

He glances at me, but all I can do is shrug.
Another bitch, by mere Holly connection.

MERLOT-FACED, HE GOES

But not before flipping her off.
"Wow," I say. "You should write
a book—*Two-Sentence Castration.*"

She laughs. *Sounds like a short book*
to me. Anyway, I was thinking about
writing erotica. Entertaining research

and all. And speaking of research,
those cute guys over there are scoping
us out. You up for a little fun?

I'm starting to wish I'd ordered
something stronger. "Depends
on what you've got in mind."

Harmless flirting. Maybe a free
drink or two. She doesn't wait
for me to agree, and all it takes

is a single filthy look—of a whole
different variety than the last one—
for the erotica research to begin.

Holly and I go out together fairly
often. But this particular side of her
is relatively new. The change is not

in the way she flirts—all wildcat eyes
and come-on smile from across the room.
The change is in her follow-through.

HOLLY IN ACTION

Is nothing short of awe-inspiring.
I would not call her flirting harmless,
however. I would call it straight
for the jugular. Except the jugular
is not located where she's aiming.

We are now sitting with Grant
and Caleb. I'm currently sipping
one very strong mojito while
Caleb gripes about congressional
reregulation. Holly, who is on

her third very strong mojito,
has hitched a leg over Grant's
knee, effectively airing out
her crotch. Hope she's wearing
panties. But if I were taking

bets, I'd guess no way. And I
can also imagine where Grant's
fingers are creeping. Half of me
is grossed out. The other half
really wants to look. Holly acts

all innocent, like nothing's going on
under the table. But everyone here,
including Average Guy, who is
sloppy drunk and leaning toward
belligerent, knows otherwise.

UNDER THE TABLE

Where voyeurs and lawyers
duck their heads, truth loiters,
obscured, in the shadows.

It's

the key to deception, central
to suspension of disbelief.
Fact, in overt disguise, is often

all

people need to embrace
lies invented as distraction.
In back rooms, filthy with

smoke

and the sweat of success,
decisions are made,
agreements entered into

and

lives change, sometimes
not for the better. In more
ways than one, eyes are

mirrors.

What does it say about
you if you can't bring yourself
to look into them?

Holly

FOUR MOJITOS

Approximately one per hour. I actually
feel okay driving home, though
I'm pretty sure I wouldn't want to get
pulled over right now. I could have let

Andrea drive. She volunteered. But I
didn't want to listen to her bitch
about my behavior. It wasn't *that* bad.
"Harmless flirting. Free drinks. Research."

That's what I said. And that's what it was.
Mostly, anyway. Grant *did* give me his card.
Told me to call. He's disgustingly good-
looking. But I'll probably lose his card.

Right at the speed limit, it's a twenty-five-
minute drive home from downtown Reno.
I manage it without drawing attention
to myself but have to admit I'm happy

when I turn off the main highway, onto
the little road through the valley. Rarely
will you find cops out here on a Friday
night. Well after one a.m., the action

is in town. Still, I maintain the thirty-five-
miles-per-hour limit all the way home.
I expect it to be dark. Everyone fast
asleep. Surprise. Not even close.

ALMOST EVERY WINDOW IS LIT

Shit. What's going on? I throw the Cherokee
    into park, pop a couple of killer breath

mints, hurry toward the door, stomach
    churning. Inside the house is a not-pretty

scene. Mikayla is on the couch, arms
    crossed, jaw set. But she's been crying.

"What happened? Mikki, where's your
    car?" Jace turns, anger evident in the eggplant

    color of his face. *Nice of you to come*
        home. I've been trying to call you—

"Sorry. My cell's dead." Not exactly
    true. I turned it off to avoid interruptions.

    Do you know what your daughter
        was up to tonight, while you were out . . .

He lets the end of the sentence dangle,
    implying something ugly. I ignore that, look

at Mikayla, who sits, granite-faced, glaring.
    "Uh . . . I guess I don't. You weren't at Emily's?"

    Yes, she was. Long enough for Dylan
        to pick her up for a party at Nevada

Flats. Someone tipped the cops.
Luckily, Stan was one of them. He brought

her home. Not the first time Jace's brother
has run interference for one of our kids.

"Well, other than Mik lying to us,
it could be a whole lot worse, right?"

Unless you want to consider underage
drinking, plus marijuana and ketamine.

"Mikayla! Tell me you're not doing
drugs." I couldn't have missed the signs.

She shakes her head. *A little weed,*
Mom. I don't indulge in the hard stuff.

A snort on the stairs makes us turn.
Believe that, you believe in Santa.

It's Trace, and Mikayla isn't happy.
What would you know about it, asshole?

I may be an asshole, but you're
a ho. I know that about you too.

"That's enough!" My head pounds. "Go
to bed, Trace. We don't need your input."

I DON'T BELIEVE IN SANTA

Was never allowed that small pleasure
as a child. My own child is still spying
on us from the staircase. "Trace! I said go."

He goes, singing an ad-libbed carol.
Ho, ho, ho. What do you know?
Who, who, who. Who would you do?

I choke back a giggle. But Jace remains
stern-faced. "I'll take care of this for
now. Mikayla, come over here."

Jace scowls. *Fine. But there will be*
consequences to discuss in the morning.
He pivots. *I'll check on Trace and Bri.*

Mikayla approaches warily but does as
she's told. Her hair is a mess, her face
streaked with heavy stripes of mascara

and eyeliner. She smells of alcohol,
and her eyes are red—from crying or
smoking or both. But her pupils appear

normal, and when her gaze meets mine,
it is focused. Present. There is something
else, though. Another scent she wears,

faint but unmistakable. "You need a shower.
And your dad is right. We can't just let this
go. God, Mik, summer vacation is supposed

to be fun. This was not a good way to kick
it off." I consider whether or not to ask if
she and Dylan are using condoms.

She goes totally stiff. *You're not going
to ground me, are you? Dylan's taking
me up to the lake tomorrow.* It's a whine.

"Pretty sure that won't happen, Mikki.
Your dad's really angry . . ." I should be
too. Maybe I will be, once I sober up myself.

"Look. You could be in a whole lot more
trouble. Go on to bed now." I get another
whiff of sex. "But take a shower first.

We'll talk in the morning." I watch her go,
all skinny jeans and seventeen, thinking
she's grown up. Believing she's in love,

hoping he loves her back, and willing
to do whatever it takes to make that so.
I get the urge to run after her, pull her to

me, daughter to mother, confide that sex
isn't the way to make a man love you.
That love and sex can, in fact, remain

independent of one another. Maybe even
should. Half of me wants to tell her all that.
The other half suspects it would be useless.

TUMBLING TOWARD EXHAUSTION

I wash my face, slather on
pricey antiwrinkle cream.
Brush my teeth. Take a pre-
bed pee. Routine. Routine.

Routine. As I slip into my
favorite nightgown, Jace
comes into the bathroom.
He takes one look at me

and scowls, etching his
forehead. *When are you
going to get rid of that
thing? It's ratty as hell.*

Still pissed. "Screw you.
It wasn't my fault she went
to the party." And I'm not
in the mood to let him take

it out on me. I go on to bed,
slither between the cool sheets.
Before long, Jace joins me.
Offers a lame *I'm sorry.* But

when he tries to touch me, I
turn away, scoot clear to one
edge of the mattress. Wisely,
he leaves me alone there.

QUIVERING RAYS

Of daybreak bring me wide awake. I thought
I might sleep later, considering what time I finally
went to bed. But no. Beside me, Jace mumbles

in his sleep. Hope whatever dreams have captured
him have tempered his anger. I slide quietly into
the silence of Saturday, early morning. Put on

my running clothes, despite a hint of hangover.
I can use a good sweat, not to mention a way
to process everything that went down last night.

Being a teen is hard, but being a parent is harder.
I mean, we're supposed to have all the answers.
Seriously? Sometimes all I have is questions.

Who am I really? What do I want? Is it too late
to take an alternate route to wherever it is I think
I want to go? And since I have no clear idea

what my ultimate goal is, how can I reasonably
counsel my children about setting their own
course? How do I teach them morals when

I'm questioning my own right now? Grant was
a delicious piece of temptation. Not sure what
I would have done if Andrea hadn't been there.

BUT ANDREA WAS THERE

So instead of Grant being a source
of guilt, I'll let him be inspiration.
I really am going to write erotica.
As I run, a story begins to percolate.

When I get home, I let myself in
quietly. The TV is on. Brianna is up.
I can hear her talking on the phone,
no doubt to her best friend, Harley.

But everyone else is still in their rooms.
I sneak into my study, find the journal
Mikayla gave me for Christmas, open it
to the first crisp white page. I write:

We leave our companions talking politics
at the table. He takes my hand, leads me
down the long hallway, out the back door
and into a pale-lit passageway. City stink
mingles with summer jasmine and his personal
scent of leather.

He tugs me away from the neon-streaked
street, to the far end of the alley. "No one
here but us," he says, pushing me back against
a rough stucco wall.

His fingers snake into my hair, pull my face
into his and when his mouth covers mine, rum
and mint flavor his tongue. The kiss I return
is not gentle, and when his body rocks against
mine, he is hard against the throb growing
faster, faster between my legs.

He is strong. My heart pounds as he wraps
my right leg around his hip, lifts. Beneath my
short denim skirt, he finds nothing but skin
and hot, wet pulsing. His fingers start there,
work their way inside. My body screams for
orgasm, but not like that. "Fuck me," I beg.

His eyes, feral, meet mine. He smiles, props
me up on his knee. Unzips his fine silk trousers,
brings the swollen knob of his cock just outside
my thrumming slit. Stops. "Say please."

I'm just about to say please when
yelling erupts in the other room.
Jace and Mik are at it. Better run
interference. First, I go back up to

the top of the page. I'll finish the story
later. But for now it needs a title.
I write: *Vanilla*, close the cover,
and stash the journal deep away.

VANILLA

Unique to its place in the world,
and to its circumstances—
an orchid, aromatic in bloom,
and elegant in its simplicity,

vanilla

grows on a demanding vine.
One flower, one fruit, a handful
of seed pods, steeped to
unparalleled taste.

Flavored

in such a way, the simplest
of puddings becomes remarkable.
Why, then, the syntactical
disconnect, when the noun
becomes an adjective, modifying

sex?

Applied to the partnered bed,
apt vanilla descriptions,
including *flavorful, aromatic,*
elegant, and *demanding*,

should be

considered desirable,
and no less so if readily
attainable. Throw in *remarkable*
and *unparalleled*, vanilla
sex needs to be sought after.

Celebrated.

And not disregarded
in favor of sleeping in.

Marissa

SATURDAY MORNING

Is no different than any other
morning in the Trask household.
While Christian and Shane sleep in,
I'm up early to take care of Shelby.
Someone has to do it. And that

someone is always me. She had
a good night last night, so after
a Pull-Ups change we move straight
into her twice-daily chest physio-
therapy. "Okay, cookie dough,

let's get on with the CPT, shall we?"
Cheerful. I am always cheerful,
or try to be. Suction first, to clear
her esophagus of overnight slime.
Then a series of chest compressions

to loosen any buildup. Front.
Flip to right side. Flip to left side.
Back. One hundred times, give
or take. Sometimes I lose track.
"Can you help Mommy count?"

I thump away, and she does her
best to imitate my "One, two,
three." They come out little
squeaks, but we both know
what she means. "Fabulous."

Relatively phlegmless today,
at least so far, I am hopeful
that the morning will remain
relatively uneventful. "Would
you like to swing for a while?"

The smile that pops out on her
face makes her look completely
human. All little girl, except
if you look real hard, you can
almost see a halo. And I think

it's growing. Coalescing.
Probably just lack-of-
sleep hallucinations. Can't
remember the last time I got
more than three uninterrupted

hours. "I'll go get Daddy to
take you outside to swing.
It's a Daddy kind of job,
isn't it, cupcake?" Why do I
keep calling her food names?

LACK OF UNINTERRUPTED SLEEP

Moved my husband into the guest room
a couple of years ago. If any guests
happen to show up, Christian would
probably sleep in his car. That's not likely.

We don't often get visitors since Shelby's
condition was diagnosed. Andrea hardly
ever comes over, and she's my sister.
Can't really blame people, I suppose.

SMA isn't pretty. And it fucking stinks.
Antiseptic and medicine and sick-
dirty linens. The odors permeate
the house. No deodorizer can mask

them. Wonder if we'll have friends
again once Shelby is . . . shit. I've got
to stop thinking like that. I glance at
the clock in the living room. Nine-

oh-two. Christian can get up, damn it.
Don't care how late he worked. It must
have been late. I didn't hear him come in.
I don't bother to knock. "Christian, could . . ."

The room is empty, the bed unruffled.
Looks like he didn't come home at
all. I could be angry. I could be
worried. But really, why bother?

IT'S NOT THE FIRST TIME

He hasn't come home, and he always
has an excuse. Big project. Too tired

to drive the fifteen minutes from work
on the south end of the city to home, in

the northwest. Still, I did promise Shelby
her daddy would take her outside to swing.

I pick up the phone. Dial Christian's cell.
Four rings, to voicemail. "Where are you?

Your daughter is hoping you can spare
a few minutes for her today. Call, okay?"

The teakettle whistles and as I pour
the steaming water into a cup, I happen

to glance at the calendar. This particular
June Saturday is marked *Claire's Shower.*

Claire and I were flight attendants together, and
though we don't see very much of each other

anymore, we did our share of high—and low—
altitude partying. She's having a baby at thirty-nine.

Lucky her. Everything looks fine, according
to her ob-gyn. Then again, in utero, Shelby

looked just perfect too. We didn't know
there was a problem until she was around

seven months old and couldn't turn over,
let alone sit up. I hope things turn out better

for Claire's baby girl. The phone rings.
Christian. *Uh . . . hey. Sorry. We're trying*

to fulfill this big contract . . . Yeah, yeah,
yeah. What counts is, *I can't make it home*

until tonight. Tell Shelby I'll play with her
tomorrow, okay? He's about to hang up

when I locate enough guts to say, "You promised
you'd take care of her while I went to Claire's

baby shower. That's at two p.m. God, Christian.
Why can't I ever fucking count on you?"

Ask your sister to watch her. See you later.
No apology. He's just gone. A white-hot cinder

flickers in my head. "Bastard!" The word slithers
from my mouth, much to the amusement

of my son, who has come into the kitchen
in search of breakfast. He laughs. *What have*

I been telling you these last few years? Dad
is *a bastard. Question is, why does he stay?*

I WAIT FOR HIM

To quit rearranging
the contents of the refrigerator.
When he emerges,

cheddar and pastrami in hand,
I look into his eyes,
search for the intent of his query.

I see only honest curiosity.
"Why wouldn't your father stay?
This is his home, right?"

Shane shakes his head. His hair,
which has grown too
long, sways like wheat in wind.

He doesn't want to be
here. Not one iota. He quit caring
about us a long time ago.

I watch him start stacking a huge
sandwich. Try to think
of a denial he'll go for. Can't quite

manage it. "He loves you.
I'm sure of it." But what I don't say
is deafening in its silence.

I KEEP SHANE COMPANY

For a while, sipping my tea as he eats.
Why can't we share more minutes
like these—almost a normal family?
I want to stay here longer, but Shelby

lies alone in the other room, waiting
for the dad who is too busy to take
her out into the soft morning sunshine.
I didn't even turn on Barney. Before

I go to her, I call Andrea, expecting
Harley to answer. She always beats
her mom to the phone and I always
hear disappointment in her voice

when it's Aunt Missy and not Brianna.
But today it's Andrea who says hello.
"Hey. What's up?" I wait several
minutes while she talks about going

out with Holly last night. Finally,
she yields to me. "Sorry to have to
ask, but I was wondering if you could
watch Shelby for a couple of hours

this afternoon. Christian was supposed
to handle it, but he has to work, and
it's Claire's baby shower and . . ."
Damn. I sound borderline hysterical.

So I know she must feel awful
when she answers, *God, what is it*
with husbands—or ex-husbands?
I wish I could, but I have to drive

to Fallon to pick up Harley at
her dad's. Steve was supposed to
bring her home, but now he says
he's got the flu or food poisoning.

If it's just bad fast food and a stinky
bathroom, it could wait, but if it's flu,
we'll all get it and . . . She pauses,
perhaps intuiting that beyond all reason

I am in tears. "Never mind. It's only
a dumb shower, and looking at baby
clothes will probably make me all
weepy anyway. Just never mind, okay?"

I half slam the phone. Not her problem.
Why should she care? "Put your plate in
the dishwasher," I remind Shane. If I don't,
I'll find it in the sink. Oh hell, I probably will,

regardless. That, stupidly, makes me
cry even harder. I've got to stop or
Shelby will get upset. And if she starts
to cry too, I'll be up to my elbows in snot.

UNEXPECTEDLY

Shane gets up, rinses his plate,
puts it in the dishwasher, then
comes over and puts a hand on
my shoulder. *I can take care of*

Shelby for a couple of hours.
You go to the baby shower.
I shake my head. "If something
happened, it would take me too

long to get back. And it's not
that important for me to go."
Mom, you never get to do any-
thing. It's really fucked-up of

Dad to load everything onto
you. She's his daughter too.
He's saying everything I'm
thinking. "I know. But it is

what it is. Right now, will you
please help me take her outside?"
Sure. But only if you stop crying.
Then he does something he hasn't

in I can't remember how long—
he hugs me. Like he loves me.
Shelby will have to wait a few
more minutes. Tears fall in earnest.

A FEW MINUTES

Late waking, you could
miss a train. But while
you wait for the next one,

your

world might start spinning faster.
Someone new saunters
off the subway and into your

life

with nothing more than
a smile at the exact right
moment. Sometimes fate

is

generous. The challenge is
acknowledging the gifts
she offers. They are

not

always obvious. At times
one appears, subtle
as a moon shadow. A smile,

the same

as a thousand other smiles,
except for the intent
behind it.

Andrea

IF I HAD TO TELL THE TRUTH

Every time I opened my mouth,
my sister wouldn't be speaking
to me right now. Because the truth

is, I could have waited a couple
of hours to go pick up Harley. Not
like her dad is on his deathbed.

But Shelby is. I see her slipping
closer and closer to her destiny.
And it's a damn hard thing to watch.

Poor Missy. She deserves a few
hours away from the overwhelming
pressure. But today, I just couldn't

take the weight myself. I feel selfish.
I feel relieved to be in my car, almost
to Fallon—a forgettable town at

the very edge of the Great Basin playa.
Farmers and Navy families. (Whose
idea was it to put a naval air station

smack in the middle of sand dunes?)
And not a few antigovernment
libertarians, one of them being my ex.

A HIGH SCHOOL HOOKUP

That's what we were, me a stoner
and Steve a defensive lineman
jock who liked getting buzzed
when he wasn't knocking down

quarterbacks. Not a partnership
made in heaven, but dating anyone
on our state champion football
team put you at the top of our

very short social ladder. I liked
being up there, even if it meant
taking a fair amount of verbal
abuse from the boy who supposedly

loved me. Back in the day, I didn't
classify getting cussed out regularly
as abuse. Maybe because my dad
treated my mom the same way.

It was normal. And so was sex,
of the unprotected variety. I had
an unforgettable senior year—
cherry popped just before Christmas.

Pregnant by Easter. Married right
after graduation. I miscarried a week
later. After I healed, I went straight to
Planned Parenthood for birth control.

Steve found work as a roofer. DMV
was hiring, and somehow I qualified.
The daily fighting began. But I refused
to admit our marriage was a mistake.

Four years into the ugly mess, for
some ridiculous reason, I decided
a baby could fix things. Harley
was like an umbrella in a hurricane.

When I had to take maternity leave,
Steve worked ever-longer hours.
He came home, relaxed with a beer
or ten. Then he took a major fall.

Back surgery. Hospital bills. Meds
for the pain. Addiction to meds.
It isn't an unusual story. But it
turned out to be his story. Mine too.

I stayed with him way too long.
At the end, the decision was easy
to make. Harley was six and in
school. I already had a decent

job, with bennies and a generous-
enough salary to pay rent, utilities,
and feed my daughter and me.
Steve didn't even try to keep us.

IT'S AN HOUR

From Reno to Fallon. At least
on the return trip, I'll have
Harley's enthusiastic conversation
to keep me from getting swept
away by a river of painful reverie.

Steve is sitting outside, smoking
with an auburn-haired woman, a few
years younger than he. She is tall,
and straighter than she should be
considering the size of her breasts

in relationship to relative body fat.
Fakies, for sure. Not that he'd care
if they're real or silicone. Not that
I care, either. Steve doesn't bother to
introduce us, so I say, "Hi. I'm Andrea."

> That's all it takes. *Harley's mom,*
> *right? God, she is just the sweetest*
> *thing. I'm taken with her, ya know?*
> Uh, yeah. She's my kid. *Oh. I'm*
> *Cassie. Cassandra, but, ya know.*

I don't exactly know much, but
I'm starting to guess a lot. She talks
about a hundred miles per hour
and weighs about the same number
of pounds. "Where *is* Harley?"

Steve opens his mouth. *She's inside,*
playing XBox 360 with Chad.

, but "Who's Chad?" Somehow,
ss the answer before it comes.

Cass's kid. When I start toward the door,
Steve says, *Wait. I have something to tell*

you. I got a job in Reno. I'm moving back
next week. I want to see Harley more . . .

Yeah, chimes in Cassie. *I told him*
a father needs to be in his kid's life.

Thank you very much, Ms. Anorexia.
"Uh. Yeah. Well, we can discuss it."

Not right now, however. I semi-storm
the door. Inside, my sweet, preadolescent

daughter is sitting practically knee to knee
with a completely adolescent boy who looks

exactly like his mother. Minus the fake tits,
of course, and plus a few zits. The two kids

are completely absorbed by some sort of gun-
fire game. "Hey, Harley. What are you playing?"

She doesn't even look at me. *Wicked*
Warfare. It's really cool. She does glance

at Chad, and I do not like her expression—
total adoration. She just met this guy, and

he's not all that, and he's way too old,
and . . . "Okay. Well, we've got to go."

Just one minute. Let me finish this
round. She keeps blasting away

at something on-screen . . . "Wait.
What are you shooting? Not kids?"

Don't worry, says Chad. *They're not*
American kids. They're Muslims.

What the hell? "Harley . . ." I keep my
voice controlled. "Let's go. Now."

Finally, she turns her face toward me, and
what she sees convinces her I'm not kidding.

She puts down the controller. *Bye,*
Chad. I'll see you soon. I only hope

she notices he doesn't acknowledge
her, except to say, *Yeah. See ya.*

ON OUR WAY

To the car, Harley goes over to Steve,
gives him a big kiss goodbye. Then,
against all reason, she rewards Cassie
the same way. When was the last time

she kissed me? A little monster, not
positive of its color, but likely green,
begins a slow nibble in my belly.
Not fair! Where was this man

through eight years of parent-teacher
conferences? Where was he when
she sang holiday carols and recited
two-line soliloquies in school plays?

As for his girlfriend, regardless
of how long she's been in his picture,
Harley never met her before yesterday.
She doesn't deserve my child's

affection. And neither does her son.
Guess we're past due for that mother-
daughter talk. Wonder if a churn of
stomach acid can kill that little monster.

HALFWAY HOME

I'm still working on how to approach
the subject when Harley saves me

the trouble. *How do I lose weight,*
Mom? She has always worn a few

extra pounds, but not a whole lot.
"Fewer calories, more exercise."

She assesses herself in the mirror.
Would you help me? Please?

"Of course. But why are you
worried about it, all of a sudden?"

I want to wear skinny jeans, like
Brianna does. They're the style.

"You and Bri have totally different
body styles, Harley. Even if you lose—"

I don't care! All the boys like her,
and they never like me. I hate it.

Where is this coming from? Oh.
"This isn't about Chad, is it?" It is.

He's really cute. And he's really nice.
And he doesn't have a girlfriend.

YIKES! MAJOR CRUSH

Her first, at least that I'm aware of.
And it happened so fast. Oh my God.
Do they all strike like rattlesnakes—

quick and venomous and relentless?
As she goes on about Chad and how
he taught her to play *Wicked Warfare*,

something he said comes back to me.
They're Muslims. "So does Chad go to
Fallon High?" Please, please say yes.

No. He goes to Reno High. Isn't that
awesome? Cassie got Dad his new job
at Terrible's, and they're going to live

together. So when I go see Dad, I'll get
to see Chad too. Isn't that awesome?
I'm on a diet as of today. Can we stop

at the store and get healthy food?
'Cause you buy too much junk food,
and you know me. I can't say no to . . .

I stop listening. Not even her chatter
bombardment can keep me from plunging
into that river of reverie. It's not that

Harley's growing up. That, I can (sort of)
take. (Minus all the "awesomes.") What I
can't take at all is Steve helping her do it.

REVERIE

Is a place to cozy into
when you're alone and
in need of understanding.
It's a familiar space

where

candles light the corridor
to yesterday. Or tomorrow.
Take the left fork to what
will be, the right into

memory.

There, in that vast,
mirrored hall where
dreams echo without
change, illusion

gains

transparency. Linger
awhile and the murky
water of recollection parts,
allowing essential

clarity.

Sometimes it happens
like that. Sometimes
you just get lost.

FAMILY DYNAMICS

Are not static. They can change with a choice.
A whim. Happenstance. Mikayla goes to a party.
Gets busted. Gets grounded. Without technology.

She actually picks up a magazine. *Time.* Sees
a story about how the Internet is changing
the way adoptees locate their birth parents.

Have you ever thought about trying this?
she asks. *I mean, c'mon, Mom. No-brainer.*

And the weirdest thing is, no. I never thought
about using Facebook to try to find my birth
parents. I've talked about searching for years.

Apparently, Mikayla paid attention. *You*
want to know where you came from, right?

Don't all adoptees? Oh, I guess some claim
not to. But how could you really *not* want
to know where you came from? Why you

look the way you do. Why they gave you away.
Threw you away. *I'll help, Mom,* Mik says.

So yeah, of course she volunteered so she'd
have a legit reason to be on the computer.
But she hasn't offered to help me do anything

since the last time we baked cookies
together. She was maybe eleven. She'll be
eighteen in less than five months. I'm betting

she'll hit the door running two minutes past
graduation. Maybe doing this research together
will help us grow a little closer before life wedges

us completely apart. *Tell me what you know*
about your birth parents. No names, right?

No names. No ages. No real clues except,
"Your grandma told me they were from Elko
and my mother got pregnant in high school."

Mama may have known more. But she wasn't
about to share it with me. I think she worried
I'd love my birth mother more. Maybe. Mama

wasn't the nicest woman. *So you were born*
in . . . God, Mom, you're going to be forty.

"Don't remind me." All the running in the world
won't fix the corners of my eyes. Laser erasure
beckons. "I can almost see the Grim Reaper."

Mom! Don't say that. She shudders.
You are not allowed to die. Ever!

MIK STARTS HER RESEARCH

I think about Mama and Papa and how
they arranged my adoption through
their church. My childhood was weighty
with Christian expectation. The kind

that makes a person never want to set foot
in a church again. The kind that bumps
a girl into teenage rebellion. Or maybe
I inherited the tendency—some hit-sixteen-

and-go-crazy-wild gene. Mikayla, in turn,
seems to have gotten it from me. What else
did I receive via DNA? My stubbornness?
Distaste for chocolate? Rabbitbrush allergy?

What roll of genetic dice gave me these topaz
eyes and burnished bronze hair? I didn't dare
investigate while Mama and Papa were alive.
But with both of them lost to cancer, I'm free

to try. Connection. The idea shimmers
like summer heat on a stretch of distant
highway. Vanishes, a mirage, within
the very real possibility of never finding it.

> *Okay, I think I know what to do first.*
> *I'll see if Elko High School is on Facebook.*
> *I can get on the computer, right?* Mik drops
> her voice. *Dad doesn't have to know.*

CONSPIRACY FIRMLY ESTABLISHED

I allow Mikki an hour on her laptop
while I return to my desktop web surf.

I'm thinking about going back to school.
I had almost five semesters in before I dropped

out to get married and have my own babies.
It wouldn't take that much to finish.

A degree would be something all mine.
Not sure why I want it. Probably won't

ever use a BA in English. But ever since
this writing bug chewed into me, I've had

a fever to put words on paper. Might as well
make sure they go down right. Uh . . . correctly.

Maybe I could even take a class this summer.
I'm looking into that when I come across this:

High Desert Muses invites all local writers
to join us for communion and critique.

Second and fourth Wednesday evenings
of every month at Starbucks in Carson City.

All writing levels and genres encouraged.
Wonder how they feel about erotica.

BEFORE I GET THE CHANCE

To call the number listed for more
information, there's a firestorm of footsteps
in the front hall. Jace crashes in, cursing

some client, only to find Mikayla
on her computer. *What the hell are
you doing online? Shut that down.*

Here we go again. And once again,
I rush to Mik's rescue. "Hang on, okay?
She's doing some research for me."

At Jace's dubious look, Mikki explains,
*Yeah, Dad. I'm helping her search for
her birth parents. Facebook is the new—*

No! Not that again, Holly. The last time . . .
He shakes his head. *I wish you'd just leave
it alone. When it all goes to shit, you turn*

*into a basket case. Even if you did find them,
what would it prove? That they still don't want
you, or would have come looking themselves?*

*God, Holly, what is it with you? You have
people right here who love you. Your family
is all you need. Why go sniffing elsewhere?*

His words are bullets. I want to shoot back,
but going to war is probably exactly what
he wants. I try diversion instead. "Bad day?"

Crap day. I don't know why . . . and
off he goes, ranting about whatever it
is his client did that's going to screw up

all his hard work. I could follow, listen.
Try to soothe him out of this mood, but
at the moment I'm wondering why

it's always up to me to offer sympathy.
"You should probably log off," I tell
Mik. "No use irritating your father more."

Fine, she huffs. *But it's so not fair.*
Why does he have to be such a jerk?
Can I call Dylan? Just to say hello?

At my hesitation, she pleads, *Please, Mom!*
I haven't talked to him in days. I need to hear
his voice. Don't you remember being in love?

Some sort of commentary? Most likely
unintended, however close to home.
"Of course I do. But I don't want your dad

to get mad at you." Her cheeks compress,
pinching her mouth into a tiny O, and
her eyes threaten tears. "Okay, but no more

than two minutes. I'll keep Dad occupied."
The O becomes a wide U before she mouths
Thank you, scurries off into the other room.

I FOLLOW A TRAIL

Of Jace's clothes, left scattered on the floor.
He's in the bathroom, so Mikki should be
okay for a few minutes. Wordlessly, I pick up
the strewn garments, take them to the laundry
room, feeling the tiniest bit traitorous.

As I clean out the pockets of my favorite
denim jacket, I find a business card. Grant
Sothersby? Oh, yes. Mr. Vanilla—the one
who I decided not to call. But suddenly
I get the urge to do just that. Suddenly,

war sounds good. A covert war—to be
more than a little traitorous. My family
is all I need? Hardly. I need to be spoiled.
Spotlighted. I want someone to tell me I'm
beautiful. Hot. Kick-fucking-ass.

I go to the kitchen. Pick up the phone.
Dial Grant's number. Change my mind.
Hang up. What am I doing? Seriously.
Plotting infidelity at my kitchen counter?
Flirting, even semi-dangerous flirting, is not

the same thing as arranging a shameless
roll in the sack. But now the phone rings
in my hand. Grant, returning his caller ID,
no doubt. I have to answer or someone
else will. "Hello? This is Holly, remember . . ."

HE DEFINITELY REMEMBERS

And now the decision seems to have
been wrested from me. We plan to meet
downtown for drinks. The unvoiced "after,
we'll see" hangs like a lace curtain between us.

Rather than try to think up a convincing
excuse, I say to Mikki, "Tell your dad I prefer
not to collect his clothes like he is six.
I'm going to a movie." She owes me,

nods wordlessly. I am all the way down
the driveway before my cell rings. *Hey.*
I'm sorry about the clothes. Are you
really mad at me? Sharp little teeth

of guilt gnaw, but not viciously enough.
"I'll get over it. I just need some time
to myself." I hang up and he doesn't call
back. Must be a sign. By the time I get

to the bar, Grant is already there, better-
looking than I recalled. As I nestle
beside him, a waitress saunters over with
mojitos. I break a smile. "You remembered."

He licks his lips, catlike. *Of course.*
You are unforgettable. Ka-ching. *I was*
beginning to think you weren't going
to call. But I'm really glad you did.

WE SHED ALL PRETENSE QUICKLY

Before we finish the first drink,
it's clear we're both here for sex.
When the under-the-table foreplay
becomes too intense, Grant pays
the bill and we walk down the street
to a cheap motel. Okay, it's a dive.
It doesn't have hourly rates, but by

the look of things, it should have.
The room smells of Lysol, and its
elderly carpet is stained with God-
only-knows-what. "Not exactly
five-star. Better check the sheets."
They look okay, are perfumed
with bleach. Guess that's really all

that matters. I make sure the door
is locked, and when I turn around,
Grant is already out of his clothes.
His body is thicker than I expected,
and hairier. Just two of the things
I have to get over as I strip to skin,
crawl into bed next to him, starved

for specialized attention. Instead,
what I get from this stranger is the
same sex waiting at home. Missionary.
Ordinary. He comes. I don't. Done.
I leave him there, dozing. Walk back
to my car, past hookers and drug
deals. Feeling cheaper than the room.

SEX WITH A STRANGER

Is an eye-opening experience.
Just when you think you know all
there is to know, come to find out
you ain't learned everything yet.

No
strings

means doing things your way,
but only if you happen to be
the top. When you're not, it means
accepting the particular brand of

sex

you're being offered, mostly
without complaint. That's when
things can get sticky, and not
just literally. Saying stop

can
be

problematic when your partner
is headlong into orgasm. Asking
for longer or gentler or once more,
with feeling, is quite often

disappointing.

Sex with a stranger can fill in
the blanks, but whether or not
you like the turn of phrase
depends on the stranger.

SWIM THERAPY DAY

Is Shelby's favorite day of the week.
I'd take her more often if I could,
but not only is it expensive, it's hard
to get her there by myself. Once

upon a time, Christian helped.
But now it's pretty much up to me
to load her into the van, strap her
into her special bed, drive twenty

miles to the one gym that allows
special therapy programs in their
heated indoor pool. The water
must be very warm because kids

with SMA have lower muscle mass
and tend to chill easily. No chills
allowed, and absolutely no head
dips below the surface. Water in

the lungs would be disastrous.
But in the pool, helped only to
float, Shelby is a manta. She can
move on her own, something

she can do hardly at all, lying flat
on her back. When she swims,
she gains the tiniest bit of control.
She transforms. Spreads her wings.

SOMETIMES I SWIM

With her. But today, her physical
therapist instructs her to lift her knees,
straighten her legs, bring her arms up

in the water. Shelby has no clue
that she is being assessed for progress
or failure. All she knows is she's having fun.

> *Hello, again.* The voice falls over
> my shoulder, a shadow. *How are*
> *things? Your daughter looks happy.*

It's Doug Schneider, another SMA
parent. When Shelby was first diagnosed,
and we were struggling to make sense of it

all, he and his wife, Ally, were so helpful—
sort of an unofficial support group of two.
"Shelby's happiest when wet, and she loves

Vivian. Hey there, Joey. You ready for
a swim?" Joey, who's type 2 and so less
severely impacted than Shelby, nods

> and holds up a hand. *High five.*
> The gesture comes easily for him,
> though the words are difficult.

"Way to go, little dude. Hey, where's
your mommy today?" Joey shrugs,
and his grin narrows. Doug leans in

close to me, speaks quietly into my ear.
Ally left. She says it's temporary—a little
time away to think. But she's not coming

back. He swallows deeply, as if drowning
words he's frightened to let surface.
I don't know what I'm going to do.

"Oh, Doug. I can't . . . I don't . . . are
you sure?" But of course he is. "I can't
believe it. Ally always seemed so devoted."

How could she? [Oh, but you know how.]
How could anyone walk away from
her child—whether or not that child

is whole? [One foot in front of the other.]
No, especially because he's *not* whole.
He's fractured. A clay pot, threatening

to break into shards. His mother should
be the glue, holding him together.
[Words are easy. Being the glue is hard.]

I still have to work, and a full-time
caregiver would be so expensive.
There's my mom, but she lives in L.A.

"I'm so sorry, Doug. Please let me know
if I can help." We both understand it's an
empty offer. No way to follow through.

ESCAPE

Ally chose it.
Can't say I haven't
thought about it, and I
ponder it all the way home.

In the backseat,
Shelby hums happiness.
She deserves every minute.
Every second. But what does

her time here
mean? To her? To me?
What would she do without
me? What would she be? Nothing

but a burden? Is
that what she is to me?
Her smallest accomplishments
bring such pleasure. Feel like gifts.

And yet, there are
times I could easily run
away from the sad soap opera.
To what, I don't know. I wonder if

Ally knew—had
some preplanned place
to go. Half of me is disgusted
by her. The other half wants to be her.

THE HOUSE IS EMPTY

When we arrive—Christian, away
on business; Shane, *Gone out with*

a friend, so the note he left informs
me. I push Shelby's stander down

the long hallway, the soft whir of
its wheels the only sound to break

the air-stealing weight of silence. I settle
her into bed and am adjusting the web

of tubes when the doorbell rings.
"Who could that be, my little mermaid?

You take your nap and I'll go see." Visitors
are rare at Casa Trask; unannounced

visitors are almost unheard of. If it's
a Jehovah's Witness, I'm half tempted

to let him in, if only to bring some sort
of dialogue into the afternoon stretching

long and longer in front of me. I've just
about convinced myself I'll come face to

front page with *The Watchtower*, so when I
open the door, I'm almost shocked to find

the first guy I ever kissed standing
there. "Drew! What are you doing here?"

The grin, spreading slowly across
his face, is well known. Well loved.

I had to run a few errands in Reno,
so I thought I'd stop by and catch up

a little. Aren't you going to let me
in? Or is your loving husband home?

Christian doesn't approve of my friendship
with Drew, who moved to Tahoe several

years ago to work at a ski resort. Or, possibly,
to reconnect with me. That's what Christian thinks,

and he could be right. Still, Drew and I are
just friends. And Christian isn't here. I stand

back from the door, blushing an apology.
"Come on in. I was just about to make some

tea." Drew follows me toward the kitchen
and I am enveloped by a fog of patchouli.

He's worn the scent as long as I've known
him and it conjures powerful memories

of sneaking off to an Oregon barn for long,
lustful (but sex-free) make-out sessions.

Sex-free, because we were only fourteen,
and though the example set for us by our

hippie parents was uncommitted rutting,
somehow both Drew and I believed in love.

And love each other we did, in that pure,
all-encompassing way that only adolescence

knows. We even talked about getting married
one day. Ridiculous, yes. But it didn't feel

that way then. I thought I'd die when my
parents decided to abandon the Oregon farm

in favor of northern Nevada suburbia. Drew
and I wrote each other faithfully for a couple

of years until the letter exchange became less
frequent. Eventually, we tumbled for other people.

When his marriage crumbled, he moved to Tahoe.
My own tattered marriage somehow remains intact.

The time-weathered constant has been the "us"
of Drew and me. Our friendship has survived

everything, including Shelby. He sees her as
I do, calls her an angel with clipped wings.

AS I FILL THE KETTLE

He asks about her immediately.
How is Shelby? Still a Barney fan?
He stands just across the counter,

throwing off his unsettling energy
and scanning every inch of me
with molasses eyes. "She will always

love Barney. And she's maintaining.
She had swim therapy today. Vivian
says she's hanging in there." I smile,

hoping he doesn't intuit my Ally
envy. *And Shane? Anything new
with him?* Small talk, to be sure.

But Drew's small talk makes me
feel like someone in my life cares.
"He smokes weed and watches gay

porn. Same ol', same ol'. Ditto,
Christian. Works all the time. Travels
too much. Sleeps in the guest room."

Drew reaches across the counter,
traces the counter of my jaw.
Sounds lonely. You deserve better.

I close my eyes at his touch.
Remember too much of our history
in that briefest of moments. Turn

toward the whistling on the stove.
"I understand why he runs, Drew.
Not that understanding it makes

it better. But I'd run away too,
if Shelby didn't need me." There.
Said. Nothing left to intuition.

Ah, but see, that's the difference
between Chris and you. He leaves
because of Shelby, but she's

the reason you stay. You have
heart. He is a selfish prick.
What did you ever see in him?

My brain rewinds to the afternoon
Christian and I met, on a Reno-
to-Dallas flight. He was young,

handsome, new at InnoTechnoVent,
and flying first-class with his boss.
I was the purser. When I bent to serve

him lunch, our eyes linked, and
something in his whispered to me.
When he slipped me his number,

I had no idea how far we would go
together—or how far we would fall.
All I saw on that day was "Potential."

POTENTIAL

That's what desert-weary
settlers saw in the river-fed
verdure they called the Truckee
Meadows. There, as they rested
before the Sierra crossing,

greed

took easy root. Build a bridge,
demand a toll, your own journey
halted east of the mountain's
stark skirts. And in its shadow,
you watch a cow town spring up,

graft

central to what it becomes
over the years—the Biggest
Little City in the West, brick
and concrete denying granite

grandeur;

harsh neon glitter fighting
the pale light of moonrise.
Quick, plastic weddings.
Six weeks to divorce.

Broken
promises,

circlets of gold, memories
tossed from the bridge
to fall into forever
beneath the pulsing rapids.

Andrea

A RAPID PULSE

That's what I've got, courtesy of the guy
on the other end of the line. He is a wad,
and I am the chief wad catcher. Guess
that's what comes with being in

the same department for twenty
years. I just wish more frequent
raises came along with it too.
But considering Nevada's budget

crunch, I'm lucky to have a job
without furloughs. I started at DMV
the year after I graduated from high
school. Figured I could retire before

I hit fifty. I'm still on track to do
that. But I've still got a dozen years
to go. And that will be an extremely
long twelve years if I keep getting wads

like this. "I'm sorry, sir . . ." Remain
polite, despite the fact that he has just
called me an *ignoramus*. Hey, it's better
than *bitch*. "But without the required

documentation, we cannot issue
a duplicate title." Wait for the rant.
Hold the phone away from your ear.
Wow. This man is really worked up.

What I have to remember is, it's all
coming from a place of deep emotion.
"Sir, I understand the car belonged
to your father. But he put the title

in his girlfriend's name. We can't just
assume he meant for you to have it
when he died." He's losing a little steam.
His energy level is dropping, along

with the pitch of his voice. "Here's
what I suggest. Go to the nursing home
and ask her what she thinks your father
would want her to do. She can't drive

any longer, anyway. Maybe she'll sign
it over to you." Maybe not, but worth
a try. And even if she says no, it's not
like he's lost much. A '78 Caddy isn't

exactly topping everyone's wish list.
Its value for him is strictly sentimental.
"You're very welcome, sir. My name
is Andrea. You can ask for me when

you call back." Full-on wad dispersal
averted. "Of course I'll remember you."
Who wouldn't? "Best of luck." And
that's why they pay me the big bucks.

I HANG UP

To a round of applause. No one
wants to deal with a wad, and we

get them much too often here
in title research. At least, being

behind the scenes, in back of
a bank of locked doors, we don't

have to worry about someone
showing up with a gun. No way

would I want to work out front.
Phone calls are a level walk in

the park. "Thank you, thank you.
I believe I've reached my nasty

customer quota for the day.
Think I'll take my p.m. break."

Our breaks are mandated—
fifteen minutes, midmorning.

A half hour for lunch. Fifteen
minutes midafternoon. Some

people smoke on the patio, but
tobacco has never been my thing.

I'M MORE

Of a once-around-the-parking-lot,
with feeling, kind of a girl, though
in summer I prefer a morning walk.

But, still June, it's not too hot yet,
and I need to burn off a little wad
stress. I'm about a dozen steps toward

> my goal when someone behind me
> calls, *Andy! Wait up!* Andy? I hate
> nicknames, especially when they're

tossed at me. Only one person
here calls me Andy—Vern Brando.
He thinks it's cool because his late

wife, Valerie, used to call me Andy.
Of course, she and I were tight in high
school and back then I didn't mind

epithets. I slow to let him catch up.
"Hey, Vern. How's things in licenses?
Any good stories lately?" He conducts

> the actual driving tests and has had
> a few close calls, not to mention many
> amusing experiences. *Always. Always.*

I pick up the pace and he launches
a relatively funny tale about a girl
who celebrated her sixteenth birthday

at DMV. She waited for an extended
period, because a parent had to sign
the paperwork . . . *not to mention,*

bring a car for her to drive. Her dad
couldn't get off work. Her mom
had taken cold medicine—twice in two

hours. She got pulled over, suspected
of DUI. Luckily, she drew a sympathetic
cop, with a ride-along who drove her over.

Mom hung tough while Daughter passed
the test, then motored both of them home.
All's well that ends well, you know?

Would that life's myriad faux pas
could all end so well. I can barely
look at Vern without remembering

him and Valerie on their wedding
day. I was her maid of honor, barely
average in royal blue, my own young

marriage already in unforeseen danger.
She was striking in ice blue, a confession
of sorts. But everyone who knew

the happy couple believed they would
weather forever. It took a delivery truck,
spinning out on sleet, to prove us wrong.

HER FUNERAL

Was the first
I'd ever been to.
Everyone there
was fractured.
Broken by her absence,
and more, by the
absolute surety that
she would never
return to us.

It was a defining
experience for me,
who knew nothing
of death. Had never
witnessed such power.

Death is omnipotent.
Or is it?

It took years to go
looking for answers.
Is death absolute?
Or might there be
some energy that does
not die? Some thread
of life that continues
beyond the grave.
What if flesh does
not, in fact, limit us?

I DON'T DISCUSS THIS

With Vern.
Neither does
he mention Valerie,
our earliest, strongest
connection, though I
suspect he wishes
otherwise.

She has been
gone for four years.
Vern is beyond ready
to move on. And I think
he'd like to move on with
me. Problem is, I see
him as hers. And

in him, I see her.
And anytime I'm with
Vern, I can't help but think
of my treasured friend, standing at
the altar in ice blue. Valerie isn't
a memory, nor is she a ghost.
She is, forever, a presence.

THE COUNTY EMPLOYEE

Parking lot is a huge rectangle,
maybe a quarter mile around.

We complete half of it at a brisk
pace, exchanging a bit of workplace

gossip—who's getting divorced,
who's sleeping with whom, who

has recently entered rehab. On the far
side of the asphalt, the tenor of our

conversation changes when Vern
asks, *So, are you seeing anybody?*

"You mean, like, seriously dating?
No. I was, but . . . didn't work out."

I spare him the grisly details, or
maybe I spare myself. I don't want

to talk about Geoff or even think
about him. "How about you?"

He shakes his head. *I haven't been*
with anyone since . . . It gets lonely,

you know? I mean, the kids keep
me busy enough. But it's not the same

as having a best friend around—
someone to confide in. To trust.

"I've never really had one of those,
not one I slept with, anyway."

I have. And I miss her. But I can't
keep mourning forever. It's toxic.

We turn the corner, and I walk
even faster, trying to avoid what's

coming next. But it's inevitable.
Hey, slow down a little, would you?

So, I was wondering if maybe we—
you and I—could see each other.

I don't know what to say. That I was
closer to Valerie than to my own sister,

and so it would feel incestuous? Am
I just being stupid? He's cute. Sweet.

Gainfully employed. But I don't think
I could ever fall in love with him. "Vern . . .

Listen. This last breakup was difficult.
I decided to spend more time with Harley,

give myself a vacation from dating." True
enough. "Maybe in the future?" Cop-out.

A COP-OUT

According to Encarta, is
a "feebly transparent
excuse for refusing to face
up to something."

Excuses,

apparently, should be
thick with honesty. Opaque
with believability. They

are

best offered up cold,
no time to invent elaborate
embellishments or

futile

misdirection. But where
is the dishonor in
fabricated justification

if

one is attempting to spare
fragile feelings?
Can deceit, not

seen

or even intuited, perhaps
be the proper choice?
A deception uncovered might
be forgiven if viewed

through

a veil of compassion.

Holly

DECEPTIONS

Come in many sizes:

Huge.

Like lying about going
to the movies, while
really meeting someone
to engage in extramarital
boffing—even if the boff
happens to suck, so isn't
even close to worthy of all
the ensuing guilt. Gack.

Big.

Like telling your parents
you're spending the night
at your girlfriend's, when
in fact you're going to a drug-
and booze-soaked party with
with your horny boyfriend.

Medium.

Like claiming you've taken
up running completely for
its health benefits, though
you know it's more about
all that positive attention.

Small.

Like writing erotica in
private moments. Dirt,
floating in your bathtub.

THE FOURTH WEDNESDAY IN JUNE

I inform my family that I'm going
out to a play with a friend. Don't
know why I feel the need to lie,
except if nothing comes of this writing

thing, it will just be another whim
lacking follow-through. My last hobby
was watercolor. I took a class and
everything. Really enjoyed the creative

process and my teacher said I had
a talent for landscapes. He even offered
to introduce me to a friend who has
a gallery. But then Papa got sick and

I quit the class and just never picked
up a brush again. Maybe someday. Or
maybe the writing will fill the same
artistic gap inside me. Who knows?

I tuck the journal with the unfinished
story deep inside my purse. Not sure
if I'll find the courage to pull it out.
Not sure I'll find the drive to finish it,

let alone keep working on the collection
I envision writing. *Vanilla* is supposed
to be only the start of a themed anthology
that I think about calling *Essential Oils*.

ON A WEEKDAY EVENING

Starbucks is pretty low-key.
Easy enough to find the *High
Desert Muses*. They're the only
group in the place. "Hi. I'm Holly.
I called . . . Betty, I think?"

I'm Betty. Welcome, Holly.
She is an older woman, late
sixties, maybe. *Let me introduce
everyone.* There are five tonight,
though Betty says the group

has eighteen members.
At the table is Sally, who is
around Betty's age. The two
of them write romance. *Bodice
rippers,* Sally claims. *Good stuff.*

Sahara is a couple of years older
than me. She's penning a memoir
about her time as revue dancer
and casino guru's wife. On the far
side of the table is Daniel, a second-

year college student, working on
a dystopian horror. And finally,
Bryan, who happens to teach English
at Mik and Trace's high school. Thus,
his drive to write teen fiction.

I sit beside Sahara and across
from Bryan. I can't help but notice
his striking green-apple eyes. Mostly
because of how they are focused on
me. *What are you writing?* he asks.

My face flares, but whether it's due
to his attention or because of what
I'm writing, I'm not sure. "Um, uh . . .
well, I'm just sort of getting into it,
but I, uh . . . started a piece of erotica."

Sally is unfazed. *Great market
for that, especially if you go straight
to ebook. Betty will be an excellent
resource for you too. She's penned
her fair share of the spicy stuff.*

My expression must say more
than I want it to because everyone
laughs and Betty says, *What? I may
be old, but my memory's still good.
And my husband isn't quite dead yet.*

Way too much information.
But hey, if she's willing to share
it, I guess I can take imagining it.
Wait. Maybe not. But I'm laughing
too. I think I like these people.

AND THEY ARE, IN FACT

Really good writers, to a one.
Bryan's contemporary young adult
novel will hit kids smack where they live.

I know, because I've got three living
there now. Dystopian horror is not my thing,
but Daniel can build an exceptional

scene, one that puts you right on the edge
of your hard plastic Starbucks chair.
When I ask him where he learned to

write like that, he says, *I took creative*
writing at Western Nevada. You should
check it out. The community college

is right here in Carson. "I definitely
will. Thanks." As a general rule, I'm not
much into romance either, but the bodice-

ripping kind could possibly make me change
my mind. And Betty's leaves little doubt
that she can write erotica. Steamy! Sahara's

writing is probably the weakest of the lot,
but she can put a paragraph together, and
her sensory details are vivid. Around the table,

the critique is accurate. Not unkind,
but not exactly easy, either. I could
learn a lot from these people.

SO WHY

When they ask if I brought anything, do
I shake my head? "Maybe next time."

No problem, says Betty. *Most people*
don't read the first time round. I hope

you come back to us. This is a good
group. You can trust their opinions.

We have fun traditions too, says Bryan.
Like going out for drinks after we finish.

Who's up for it tonight? His head rotates, person
to person. But only Sahara says, *Heck, yeah.*

The smile she gives Bryan makes me think
they've got something going on. But when

he looks at me with those riveting eyes,
I find something beyond friendly attention

there. Heck, yeah. "Sounds like fun." As we start
toward the door, Bryan falls in so close behind

that his breath falls over my shoulder, teasing
the pulse in my neck. He wears some delicious

woodsy scent. Stop it, Holly! Never again,
remember? That's what I promised myself after

that disappointing night with Grant. So why
am I more than a little interested in this game?

IT IS A GAME, PURE AND SIMPLE

And likely dating to Victorian
times. I'd say all the way back to
the Neanderthal era, except primitive
people had no use for flirtation.

We meet up at Kentucky Kate's—
as the name implies, a country-
flavored tavern. Jace and I used
to come here once in a while.

Don't ask me why. Country
isn't really my thing, or Jace's,
either. We enjoyed slumming
it, I guess—cheap beer, with

peanut chasers, toss the shells
straight onto the wooden floor.
The place hasn't changed a bit.
There's an open booth in back.

I slide into one seat, Sahara
into the opposite, leaving Bryan
with a choice. He sits across
from me, which might disappoint

me, except his long legs end up
knee-to-knee with mine. *What's
your pleasure, ladies? I'll go to
the bar. Service can be slow here.*

He nods toward the cocktail
waitress, who must be at least
seventy, but is completely charming
in a short, frilly square-dancing dress.

When he goes for our drinks,
Sahara starts peppering me with
questions. *How long have you
been writing? Married? Have kids?*

She is bubbly and enthusiastic,
which normally might bother me,
except she makes the conversation
all about me. Most women like to

talk about themselves. By the time
Bryan returns, three margaritas
in hand, Sahara could fill him in
on my pertinent stats. She doesn't.

She redirects the conversation
until it's all about him. Will he get
a cost-of-living increase? Is his
job safe? How's his wife? The last

question makes me scope out his
ring finger. It's bare. But so is mine.
Sahara's cell warbles. She glances at
the caller ID. Decides to answer.

IT'S HER MOTHER

Who needs her help *right now,*
despite the late hour. Sahara
apologizes, polishes off her drink,

and goes. Leaving Bryan and me
all alone. Well, except for the bar
full of cowboys. He acts like there's

no one else around, however, all
his attention lasered directly toward
me, courtesy of those incredible

eyes. He's got an amazing smile
too. Every now and again, our hands
brush as we reach for peanuts.

The energy exchange is real.
Palpable. I go ahead and give him
a brief rundown on my family.

He talks about his accountant
wife with little emotion. When
he discusses his students, though,

he comes alive. I watch his mouth
when he speaks, wonder how he
kisses. I'm aware of his scent—that

evergreen cologne over warm male
skin, a heady combination. The deep,
dark forest folds in around me.

IN THE DEEP, DARK FOREST

Where treetops dodge
the slanted light, wind
loses voice midst the silent
creep of shadows and

all

creatures shed their skins,
disclose the luminescence
within. In that hallowed place,
truth is survival, and so

secrets

scatter, lie exposed upon
the leaf-strewn loam, carrion.
There, in the belly of time-
wearied woods, façades

are

peeled away and the fruit
that lies beneath may be
elegant or insect-ridden.
Integrity and sin will be

revealed.

Marissa

THE FOURTH OF JULY WEEKEND

Doesn't mean much to me, except
Christian will be spending time at home,
like it or not. Coming off a three-day
business trip to New Orleans, he isn't in

a hurry to say good morning. He's asleep.
Or is he? A strange noise leaks from
the intercom. Singing? In Shelby's
room? Yes, and it's definitely Christian.

Blackbird singing in the dead
of night. Take these broken wings
and learn to fly . . . He used to sing
that song when she was a baby,

back before we had any idea that
something was wrong with her.
But it's been years since I've heard
him so much as hum, and lately

he barely even talks to her. A massive
lump forms in my throat. Coffee.
That will wash it down. The kitchen
is relatively cool for July. Our usual

stifling heat wave hasn't hit yet. In fact,
most of June was misty cold. Not Nevada weather
at all. I would have welcomed the gray.
But moisture isn't good for Shelby.

Through the intercom, I hear Christian
take on morning CPT, another job
he almost always avoids. *Okay,
little girl. Let's play some drums.*

Shelby does her best drum
impression as her daddy thumps
the crud loose from her lungs.
She must be in heaven, having

so much masculine attention.
God knows it's been a hell of
a long time since I've had any.
Not that I'd know what to do with it.

I sit at the counter, elbows against
the cool granite, looking out
the window at the mountain's
steep angles. The Sierra drew

my parents here three decades
ago. It has long been a presence
in my life. There are people who live
without mountains, but I'll never be

one of them. There are people who
live without spouses and children.
I'm not so sure I could never be
one of them. I almost am now.

I DRINK MY COFFEE BLACK

And I brew it strong. *The way coffee*
was meant to be, my dad told me

the first time I tried it, *with* sugar
and way too much cream. I miss

Mom and Dad, who opted for
a nomads-in-an-RV lifestyle some

six years ago. Right before I got
pregnant with Shelby. They swing

through the area a couple of times
a year, reliably including Labor

Day weekend. They are Burning
Man devotees, don't ask me why.

God-awful hot on the playa in
early September. And dusty. Dirty.

No, that celebration of the carnal
is definitely not for me. But they've

gone every year since 1993.
This year, they decided to summer

on the West Coast, so they'll stop
by any day now, en route to California.

I should probably check my email,
see if they've sent any updates.

They refuse to keep a cell phone,
but Mom has a laptop and whenever

Dad spies a Starbucks, they stop
for coffee (*the way it was meant*

to be) and free wireless. That's my
parents. Too chintzy to spring for

cell service, but willing enough to
pay for overpriced but good coffee.

I take my strong-brewed, supermarket-
brand coffee to the little dining room

nook where my computer resides.
This dinosaur Dell has been my main

source of sanity for the past four
years. If I have to be sequestered at

home, at least I have a way to bring
the world to me. One day I'll venture

out into it again. But for now,
cyberspace will mostly have to do.

MY INBOX

Is relatively empty. There is a message
from Mom: *In Elko. Spending a day*
in Lamoille Canyon. See you soon.

Spam message. Spam message. And
one from Drew. *Have you seen this?*
There's a link to an article about

a new drug that the FDA has approved
for clinical trials. Stem cell research
and molecular therapy have focused

quite specifically on SMA and in recent
years have produced some promising
leads. This one is a motor neuron

replacement product, derived from
embryonic stem cells, and it looks
like it could be the miracle so many

SMA parents have been not so patiently
waiting for. "Christian! Come here!"
Expectation surges through my veins,

making my heart work really hard.
This probably couldn't "cure" Shelby,
but it might make her better. "Christian!"

What is taking him so damn long?
Has he gone deaf? I push back from
the computer, speed-walk down the hall

to Shelby's room. "Christian. Did you
hear me? I need to show you something." He is sitting beside the bed,

tumbler in hand, watching a Thomas
the Tank Engine DVD with Shelby.
She doesn't seem to mind the smell

of scotch, but it makes me want to gag.
I fight to keep my voice steady. "Christian,
can I see you for a minute, please?"

What? He looks up at me with droopy
cocker spaniel eyes. *Oh, okay. Daddy*
will be back in a little while, baby.

Not in that condition. I nudge
him toward the dining room.
"It's not even ten in the morning,

and you're drinking? Not only that,
but getting drunk right there beside
your daughter's bed? Are you crazy?"

He pours himself into a chair, puts
his glass down on the table, leans
his head into his hands. Says nothing.

BUT THE WAY

His shoulders tremble, like boulders
in an earthquake, tells me he has fractured.

I should go to him. Put my arms around
him. Tell him I love him. But I don't

know if that's true anymore. "What's wrong
with you?" Colder than I meant it to be.

Several silent seconds pass. Finally,
he straightens. *What isn't wrong?*

He reaches for the mostly empty glass,
helps himself to the last swallow.

She's failing, can't you see that? And
there's nothing we can do but watch.

"No. I was just reading about this new
drug. It's still experimental, but—"

Stop it! Just stop, Marissa. Every fucking
time some new treatment comes along,

you get your hopes up. I used to let you
get mine up too, but not anymore.

"We have to hope. Every day she's still
here brings us that much closer to a cure."

God, you sound like you're soliciting
donations or something. His voice

keeps growing louder. *Look, even if*
that new drug turns out to be a cure,

Shelby's not a good candidate for
treatment. You know that as well as

I do. If it's still experimental, they'll
look for kids with the best chances of

improvement. They need poster
children, to keep the funding coming.

He gets up, takes his glass into
the kitchen. Through the doorway,

I see him refill it. "That's not going
to make things better." So why do

I suddenly want one myself? Anger
crawls up my neck like an insect.

A buzzing, stinging wasp. "Did you
fucking hear me? I said—"

A DOOR SLAMS

At the end of the hallway.

Everyone between here and
Reno can hear you, Mom.

Shane stomps into the room.

If the two of you have to fight,
can you keep it between you?

He pokes his head into the kitchen.

Seriously, Dad. Mom's right.
What's wrong with you?

Christian mumbles something.

Yeah, well, says Shane. *Life pretty*
much sucks and then you d—

He stops himself. Moves closer.

Lowers his voice. *What's the point*
of arguing? He wants to wallow.

"I don't understand why he—"

Shane interrupts me. *Not so hard*
to figure out. It's all about guilt.

ABOUT GUILT

It's

something learned
in childhood—this nibbling
of conscience that begins
with denial—*I did*

not

push my little brother out
of the swing. No contrary
evidence, you think you've
gotten away with it until

an emotion

you don't quite understand
percolates inside of you—
an acidic brew that churns
until you make the decision

to

confess those bruises on
Junior's forehead are,
indeed, because you shoved
a little too hard. Choose to

ignore

it, and guilt will inexorably
corrode, chewing flesh and
soul until it bleeds you out.

Andrea

CAMPING WITH MY PARENTS

Was never exactly fun. But at least
now they have an RV. When Missy
and I were kids, we had to rough it.
Sleeping bags on the ground,
under the stars. Mom and Dad

rated the scruffy tent so they could
have scruffy sex on their scruffy
air mattress. Marissa and I got to
hear it all. Nice. Especially the sort
of decrepit howl Dad always did

when he finished the deed. Some
things you never forget, no matter
how hard you try. I'm pretty sure
they don't still have sex, but maybe
I should ask. Harley and Brianna

are supposed to sleep inside the trailer,
on the sofa bed. I still get a sleeping
bag on the ground, under the stars.
Or maybe the backseat of my car.
Especially if there are bears at Prosser,

and I'm pretty much thinking there
must be. Which makes me wonder how
many bears prowled close by Marissa
and me while Mom and Dad indulged
in a little growl-and-howl nookie.

I DON'T MENTION BEARS TO HOLLY

We sit at her neat kitchen table, waiting
for Harley to help Brianna pack for
our overnight excursion into the not-

quite-wilderness. I said yes to Holly's
half-ass coffee, though I promised Dad
I'd stop by Starbucks in Truckee before

heading north on the highway to Prosser
Reservoir. "Harley and I are doing Fourth
of July in Sparks. You guys want to join us?"

Sounds fun, but we've got Aces tickets.
Baseball and fireworks. Can't get much
more "God Bless the USA" than that.

Trace stomps into the kitchen, carrying
a book. *Mom. You left this on the patio.*
When did you start reading this crap?

Holly laughs. *I wouldn't call it "crap,"*
exactly. But it's definitely not great
literature. She shows me the not-lit

in question. The cover pictures a cowboy
riding a horse under a full moon, juxtaposed
with a schoolmarmish woman in a low-cut

dress. "*Widows along the Trail*? What *is*
it, exactly? A western romance? When
did you start reading that crap?"

She glances toward Trace, whose head
is completely immersed in the fridge.
Drops her voice very low. *Remember*

I told you I wanted to write . . . She mouths
the word *erotica. Well, I joined a writers'
group and two of the ladies write romance.*

Some of it's pretty . . . whispers, *steamy.
I've been looking into it—reading a little
of it—and I think I could write it too.*

She looks at me expectantly. I'm not
sure how to respond, though. "Wow.
I thought the writing thing was a joke."

Trace emerges from the refrigerator.
*Oh, no. She's serious about it. Like
she was serious about painting.*

And before that, ceramics. And before
that, hydroponic gardening. And before
that, hosting fantasy birthday parties.

This is different, Holly insists. *Because
I could actually make money writing.
At least, eventually. I mean, I have to*

*get good at it. But I'm willing to work
hard. Wouldn't it be cool to get paid for
making up stories about . . . you know?*

THAT EARNS

A major eye roll from Trace,
who clomps across the polished

tile to the table, nibbling a cold
chicken leg. *You want to write*

racy books, Mom? Why not a nice
paranormal? Or maybe zombies.

Oh, says Holly, *they have those too.*
They're not all *westerns, you know.*

I think she missed his point.
"Not sure I'd want to read about

hot zombies. I mean flesh eaters
aren't exactly what I'd call sexy."

Guess it depends on what kind
of flesh they're eating. Deadpan.

I spit my mouthful of coffee
halfway across the table.

Trace! But Holly's laughing too,
as she hands me a paper towel.

He rolls his eyes back and forth
between us, grinning. *Just saying . . .*

WHEN DID HE GROW UP?

When was the last time I really
looked at him?
talked to him?
acknowledged him?

He used to tag along sometimes
on the girls' playdates.
to the girls' parties.
with the girls to the movies.

Seems my view of him has been
filtered through the girls.
colored by his mother.
distanced by distractions.

Somehow, over the past decade
he has stretched tall.
he has muscled up.
he has come into his own.

And all that makes me wonder
what else I've ignored.
what else I've slept through.
what else I've missed.

While I let my own life slip away.

AS I MUSE

Jace cruises into the kitchen,
polished brass hair sleep-tousled.
He is shirtless and wears only

a thin pair of flannel shorts
beneath his smooth-skinned

chest. He comes over to Holly,
kisses her cheek, draws his
black walnut eyes even with mine.

Morning, ladies. Then, to Holly:
Thanks for letting me sleep in.

Trace is the image of his father,
except for the narrow high-bridged
nose inherited from Holly. He says,

*Did you see what Mom's reading,
Dad?* He's a trouble caster too.

Jace picks up the book, opens
it, turns to a page somewhere
about halfway in. Skims it for

a second or two. *Holy lima beans!
Hope you're picking up pointers.*

Holy lima beans? Half amusing,
half confusing. And very Jace,
whose Kansas roots cling to him,

though his parents moved him west
as a kid, close to forty years ago.

He puts down the book, heads
toward the coffee maker, and
I can't not notice the attractive

outline of his butt beneath his clingy
shorts. He pours a cup of brew, and

as he turns, I have to force myself
to look higher than his waistband.
God, I'm almost as bad as his wife.

Then again, I do have an excuse,
because while she has easy access

to regular sex, I most definitely
do not. I haven't slept with a guy
in six months. I'm getting a wee bit

antsy. "Those girls should be about
ready, don't you think?" I take

my empty mug to the sink. "Trace,
would you mind rounding them up
for me? We really should be going."

The "round them up" remark reminds
me of Holly's book. Pointers, indeed.

FROM HOLLY'S PLACE

To Truckee will take over an hour,
the three of us and our overnight
stuff pretty much crammed into
my elderly Subaru. The girls sit

in back, annoyingly thirteen—
whispering,
giggling,
waving at semis,
discussing boys.
The main boy being Chad, who's—
almost seventeen,
like, really cute and buff,
on the basketball team,
amazing at gaming.
Funny. I remember him with—
greasy long hair,
a face full of zits,
basketball height, but
not much in the way of muscles.

For some idiotic reason, that
makes me think of Jace, half
naked in the kitchen. He's not
exactly "buff" either, but that

didn't detour my inappropriate
semi-lust for his pretty-damn-
good-for-a-guy-his-age's body.
I really need to get a [sex] life.

I TRY TO TUNE OUT

The backseat boy chatter.
The highway begins to wind
up the mountain, and I'm really
glad I'm driving. The last time
I rode shotgun along this stretch
I almost asked Geoff to pull over.
He would not have appreciated

puke-spattered leather upholstery.
That man was unreal. Charisma,
personified. At least until he had
a drink or two, and then he was
anything but charming. Geoff
was, in fact, the guy who made
me swear off men for the past

several months. No sex, not even
amazing sex (and it was that),
is worth the kind of verbal
abuse that man threw at me.
To top it all off, I found out
he's married but he expected me
to stay with him. Uh . . . right. I put

an immediate end to it. To us. To
amazing sex, or any sex except
the battery-operated kind. But
while that might take the edge
off, it only whets my appetite
for a more impressive menu. Solo
orgasm isn't even a decent appetizer.

THE MENU

At the Cottontail Ranch is five-
star-rated by politicians and
rock musicians and well-heeled
truckers, heading east from Carson
City. Porn princesses serve

Hand Job

and pretzel snacks, along with
fifteen-dollar drinks. Order
appetizers from column one:

Girl-Girl
Massage (Give or Get)
Oral Delight.

Everything is à la carte,
with entrées from

Around the World:
Full French
Asian Wet
Neapolitan.

While your main course
is prepared, you can enjoy a

Vibrator Show.

Front-row seats run a little
more, but you don't want a

Half-and-Half

view. Finish your meal with a

Whipped Cream Party
Champagne Party

or maybe just a little

Love at the Y.

Holly

RUNNING IS A CURE

And not only for stress and blubbery
butts. It also alleviates writer's block.
Can't believe you can get stuck writing
sex scenes. Then again, since most

(make that all) of the sex I've had for
the past couple of years has been
pretty uninspired, trying to write
a believable orgasm is taking a lot

of imagination. Jace said he hoped
I'd pick up pointers from my current
reading. I felt like telling him he should
study the book as a sort of refresher

course. Can't remember the last time
he went down on me. Cunnilingus
is barely even a memory. Maybe
I need a girlfriend. One with an active

tongue. I've never been with a woman.
Should I put that on my prefortieth
birthday wish list? Where would I even
find one? On craigslist? Nah. Too

many crazies. I could pay for one,
I suppose. Take a little trip out to
the Cottontail Ranch? Oh my God.
What's wrong with me? Hormones?

MORE LIKELY

It's too much erotic romance
reading. I push myself harder
uphill, lusting only for solid
thigh muscles. My own, that is.

I got a bit of a late start this
morning. It's nine-ish, and
the mercury must be approaching
eighty-five. Sweat rains from

my face and soaks my sports
bra and shorts. The temp will
climb close to a hundred by late
afternoon, but it should cool off

to just about right when the sun
goes down. A great evening for
Reno Aces baseball and Fourth
of July fireworks on the river.

Jace is a huge baseball fan.
He hoped Trace might take up
the sport, but the only one of
our kids who gives two hoots

about baseball is Bri. Go figure.
She even played Little League,
until she decided she liked boys
too much to kick their butts at ball.

SMART GIRL

Takes after her mother, who
is currently downshifting for
the final long uphill driveway

push. I reach the top, winded and
dripping. Excellent run. I need
water and coffee, in that order.

As I reach the back door, I can
hear voices. Okay, the neighbors
can probably hear them. Jace

and Mikayla are at it again. I half
consider backing away and letting
them yell themselves into a stupor.

Better not. I push through the door.
"What is going on? Do you two know
any other way to communicate?"

Mikki is flushed, sour cherry
red. *Dad says Dylan can't come
with us to the game tonight.*

You're still grounded! yells Jace.
*Grounded means no proximity to
your boyfriend, who, just by the way,*

*is the reason you're grounded in
the first place. Why is this even
an argument?* He looks at me for help.

Why must they always plop me
smack in the middle? I want to
argue for Mik that it's been almost

three weeks. Well, two and a half,
anyway. But if I make Jace look
like the bad guy, the whole day—

and evening—will be miserable.
He doesn't much like having
his authority questioned. Not by

the kids. And not by me. "Honey,
this was supposed to be a family
evening. Dylan probably has plans—"

*He does! He planned on hanging
out with me. Please, Mom. I haven't
seen him in weeks. He'll buy his*

*own ticket and everything. Don't
you get it? I have to see him.
I . . . I . . . am in love with him.*

Jace snorts. *You don't know the first
thing about love. And if you believe Dylan
is in love with you, you're crazy.*

*Shut up, Dad. You think you know
everything.* And now she shatters.
Why are you so fucking mean?

OOH, BAD MOVE

I jump in immediately. "You apologize
to your father right now, Mikayla Jean."

Please, please
apologize. If
you don't, he's
going to plant
his will deeper.

The two of them sit there, arms crossed.
"You want to get ungrounded, don't you?"

Plum-faced, jaws
rigid, the two of
them look so much
like each other
I want to laugh.

Jace starts to blow, but I shake my head.
"Won't happen unless you say you're sorry."

Her shoulders
drop and her hands
fall to her sides.
But still her eyes
glisten anger.

Sorry. It almost sounds like she means
it. *I shouldn't have said "fucking."*

NOT EXACTLY AN APOLOGY

So I'm kind of blown away
when Jace's anger dissipates

in a cloud of inappropriate
laughter. "What's so funny?"

It takes a few seconds for him
to hiccup to a stop and say,

She just reminds me of me is all.
I once said something similar to

my dad. The main difference
being, he kicked my ass. I don't

guess I feel the need to kick
your ass, Mikayla. But regarding

Dylan and the game, my answer
is still the same. And until you show

us a little respect, as far as I'm
concerned, you're still grounded.

Her fuse quite obviously lights
again, but Jace doesn't stick

around for the explosion.
He leaves the disarming to me.

I'VE ALWAYS CLAIMED

My kids could come to me, tell
me anything, and I'd welcome
the conversation. But words
do not find me easily now. So
when I tell Mikki, "I'm really

glad you and Dylan are in love,"
I listen to her go on and on about
how sweet he is instead of saying
what I know I should: don't hurry
away from us, daughter; don't rely

on a boy for love, when we have
more than enough for you right
here, and he will probably break
your heart. When she finally has
to catch her breath, I can't believe

I hear myself say, "I'll see what
I can do about ungrounding you."
And listen to another volley about
summer beaches and bike rides
with Dylan instead of warning

her: being in love doesn't mean
you're required to have sex. And
while sex is most certainly enhanced
by love, love isn't necessarily better
just because it comes with a penis.

GAME TIME

Is seven p.m. To beat the crowd, we arrive
at five thirty. The team is autographing.

Bri goes all fan girl. *Please, please, please,*
can we get them? I especially want . . .

She rattles off some names I've never heard
of. How does she know them? Jace and Trace

are more interested in hot dogs, so
I volunteer to stand in the signing

line with Bri. Mikayla promises to
meet us at the seats after a restroom

run. I watch the progression of signature
seekers. Most are younger kids with parents.

But there are also several college-age girls,
and they're probably looking for phone

numbers beneath the players' names.
Can't blame them. A couple of these guys

are really kind of amazing, especially
this one. Number thirty-two. Who smiles

at Bri while fondling me with barely
blue eyes. When we turn away, she says,

Hey, Mom. I think he liked you, with
something approaching awe in her voice.

We find our seats, and while we wait
for the rest of the family, my dirty

little brain starts composing a new story:
Big Bat Groupies. Starring number thirty-two,

and opening in the home team locker room.
I've got him just about down to his jock-

strap when the boys arrive, loaded down
with goodies. *Where's Mikayla?* asks Jace.

I pull my head out of number thirty-two's
pants. "I haven't seen her, but I could use

a potty break myself. I'll go look for her.
Don't eat my hot dog." It's a hike to the ladies'

room. I don't see Mikki anywhere, but on
a sudden hunch, I circle the grandstands,

to the rapidly filling grassy hillside above
right field. And, of course, my suspicions

are confirmed. Right there, back to me,
is my older daughter, kissing Dylan Douglas.

A DAUGHTER

Is a rainbow—a curve
of light through scattered
mist that lifts the spirit
with her prismatic presence.

Is

a shadow—a reminder
of something brilliant
ducking out of sight, too
easily drawn away. She is

an

aria, swelling within
the concert chamber, an

echo

reverberating across
a miniature sea.
She is a secret,
whispered, a hint

of

what we cannot know
until it finds us.
She is a sliver of her
father, a shard of

her mother.

A daughter is a promise,
kept.

Marissa

AN UNINTENDED BENEFIT

Of buying this old house, perched high
in the Reno foothills, was it came
with a giant deck that has a spectacular

vista of the city. It's especially lovely
at night, when windows light in quick
succession, glittering gold like fairy dust,

and multicolored neon creeps up tall
casino walls. And on certain evenings,
when the city fathers so decree,

they shoot fireworks over the concrete
below. New Year's Eve, usually.
And always on the Fourth of July.

Most locals have to drive to see them,
fighting for parking and a view location.
But all we have to do is step outside

the sliding glass door and settle into
our comfortable patio chairs. When Shane
was little, we hosted fireworks parties

for his friends. And our friends. Back
when we still had friends. When we still
had each other. Too much heartbreak ago.

TONIGHT, FOR THE FIRST TIME

Shelby will watch fireworks.
Even in July, evenings here
can be cool. Or windy. Neither
is good for lungs battling

to breathe. But tonight is warm
and breeze-free. So Shelby and
I will have our own fireworks
party. Shane is off with some new

friend. Could be a boyfriend,
I suppose. Other than the usual
"safe sex, please" warnings, I try
not to probe too deeply into that

part of his life. I don't need, or
want, the details. Would I feel
differently if he were straight?
Maybe. But seems to me a father

would be more interested in his son's
sex life than a mother would. I don't
think Christian wants to know the details
of our gay son's sex life either, though.

When Shane came out two years
ago, Christian kind of turned his back
on him. Of course, by then he had
long since turned his back on me.

WHEN I LET MYSELF THINK

About it, sometimes I get angry.

Other times, I mostly feel numb.

But every now and again, sadness

descends, bone-brittling cold,

a deep of winter hailstorm, and

I am defenseless in the face of it.

I look through the polished glass

at my husband, asleep on the couch.

There, lost in sleep, his face wears

no worry, and I glimpse a ghost

of the man who wrote me love letters.

Time has stolen more than sonnets.

I SLIP PAST HIM

And down the hall to Shelby's room.
When I come in, her eyes turn
eagerly away from *Cinderella*
and toward me. "Are you ready
to see fireworks?" It takes several

minutes to maneuver her out of
bed and into the stander. She weighs
next to nothing. I could fold her
like a pie crust. She is a dryad,
soon to return to her sacred woods.

"It's a beautiful night. Perfect
for sharing. Oh, look. Shelby's got
wheels." She smiles at the old joke,
and we're off on our adventure.
As we roll past Christian, still snoozing,

Shelby points and sings something
very close to *Daddy*. The word
drops gently into whatever dream
he's maneuvering, because his body
responds with a definite twitch.

"Daddy's sleeping," I whisper.
"He had a very hard day." Not true.
He spent the morning working in
the study, then started on the whiskey
at lunch. Home, sweet home.

IT REALLY IS GORGEOUS OUTSIDE

Not quite nine o'clock, the evening sky reminds
me of agate—black, swirled with auburn

and indigo. Stars scatter across the breadth
of it, though you can see them best above

the mountain, away from the distraction
of the city's lights. "Look, Shelster.

There's the Big Dipper. See how it's shaped
like a giant spoon?" Her eyes glitter,

and she holds her palms toward the heavens,
as if trying to catch any small falling piece

    of them. *Pri-ee*, she says. Pretty, and
    I think I must show her more prettiness,

sooner rather than later. We sit for several
minutes, soaking in the honeysuckle

perfume as the night grows dark enough
to light the fuses. And finally, they do.

Shelby's eyes grow wide with delight
as the sky bursts with color. Red. Blue. Green.

After the second mushroom of light, the door
opens and, sleep-mussed, Christian comes outside.

Fireworks. I almost forgot about them.
May I join you ladies? He pulls a patio

chair over beside Shelby. Reaches for
her hand. I am without words. Without

breath. Afraid to even try and breathe,
because if I do, this unexpected moment

might vanish into ether. We are too far
from the source to hear the percussions,

so we sit in semi-silent awe of the aerial
beauty, the exception being Shelby's barely

there *Ooh. Pri-ee*'s. I hold her other hand,
and we are a three-link chain. For the first

time in a very long time, we don't feel
broken. The twenty-minute display ends

too soon. A slight breeze now blows over
the hills, and I must take Shelby inside.

"Okay, little girl. Time for bed." I hope
she dreams of fireworks and unbroken chains.

BEDTIME ROUTINE ACCOMPLISHED

Shelby is well on her way to Dreamland.
I leave her with a kiss on her forehead.

It's almost eleven, and Shane still
hasn't come in, though his curfew

is fast approaching. I think about
waiting up for him, but Christian is here.

Might as well let him play the part
of disciplinarian. I can hear him in

the kitchen, so I go to join him
there. When I slip into the room,

he turns from the counter, two drinks
in hand. *Thought you could use this.*

What the hell. Maybe just one.
I take the glass. "Thanks. And thanks

for tonight. You made Shelby very
happy." I try a sip—cognac, neat.

My favorite, once upon a time.
He remembered. That surprises me.

Christian gulps his own drink. *She deserves*
happiness. Glad she saw fireworks.

And now it starts to feel awkward.
I take a bigger sip, enjoy the slight

burn, and the pleasant way my head
is starting to buzz. Call me a lightweight.

"Okay, well, I'm going to bed. Shane
is a little late. You might want to call him?"

Christian agrees and I go to my bedroom,
finishing my drink on the way. Before

I do anything else, I turn up the volume
on the intercom. Just in case. Brush my teeth.

Wash my face. Slip out of my clothes
and between the black satin sheets—my own

bedtime routine accomplished. Brain
pleasantly fuzzy, I slide toward sleep.

And the door opens. Shuts. Footsteps
cross the floor. It's Christian. "What's wrong?"

Nothing. The covers lift and he finesses
into bed. *I wanted to sleep in here. Okay?*

My first instinct is to tense. But then
a deeper, needier instinct takes over. "Okay."

HE SMELLS OF WHISKY-BEADED SWEAT

But permeating that is the scent
of male. Testosterone or pheromone,
wherever it is carried, it cannot be ignored.
Though his back is to me, I reach for
him, and when he turns, I throw myself

into his arms and we are kissing with
a ferocity that only strangers share.
His hands snarl into my hair, pin
my head to the pillow as his mouth
travels my neck, teeth and tongue working

in unison, to the taut knots that are my nipples.
He grows rigid against my leg and I sigh
but say nothing, afraid words will wake me
from whatever dream this has become.
One hand comes loose from my hair.

It moves down between my legs, finds
undertow. One finger, two, go inside me.
Three. Plunging. I am close but fight
cresting with all I have. He licks along
my torso, and his face seeks the V

between my thighs, tongue joining
fingers. This is something remembered.
But when he pushes inside me, the intensity
of his thrusts is nothing I've ever known.
Who is this man? Does he belong to me?

WHO IS THIS MAN?

In the glass, he is a stranger,
yet his scent is familiar
and the hand at your elbow
feels proprietary there.

What

this means, you do not know,
so you walk a little faster. But
he keeps pace. The hair at
your collar pricks, though you

are

not in danger. The hour
is busy, the sidewalk
crowded. All you have to
do is scream. But before

you

open your mouth, his velour
voice calls your name, stirring
leaves of memory, coaxing
them to float, and now you're

afraid

they won't. When you turn
to study his face, something
in the way he looks at you
makes you search for the *us*

of

you, buried in the deep
of his eyes. Yes, you knew
him once, but he is a changeling.
Metamorphosed. And you run.

Andrea

THE PROBLEM WITH HEALTH KICKS

Is they work best if everyone living
under the same roof shares them.
Honestly, I'm proud of Harley and

how she dove headfirst into the whole
eat-right-and-exercise-daily thing.
We even found her a special summer

program: Healthy Eating + Exercise =
Live Longer, or HEELL, which is
supposed to read "heel," not "hell."

And hell is kind of what it's become.
Because the thing about programs
is someone has to facilitate them.

And for Harley, that someone is me.
I am her HEELL sponsor, I guess.
Which means trying to fulfill her request

that we eat all organic. But Sak 'n Save
is between work and home, while
Whole Foods is twenty minutes out

of my way, not to mention out of my
budget. Hope she never discovers
I'm saving containers and bags marked

organic and putting regular produce
inside them. Hell hath no fury like
a scorned farmers' market devotee.

MY SECOND JOB

As her facilitator is helping her
count calories, fat, and sodium

content in every foodstuff that
goes into her mouth. Oh yeah,

and into my mouth too. Who knew,
in a regular one-patty fast-food

cheeseburger, with condiments,
a person consumes:

Calories	359	
Fat calories	178	
Total fat	19.8	grams
Saturated fat	9.2	grams
Sodium	976	milligrams

And you don't even want to look
at french fries or a Big Mac.

Fast food is now officially excised
from our diet, as is "anything white."

Meaning potatoes, pasta, rice, or bread,
except for whole-grain particleboard.

Dessert? Sure, as long as it's sugar-
and fat-free. I've taken to keeping

a big bag of M&M's in my desk.
Hiding candy from my kid. Nice.

AND THE BEST THING OF ALL

Is the exercise program.
Harley is up before dawn

every morning so she can walk
or take a long bike ride before

it gets too hot. Worse, she wants
me to come along. *Please, Mom.*

You could drop a few pounds
too. And exercise is more fun

if you don't have to do it all by
yourself. Anyway, I want you

to live a long, healthy life. That
one got to me a little. I do breathe

too hard after an uphill chug,
and my heart beats way too fast.

So I'm awake with the sun,
trying my level best to keep up

with my thirteen-year-old
daughter. My only hope seems

to be that she'll grow tired
of the rigid routine. It's only

been a couple of weeks. Right
now, she's still going strong.

RIGHT THIS MINUTE

She's going strong at her summer
program and I am on my lunch
break. I brought a nice chicken
salad from home—low-cal dressing

and all. But because I can't help
but rebel at least a little, I am at
Starbucks, where I will indulge
in a "Caramel frappuccino . . .

Okay, make it light and . . . skip
the whipped cream." Damn. Good
habits will rub off on a girl, if she
isn't careful. I take my change

and am putting it away when
someone behind me says, *Hello,*
Andrea. It's been a while.
The voice—Geoff's voice—tugs

on a string of emotions. None
I can't smile my way out of,
however. "Yes, it *has* been a while."
I move sideways to let him order,

and as the barista pours his
large coffee, the darkest roast
you have, I collect my too-sweet
dessert-substitute frappuccino.

MOMENTS LIKE THESE

Are awkward. I don't know what
to say. Whether or not just to turn
away, find a seat, and expect him

to leave me alone. He saves me
worrying about it. *May I join you?*
I'd love to catch up a little.

I shrug. "Sure." He leads me to a table
for two by the window, and it feels
all déjà vuish. Except he's drinking

Seattle roast instead of Grey Goose.
We sit, studying each other for
several hushed seconds. He looks

clear-eyed, and somehow softer
around the edges, like he's shed
an armored shell. Someone has to

break the silence. *How have you*
been? And how is your daughter?
Nice of him to ask about Harley.

"I'm fine, thanks. And Harley is
thirteen. Which pretty much tells
you all you need to know." Chitchat

definitely sucks. "What have you been
up to?" Go ahead. Ask him. "And
how's your wife?" A Russian transplant.

He winces. Sips his coffee. Finally
says, *Marina and I split up.*
She couldn't take the drinking . . .

or how I acted when I drank,
I guess. He pauses at the way my
head is bobbing. *I'm six weeks sober.*

When Marina walked out, I had
a come-to-Jesus. He stops again,
perhaps hoping to find me still

nodding. "I'm sorry about your wife,
Geoff. Are you sure it was . . ." I'm
embarrassed to finish it. Or even

admit I might have played a part
in their breakup. But he says, *It had*
nothing to do with you, if that's

what you're thinking. She never
found out about you at all. No,
she left because of how I treated

her. I've had a lot of time alone
to think about things, and I realize
I wasn't very nice to you, either.

Now he reaches across the table,
slides his hand over the top of mine.
Looks into my eyes. *I'm sorry.*

HE SOUNDS SINCERE

But liars often do. I pull my hand
away. "It's okay. I'm over it." Mostly
true. Except for that annoying voice
inside my head that keeps insisting

the only part of me men want to
cherish is the welcome mat just
south of my belly button. And this
man was instrumental in making

me feel that way. *Look. I said*
some really ugly things, but I hope
you know it was the booze talking.
Alcoholics tend to be assholes.

That makes me smile. "Can you
please tell that to my ex? He doesn't
seem to get it." He definitely didn't
get it on the Fourth of July, which

Harley insisted we share with
him, Cassie, and Chad. Poor young
man had to escort a thirteen-year-old
sort-of-but-not-formally stepsister,

not to mention one who's really
crushing on him and is so too young
to be seen with, to and from the food
and drink stands. Meanwhile, Steve

and Cassie were tying one on,
while I (who wished I could)
got to play the adult in the group.
Considering how childish Steve

and his girlfriend acted, somebody
had to. But it wasn't exactly my job.
Next year, fireworks will just be
Harley and me. Please, God.

I thought your ex was pretty
much out of the picture, says
Geoff, interrupting the unpleasant
flashback. *Is he bothering you?*

"Well, yeah. I mean, he bothers me
a lot. But he's not messing with me,
except he moved back to Reno and
Harley wants to see more of him."

He grins. *Does that mean you*
might have a few more spare
evenings for things like dinner
and dancing? Is he actually

saying he wants to ask me out?
Apparently, he is. *I know I don't*
deserve another chance. But I hope
you'll consider giving me one.

ANOTHER AWKWARD SILENCE

I really don't know what to say.
So I glance at my watch. "Oh.

I need to be back at work in, like,
five minutes . . ." True statement.

"I'll think about it, okay?" I stand,
and he does too. "I am sorry about

your wife. But I'm happy it made
you take a look at yourself. Be well."

As noncommittal as I tried to make
it, he asks, *So, can I call you, then?*

"Uh . . ." Be firm. "I guess so."
Wow, way to be firm. "But no

promises." Okay, a little better.
Out the door. Into my car. Drive

six blocks to work. All the time
remembering his alcohol-fueled

rages. The awful names he called
me. The way he lied to me. The way

he lied to his wife. His lust-filled
eyes. (Okay, that was kind of a turn-on.)

But turn-on or no, the rest counted
more. There will be no second chance.

TURN-ONS

Are personal. One woman's
Adonis is another's Puck, and
a few open-minded fairies
might even find him to their

taste.

Curly hair. Straight hair. Zero
hair. Chest hair? A must for
some, and yet for others it

is

a deal breaker. Younger lover?
Older? On one hand, youthful
stamina is a powerful lure;

on the

other, experience might trump
it, especially in matters
regarding proper use of the

tongue.

Scent? Is sweat disgusting or
intoxicating? Cologne—leather,
forest, some exotic spice, or a hint

of the

sea? And as for flavor, a swift
lick of salt may be repellent or
aphrodisiac. It's all up to the

taster.

Holly

WHAT'S ROTTEN

About uncovering a child's deception
is that no matter how much you'd
like to overlook it, you really can't.

Which wouldn't be so bad, except
when you're not exactly innocent
yourself. Regardless, poor Mikayla

is liable to stay grounded all summer
at the rate she's going. Catching her
with Dylan at the game was unfortunate.

I thought about letting it go, and might
have, except when Dylan noticed me
watching them and sputtered their kiss

to a stop, Mikayla looked at me with
such defiance that it basically pissed
me off. I'm only human, and a human

parent at that. Dylan read me
perfectly. Gave her another quick
kiss. Evaporated into the crowd.

When I gestured for her to come
with me, I thought she just might
follow Dylan instead. But she chose

obedience. Not sure if she thinks
it was worth it or not. I confiscated
her car keys. And her cell phone.

And she's just so bored. Maybe
what she needs is a part-time
job. Something to keep her mind

busy and off Dylan. At the moment,
the most exciting thing about her
life is sparring with her brother, who

makes every effort to approximate
a burr, working its way into her
hide. The bickering is relentless.

Someone has to referee, not to
mention make sure Mikki plays
by the rules. Mostly, it's been me.

I can hardly wait to escape
the house tonight, the second
Wednesday in July. Maybe I'll

even read a little of my writing.
Beyond that, I'm really looking
forward to seeing Bryan again.

SO I'M A LITTLE DISAPPOINTED

That he isn't at Starbucks tonight.
In fact, it's all women—Betty, Sally,
Sahara, a younger girl, and me, in a micro-
mini that will go unnoticed by Bryan.

Welcome back, Holly, says Betty.
You remember Sally and Sahara.
And this is Grace. I hope you brought
something to read tonight. I don't

know about everyone else, but I
wouldn't mind listening to a little
erotica. It's been a little chilly
at home, despite the hot weather.

Everyone laughs, which only makes
my face burn hotter. "I brought some,"
I admit. "But I don't want to go first!"
That isn't a problem, as group protocol

dictates we start with the youngest
member. Grace reads a tolerable
ten pages of wizards and warriors.
Not my thing, so I don't feel qualified

to comment, except to say, "I could
really visualize the world you created.
And Lambert sounds really hot."
Betty has more to say about unwieldy

sentence structure, something
I struggle with myself, so I listen
to her suggestions with interest.
As the second youngest here,

it now becomes my turn. Oh, why
not? I extract the journal from my bag,
start with an apology. "It's really rough,
and it's the first thing I've tried to write

since college." Everyone encourages
me to continue, so I launch into *Vanilla,*
read the whole thing, lowering my voice
when I come to the words "fuck" and "cock."

Don't worry, says Sally. *No one's*
listening, except for everyone within
earshot! I think that couple over
there are going to go home to bed.

Not a bad piece of writing, Betty
says. *A couple of suggestions.*
Consider writing third person, so
it sounds less autobiographical.

And if you have kids at home,
you might think about writing
only on your computer and locking
your files. The journal is a bust.

NOT SURE IF SHE MEANS

She thinks it *is* autobiographical,
but either way, she's probably right
about both the third person and

the journal. "Thanks. I'll keep that
in mind." After a few more pats on
the back, we move on to Sahara,

whose memoir is every bit as spicy
as my attempt at erotica. Wow.
She has lived a fast—and painful—

life. When she finishes this chapter,
a humiliating episode of abuse at
the hands of her ex-husband's father,

we are all speechless. Sahara looks
each of us in the eye. *I know it's hard*
to believe. But every word is true.

Oh, I believe it, says Betty. *That*
must have been extremely difficult
to relive, let alone write. Brave girl.

Major understatement. Respect
blossoms for this woman, who
has survived more than I'll ever face.

I can hardly concentrate on bodice
shredding and passionate lovemaking
in a corporate boardroom. But I try.

POST-CRITIQUE

Sahara invites me to her place.
It's quiet, and the alcohol is free.

She lives in a pricey subdivision,
in a perfectly kept three-thousand-

square-foot Mediterranean-style villa.
The spoils of war, she calls it, and

considering what she read tonight,
that sounds accurate. Inside, it's painted

in warm colors, and original artwork
hangs on the walls. All in all, it is tasteful

but comfortable, with overstuffed leather
furniture, modern electronics, and lots

of greenery. *Make yourself at home.*
She lights several scented candles.

*Do you drink wine? I've got a nice
cellar.* I ask for red, and she pours

a pricey pinot noir into a couple
of Riedel glasses. Everything about

Sahara is a complete surprise.
Including the way she sits next to

me on the loveseat, though there's
an entire empty sofa beside it.

She draws her long, suntanned
legs sideways up beneath her, so

> that her bare knees kiss my leg.
> *I liked what you read tonight.*
>
> *Was that fact or fantasy?* She sips
> her wine and appraises me with frank

eyes. "A bit of both, though the fact
didn't measure up to the fantasy."

> She smiles. *It rarely does. I thought*
> *marrying into gaming royalty*
>
> *would make me a princess. But I was*
> *just a concubine, with benefits.*

"I'm sorry," I say, and I mean it.
"But you would never know it, just

to look at you. You seem so together.
And writing a memoir. Wow. That's . . ."

> *Probably really stupid. But even*
> *if I never try to get it published,*
>
> *the writing has helped me sort*
> *through the bullshit, you know?*

We drink wine—one bottle, two—
and discuss bullshit, though hers

outweighs mine, one thousand to
one. I am conscious of the thick

scent of candles—apple custard—and
the silk of her skin, where her knees

have lifted the small hem of my skirt
and now rest against exposed thigh.

She is talking about dancing—how
the girls so valued for their beauty

quite often have low self-esteem,
something men eagerly take advantage

of. I am tipsy as hell when I sputter,
"I heard lots of those girls are lesbians."

Some are, though many more are bi.
Being with other women is easy.

Fewer demands. Better orgasms.
At my doubtful look, she says, *What?*

Don't tell me you've never . . . really?
She rocks up onto her knees. *Want to?*

I know nothing about being with
a woman. I rely on her—and instinct.

IT GOES INTO MY JOURNAL FIRST-PERSON

I can move into third during revisions.
Not that I'd change anything else.

Hyssop and Rose

She is bold, kissing me without clear invitation,
or maybe I did invite her somehow. No matter.
I can't help but kiss her back. Her pout is yielding,
her tongue, the gentle flick of a serpent, testing.
And she tastes of berries. "Lie back," she says.
She lifts my top, licks me from my navel
upward, her hair a soft trickle over my belly.

It smells of summer—hyssop and rose,
a hint of grass. I close my eyes, give myself
up to the carousel whirl—slick gloss lips and
practiced tongue, circling. Circling. Lifting
me close and closer to the horizon. And when
she goes down on me, there is an eloquence

no man could match, and I understand why
she said being with women is easy. Naïve about
how to give back, all I have to do is try. I reach
into my psyche, tap some ancient well of instinct.
In the same way that she carries me skyward,
I sample her salt, bring her to climax, find
immense satisfaction in reciprocal flight.

SATISFACTION

There's a reason why
Mick Jagger sang about
a lack of gratification.
If he couldn't get none,
back in the day,

who

might reasonably expect
that they might? Anyway,
what the Stones forgot
is that even if a person

can

find plenty of girly action,
the desired result
is only good for so long.
You can have sex for hours,
with multiple partners, orgy-style,

get

off until you're downright
sore. But rest up for a day
or two, restore bodily fluids,
rebuild desire, you'll want

some

more. Satisfaction is transient—
an interim state of mind.

TRANSIENT DESIRE

Is an unfortunate thing, at least
if your partner is on a different
trajectory. I had pretty much

given up on sex, after such a large
span of time with zero interest from
my husband. Then, one transcendent

evening brought it all back to me—
the power in a kiss; the coax of skin;
the brilliant bolt of love in crescendo.

Pragmatism should have told me not
to believe one night of fireworks
meant anything at all. Christian is still

just as driven. Still goes to work early.
Comes home late or not at all.
Still sleeps in the guest room, and

he hasn't returned even once to the bed
I still refer to as "ours." Guess I could
look at it as a one-night stand, something

I've never done. Does every one-night
stand make you feel so used the next
day? So unworthy of love? So alone?

ALONE ENOUGH RIGHT NOW

To make me seek refuge in
the figurative arms of my computer.
At least it's warm. There's an email
from Drew, giving me the lowdown
on his fishing trip. CAUGHT MY LIMIT.

WISHED I LIKED TROUT. DO YOU? I'VE
GOT PLENTY IN THE FREEZER. Why do
people who don't care for fish go
fishing, anyway? I write him back:
ADORE IT. BRING SOME OVER. I'm not

especially wild about trout. But I do
enjoy seeing Drew. Next I come to
ITV's quarterly newsletter. Often
I hit delete immediately, but this
one has Christian's name prominently

featured in the front-page headline:
VP CHRISTIAN TRASK ANNOUNCES
GAMRICH, THE FUTURE PERSONAL
IN-HOME GAMING SYSTEM.
The article goes on to describe how
the gaming system will revolutionize

gambling. People will be able to lose
their paychecks (uh . . . play for big
bucks) in the privacy of their own
homes. And they'll be able to do it
on their flat-screen TVs, much like

they now play Xbox and Wii.
InnoTechnoVent, with Christian at
the helm, leads the charge toward
in-home gaming. All it will take
is a little tweak of the current law.

Working on that is the company's
imaginative young lobbyist Skye
Sheridan, who, according to the
newsletter, JOINED ITV IN 2006
AND IS, SAYS TRASK, "A RISING STAR."

Unbelievable. I haven't heard one
word about GamRich, though
it has been in development for
quite some time. I understand
now why Chris has been so busy.

Distracted. Absent. But there was
a day, not so long ago, that he'd
have shared this kind of news
with me. Kept me in the loop,
updated me on its progress.

And if everything is going so well,
why doesn't he act excited? Why
doesn't he come home at the top
of the world? Why does he hit
the bottle and loiter inside it?

I FINISH MY COFFEE

Think about hitting the treadmill.
Scrap that. It's a nice morning.
I'll take Shelby out for a walk.
We both could use a little fresh

air before the breeze lifts summer
pollen, stirs it into the afternoon.
Shelby is currently hiking with
Dora the Explorer, but I know

she'll prefer the real deal. "Hey,
sugarplum. Mama could use some
exercise. How about we go for
a little stroll? It's pretty outside."

She answers with a big grin
and a small *Ow . . . si . . .* As I begin
the complicated routine of getting
her dressed and into her stander,

her smile stretches wider and
wider. I think, for the umpteenth
time, how lovely she is when
her essence escapes the bounds

of exterior handicap. Shelby
is a sprite. A wood nymph, in
disguise. Who could guess, by
looking at her, the mystery within?

IT'S NOT A NICE MORNING

It's absolutely perfect—temperate
air, hovering under blue topaz
skies, scalloped with puffs of clouds,
the kind you find pictures in.

"Look, Shelster. See the sailboat
in the sky? And over there—that's
a teddy bear. Do you think it's made
of cotton?" She knows cotton balls.

Shelby looks up, tries to figure out
what I'm talking about. She giggles.
C-ow-d. A good approximation
of "cloud." Now she points. *G-o.*

"Go? Well, okay, if you say so."
We swing down the sidewalk,
toward the hem of the mountain.
Though we live at the top of a hill,

the walks here are relatively level,
making for easy pushing. Front
yards are striking in summer bloom.
I tell Shelby, "Every flower has a name.

There's Rose. Coreopsis. And that one's
Lily. Ooh. Can you smell the perfume
they're wearing?" We are steeped in it,
and in the green scent of grass. Today

is one of two sanctioned lawn
watering days, and sprinklers chirp,
wasting just a little in a fine mist.
Shelby laughs at the cool, settling

against her sun-warmed skin.
We walk at a decent pace (might as
well ratchet up my heart rate), past
neighbors, working in their gardens.

I wave, and most smile as they return
the gesture. But now we round a corner
and almost bump into an elderly poodle,
pulling his elderly owner along.

She stares at Shelby, openmouthed.
My first instinct is to snap, "Didn't
your mother ever tell you staring
is rude?" She hurries on, and I force

my temper onto a back burner. "See
the birds, Shelby?" Robins. Sparrows.
Jays. I am not monster mommy. "Oh and
look. Those are insects." Dragonflies.

Butterflies. Bumblebees. Shelby tries
to repeat the words. If I close my eyes,
she is almost normal. And I am a regular
mommy, out for a stroll with her daughter.

ALL SENSE OF REGULAR

Comes crashing down with the approach
of a raunchy little car. Not sure what

kind, only that it has seen much better
days. It is in dire need of a muffler,

but its noisy exhaust has a hard time
competing with the deep bass rumble

spilling out the window, along with
a good deal of smoke. When the car

draws parallel, slowing to assess
Shelby and me, the smell of marijuana

is overpowering. Five teens are inside.
One ducks down in the backseat.

"Shane?" I say out loud, though he
can't possibly hear me past the radio.

The kid riding shotgun pokes his head
out the window. *Holy shit. Check out*

the retard. Or maybe it's an alien
from the planet Ugly-As-Uranus.

Hey, do aliens dig weed? He takes
a big drag, exhales out the window,

and the driver punches it. The ugly
car does its best to accelerate.

"Shane!" I yell, knowing it's stupid.
"I can't believe . . ." But they're gone.

Shelby, of course, has no clue what
just happened, or how hateful those

words were. Her attention returns
to a painted lady butterfly, floating

by on a gentle current of breeze.
I, however, am seething a nasty brew

of anger and hurt, plus a shot or two
of incredulity. How could Shane be

a part of that? He is many things, but
I've never known him to be cruel.

"Okay, Shellcake, we'd better go
home. The wind is coming up."

We reverse direction, walk away
from the sun, into our own shadows.

WISH I COULD BLAME THE WIND

For the way my eyes look
by the time we get home.
Red. Puffy. Underlined by
thick, dark smears. I take
Shelby inside. Settle her back
in bed. Vacuum her lungs
with the cough assist, a bit
of precaution. As I finish,
I hear footsteps and anger

threads its tentacles through
my veins, pulses. "Mama
loves you, little explorer."
I'm careful to close the door
behind me before rushing
down the hallway. "Shane!
What in the hell—"
I skid to a stop at the sight
of him—hair disheveled and

tee shirt torn. Blood drips from
his nose and split-wide lip. One
eye is swelling closed and will
wear a raccoon-style bruise
tomorrow. Before I even ask,
he says, *I stood up for her.*
Told him he was a no-good
shit-leaking asshole. He's pretty
good with his hands, though.
I think I might need stitches.

STITCHES

Would that you could
repair every injury
with needle and thread;
that the right stitch in

time

might salvage a friendship
torn by betrayal, or
a career ripped by backroom
politicking. But life

doesn't

offer that option. Nor
can we patch a marriage
worn thin with age,
zero reason, zero

rhyme

to the discontent. No,
we have little choice
but to lick our wounds,
bind them tightly

with

resignation, and move
on, certain only that
a stitch in relative time
isn't always able to save

nine.

TIME IS RELENTLESS

In its forward march. And while
science insists it's impossible, anyone with most of their brain will say
that time picks up speed as you age.

One day pours into the next,
fills a week. One week spills
into the next, completes a month.
One month surges into the next,

swells into a year. One year
overflows into the next, and
the next thing you know, you
are up to your neck in decades,

no way to work your way out
of them. No way to cycle back
through them and change what
you would, if only you could.

If you only knew that from
the start, and believed it, how
differently you might mold those
years, day into week into month.

ALL IT TAKES

To make you start thinking
about time is three birthday
cake stickers, decorating a
single month on the calendar.
August is still a few weeks out,

but there will be many candles
upon a trio of cakes. Holly's
fortieth falls on the ninth, and
she is the definition of a Leo—
Confident. Adventurous. Proud.

Melodramatic. Pretentious.
Not that I follow astrology.
But Mom and Dad do, or at
least they used to. My birthday
is the last day of the month.

That makes me a Virgo. Dad
always said I fit the description—
someone more comfortable
with routine. Reliable. Helpful.
Inflexible. Skeptical. The reason

I know about Leos is because
Missy's birthday is the twenty-
first, which puts her on the cusp.
A little Leo, a little Virgo. Together,
more than a little schizophrenic.

HER SON MIGHT BE SCHIZO TOO

Most of the time, Shane's placid
as pudding. Today, however, he got

into a fight. Missy had to haul him
off to emergency to get his lip stitched.

She called me at work, close to panic.
Her voice was a loud staccato.

> *P-please, Andrea. You h-have to*
> *c-c-come. R-right now. I tried*
>
> *to get h-hold of Christian, but he's in*
> *a meeting and c-can't be disturbed.*

I took an early out, hurried to Reno
from Carson. By the time I got here,

forty-five minutes later, Shane looked
pretty awful. But it was clear to me

that he'd be fine. Missy doesn't need
more drama. Why must she create

unnecessary hysteria for herself? Kids
get stitches all the time. Okay, Harley

probably never will. That girl is too
much like me—cautious, to a fault.

RIGHT NOW

She and Brianna are hanging
out, and though they think they're
totally sneaky, I happen to know

they're cooking up a birthday
surprise for Holly. Thirteen-year-
old girls aren't great at secrets.

In fact, they pretty much lay it on
the line. And when they think
they're whispering? Not so much.

I didn't really have to eavesdrop.
Forty is, like, so over the hill,
I overheard Brianna say.

She can't be that old, said Harley.
No way. She paused to consider.
Maybe she's lying about her age.

Brianna thought about that for a
second. Cracked up. *If you lie about
your age, you don't say you're older.*

Oh, said Harley, all serious. *Yeah,
I guess you're right. At least, not
when you're over twenty-one.*

IT WAS ONE OF THOSE CONVERSATIONS

That hinted at what the girls will
be, once they hit maturity. They
are so close now, it scares me.
I'm happy that Harley has
Bri. It's not like she's

her only friend, but
she's the only one she has
bonded with quite so tightly.
In that too, Harley is much like
me. One really close friend is worth

ten decent acquaintances.
Especially when you're plotting
something like a surprise party. It's
a big undertaking, particularly for a kid
Brianna's age. The girls are creating lists.

Guest list. Food list. Decorations list.
It's totally sweet of Bri to dream it
up, though I'm not sure she can
pull it off. All the giggling and
whispering will likely give

them away. But at least
they've got something to talk
about besides boys in general and
Chad in particular. If I hear Harley call
him *walking, talking awesome* one more time . . .

A FEEBLE COUGH

Rattles the intercom. Shit.
I hurry to Shelby's room.
"Hey, baby. It's Auntie Andrea.
Let's take care of those lungs."

I haven't actually done this
myself, but I've watched Missy.
Let's see. Antibacterial for my
hands. Turn on the cough-assist

machine. Check the pressure.
Damn. What should it be? It says
thirty/thirty. Is that right?
My hands start to shake. What if

I screw this up? As I stand here
stupidly, Shelby tries to cough
again. The problem is, she can't
cough well enough to bring up

whatever mucus is tickling
her alveoli. The cough assist forces
air into her lungs. Draws it out
again. Pressure in, thirty, pressure

out, thirty? It will just have to
do. Wait. What's this other
machine? God, I should know
the routine. Suction. Yes, that's it.

Shelby looks at me helplessly.
"It's okay, honey. I've got it
now." Please, God. Let me have
it now. I start to put the mask

over Shelby's face. Count.
I'm supposed to count to . . .
was it five? *Move. I've got it.*
Christian pushes between me

and the bed, jerks the mask
from my hands, goes to work,
coaxing green crud from his
daughter's lungs. As it gurgles

into her mouth, the second
machine sucks it out, carries
it off. Disgusting. Fascinating.
Wait. "Can I do something?"

Christian shakes his head.
Like what? It's under control.
It seems to be. He's cool. Efficient.
Shelby relaxes as her breathing eases.

I am, approximately, an idiot.
Then again, I would have
figured it out. Nerves got me.
But I wouldn't have given up.

BRAIN CRAMMED

With conflicting emotions,
I back out of the room, wander

into the living room, stand looking
out the sliding glass door at their

breath-stealing view. Some people
would be envious of this beautiful

house. At least, until they peeked
beyond the façade and into these rooms,

emptied of happiness, vacuumed
of hope. Despair hangs heavily

here, like the ocher velvet draping
the windows. I haven't seen Shelby

in a while and, even beyond her
breathing trouble, she looks thinner.

Transparent, almost. Barely there.
And yet, her will to live is palpable,

an entity unto itself. She is a flicker
surrounded by very dark shadows.

ONE OF THOSE SHADOWS

Drifts down the hall, tries to
overtake me too. *Why would she*
leave Shelby alone with you?

Keep. Temper. In. Check.
"She didn't have much choice.
You 'couldn't be reached.'"

Christian and I are like vinegar
and baking soda. Bad interaction.
"Important meeting, I take it?"

It was, in fact. So . . . The words
seethe from between his teeth.
What was the emergency, anyway?

He doesn't know? "Shane, playing
David to some kid's Goliath. Only
this time the Philistine conquered."

Chris registers zero concern.
Instead, all he shows is contempt.
What crawled under his skin? Idiot.

Bite. Back. Anger. "Apparently,
he was sticking up for Shelby.
Does that make him an idiot?"

Considering he's at the ER, yes.
This philistine has lost all compassion.
You can go now. I've got it covered.

THE PHILISTINES

Of biblical fame were much
too bold for their britches—
er, kilts—eschewing their lovely
Greek isle homes in a bid
to conquer Egypt. A very

big

ambition, not to mention
irrational, iron or no
iron. Next they set their
sights on the Israelites,
sending forth armor-clad

dudes,

led by a hulking giant.
But a half-naked kid managed
dead aim into his brain
with a slingshot. You might
expect that Goliath's fatal

tumble

might make them reconsider
their master plan for world
domination. But no. Battle
after battle, they went down
to defeat, until they crashed

hard

beneath the feet of Babylon.
Proving, then as now,
some people never learn.

SOME KIDS NEVER LEARN

You try and try to cut 'em
 a little slack, and the more
rope you give them, the more

determined they become to
 burn themselves with it. Case in
point, as she has been for months,

is my brash daughter, Mikayla.
 Here, I finally talk Jace into
ungrounding her, and what's

the very first thing she does?
 Totally disregards our imposed
midnight curfew. And not by

a few minutes. No, she comes
 bopping in three hours late.
Like she had no clue we might

be waiting up? Parents to Mikki:
 this was a test. One you failed
miserably. Which means, dear

one, you are sequestered
 again. Which is, doubtless,
a good thing. Less contact

with Dylan means less chance
of a summer STD. One can only
hope. Today, at least, she'll escape

her room for a barbecue at Jace's
parents' house. Whoopee. Wish
I could come up with a good excuse

not to go, but I've skipped out
on the family bonding thing too
many times in the past few months.

I'm putting together my not-quite-
world-famous potato salad when
Mik sweeps into the kitchen. *Mom!*

She sock-slides across the floor.
Guess what! I found someone
who might know your parents.

Something like dread plummets
into my belly. Not the reaction
I would have expected. I turn

from my onion peeling. "Really?"
Mik, who quivers excitement,
misinterprets my watering eyes.

Don't cry, Mom. It's only kind
of a maybe right now, but
I think it looks good. This lady

used to be married to this guy—
Leon Driscoll—who graduated
from Elko High in 1970. She says

his little brother got a girl in
his class pregnant the same
year. Could be a coincidence,

but I don't think so. She gave
me this Leon's email address.
I'm hoping to hear back soon.

Mikayla sucks in air, waiting for
me to say something. "Sounds
promising." It's the best I can do.

Mik deflates like I popped a hole
in her. *But aren't you excited?*
Look how close we're getting!

"Only maybe," I correct, dissolving
her smile. "Oh, Mikki. I don't mean
to seem ungrateful. It's just . . . scary.

I don't want to get my hopes
up until we know for sure. But
thank you for doing this for me."

I OPEN MY ARMS

And she accepts my hug, but only for
a millisecond. *Jeez, Mom, you smell*

like onions! You'd better wash your
hands with lemon juice. It's an old

remedy. *In fact, you'd better shower*
with it. At least she's laughing.

When her face lights up like that, I can see
her as a toddler—all smiles and wonder.

What happened to my cherub?
Is her halo still there somewhere?

"Okay. I should be finished here in
a half hour or so. Will you let your

father know? He's giving Tick a bath."
Poor dog was long overdue. I watch

my daughter's exit—all willow branch
legs and exaggerated hip sway. Where

did she learn that? I return to KP duty,
mixing in mayonnaise, mustard. Sweet relish.

Salt. Pepper. All without a taste test.
I'll trust my instincts. And skip the calories.

THE SENIOR CARLISLES

Live a couple of miles away, on a sprawling
five-acre ranchette, complete with a barn
lacking horses and a pool they hardly ever

use, except when we come over. The kids
head straight for the backyard, where
they're greeted by a matched pair of lion-

sized Newfoundlands. I can hear Brianna
screaming about dog spit. Jace barrels through
the front door, not bothering with the bell.

Anybody home? he yells. I follow him
into the vaulted-ceilinged hall. Sunlight
cascades from high windows, flooding

the Italian marble floors. I've always loved
this house, but not the way I feel when
I'm here. I'll never forget the first time Jace

brought me home to meet his parents. Not
sure if they expected something different in
the woman their son would fall for, or if they

were just a little jealous of Jace's obvious
attention to me. But that initial iced reception
set the tone for our relationship ever since.

In here, calls Marion, powering us
toward the kitchen. She is busy, putting
marinade on fat chicken breasts. *Henry's*

out back, deslobbering Brianna. Grab
a drink and take a dip. The water's perfect.
She barely glances in my direction as I set

the Fiestaware bowl on the counter.
Oh, you made potato salad again. Thank
you, dear. How can anyone so readily

make the word *dear* translate as "bitch"?
Help me! "How have you been, *Marion*?"
I try to make the name Marion translate

as "bitch." Don't think it worked. *Not*
bad. The arthritis has affected my golf
game a bit, but I'm trumping Henry.

Well, yeah. Henry's still carrying a full
client load at work. He's lucky to find
time for golf at all. "That's great, *Marion*."

Ha. That one almost sounded like "bitch."
Jeez, Holly. Grow up, would you? Marion
leaves the chicken to soak up the sauce,

washes—no, scrubs—her hands, including
using a brush to go under the nails. *Anything*
new with you? she asks, expecting me to say no.

I'm not about to discuss my writing, or
the search for my birth parents, so I guess
she won't be disappointed. "Not really."

SMALL TALK ACCOMPLISHED

I excuse myself for a bathroom
break, try unsuccessfully not to
look at the photos studding every
wall—a family history not only
complete but also celebratory.
Jace and his brother, Stan, at each
stage of growth. Henry, Jace, and
and Stan, fishing. Marion, cutting
flowers. The whole clan, skiing,
camping, traveling cross-country.

Mama

never

hung

a single

picture.

Papa

never

touched

a drop.

I detour to Henry Carlisle's well-stocked bar.
Four fingers of Dewar's might make this day
possible to wade through. I gulp pointer finger.
Wait for the brittle buzz before going outside
to observe today's chapter of Carlisle history in
the making. Jace and Henry talk law at the big
picnic table. Marion chides Mik for tanning sans
sunscreen. Trace and Bri race laps in the pool.

Beneath the barbecue smoke
lingers the perfume of fresh-
mown grass. The sky is a blue
so deep no single crayon could
replicate it. The Newfies pant
in the shade of an old maple.

You couldn't write a more
ordinary slice of Americana.
Jace is smiling. The kids are
laughing. And all I want to
do is find a quiet chair where
I can power down Dewar's.

I SCOOT INTO A LOUNGE CHAIR

Beneath the pergola, protected from
UV threat. Slide on a pair of shades.
Lean back, close my eyes, welcome
the smog of alcohol, hope it will soften

the grip of jealousy. Jace and I have been
married twenty years. But I have never
felt like a vital part of his family. There
is only one photo of me hanging on

his mother's walls—an uncertain bride
and beaming groom, surrounded by
our wedding party. In it, Marion appears
every bit as disquieted as I. I've always

wondered why she chose that one.
I mentioned the dearth of my photos
to Jace one time. His first reaction
was to deny it, but upon wall inspection,

> he had to admit I was right. Then he
> excused his mother like this. *Well, you*
> *have to admit you don't exactly insist*
> *on posing for snapshots with the fam.*

Laid it right back on me. Truth is,
he was right. The problem with wanting
too much to be a part of something is
knowing you very well might be rejected.

WHICH IS WHY, I SUPPOSE

I am trying so hard to impress
myself. If you reject yourself,

for whatever reason, it's time
to rethink. Reinvent. I watch

Trace and Bri play in the pool, still
children in essence, despite maturing

façades. I want to tell them not to
hurry. Adolescence is the beginning

of the end because the moment
you fall in love, you give away

the best part of yourself. I look at Mik,
who I know has already made

that decision, and I want to tell her
to take it back. Dylan will keep that

part of her, no matter where the future
leads them. I look at Jace, who I gave

the best part of myself to two decades
ago, and though I think he must still

carry it in his heart, I can't help
but want to take it back. If I could,

would I give it away again?

NO TAKE-BACKS

Regrets are like molecules.
We're all made up of a lot of them.
They are elemental. Building
blocks. The foundation of memory.

You

can dawdle in the past, allow
it to shadow you, or you can
walk forward into the light
of tomorrow. But you

can't

altogether disregard what has
already been—byways chosen,
detours taken. The misbegotten
decisions you can never

reverse,

but only by sorting through
them can you find where
you took the wrong turns
and gain proper perspective.

Time

is a parabolic lens,
bringing hindsight into focus.

PERSPECTIVE

Is something gained with experience.
A byproduct of living. Back-paddling
through time, trying in vain to slow

the current-driven journey. But we
just keep moving forward toward
our destiny. Never really in control,

despite our best efforts to manipulate
outcomes, because no one makes it
through untouched by the will of others.

Perspective might have hinted that
leaving Shelby with Andrea while I took
Shane to the ER would lead to a bad

situation—one that managed to wedge
Christian and me even farther apart.
Do you not have a lick of sense?

he demanded. *Your sister has no clue*
what to do for Shelby when she starts
to aspirate. If I hadn't come in . . .

I should have kept quiet. Instead,
I stabbed back, every sharp word chiseling
a well of silence we have yet to climb out of.

ALL DECKED DOWN

In cheesecloth-thin jammies,
I'm sitting alone in the kitchen,
trying to avoid scalding my tongue
on my first cup of coffee, when
Shane shimmies in. He takes one

look at me. Scowls. *Jeez, Mom,*
how old are those pj's? He goes
to the cupboard, extracts a mug.
Anyway, you gotta get dressed.
Gram and Gramps are coming over.

First I've heard of it. "How do
you know?" I watch him pour
coffee, add too much sugar and
a big splash of milk. Definitely
not his grandfather's style.

Gram and I have been talking.
We don't think it's good for you
to stay home so much, so Gramps
and I will watch Shelby while you
ladies see a movie and go shopping.

Shane arranged this with my mom?
My son is full of surprises.
"I think you've been watching
too much Lifetime." But it pleases
me that he's worried about me.

Still, my first instinct is to argue.
"I'm not sure . . . ," I start, but the way
his expectant look flatlines makes
me reconsider. "Well, maybe just
the movie. Shelby is a big responsibility."

I know, Mom. One you handle
all the time, without much help.
Gramps and I can take care of
her for an afternoon. I promise
she'll be just fine. He smiles, and

I glimpse a ghost of the child
who used to race me across
the playground. The one who
loved to swing and always begged
me to push him higher. Longer.

I have to admit I'm starting to
feel like a hermit. At times, like
a lunatic hermit. "Okay, you talked
me into it." It will be nice spending
some time with Mom. Even though

she very well might be the one whom
I inherited "lunatic" from. She's what
some call quirky. "I'll go clean up.
And Shane? Thank you." Suddenly
I don't feel completely unloved after all.

AN AURA OF NERVOUS

Excitement bubbles from me as I shampoo
my hair. Shave my legs. Exfoliate my face.

I feel like a teenager, getting ready for a date.
Okay, it's a date with my mother. But still.

A movie. In a theater. I don't even know
what's playing. When was the last time

I saw the inside of a theater? It was . . .
I can't even remember the movie now,

but it was a *real* date, with Christian. And after,
we went to dinner. And after that, we came

home. Drank too much wine. Had amazing
sex. The next thing we knew, I was pregnant

with Shelby. For the ensuing months, much
excitement. Happiness unfathomed. Until . . .

Until no more movies. No more dates. No
more afternoons with friends. They peeled

away, one by one. And who could blame
them? Who wants to hear about a baby who

will never walk? A child who will never talk?
A daughter who will never wear a wedding gown?

GETTING DRESSED

Takes a while. I'm not much
into fashion anymore. At home
I wear jeans or shorts and tee shirts.
In the winter, sweats. My rare
trips out are generally for

appointments. Groceries.
No need to look decent for those.
Everything I own is years old. Guess
I could use some new things after
all. I dig through my closet,

find a simple sundress
that I used to love. It hasn't left
its hanger in a very long time, but it
still fits okay. I comb my hair,
which could use a trim,

smooth lotion over too-pale
skin. A little makeup might help,
but all I find in the drawer is lumpy
foundation, dried-out mascara, and
a sift of peach-colored blush.

At least my cheeks can have
color. I give each a soft upward
stroke, trying not to chide the woman
who stares back at me from the far
side of the mirror. Not easy.

I EMERGE

From my room, looking half-
　　　　way okay. A low-key thrum

in the living room tells me
　　　　Mom and Dad have arrived.

They've been camping nearby
　　　　for a couple of weeks now,

but this will be the first time
　　　　I've seen them since their last

trek out west. Three steps
　　　　down the hallway, my eyes find

them. Dad, his salt-and-pepper
　　　　hair braided long down his back,

looks every minute of sixty-three
　　　　years old. Mom has aged better,

though she worries no less.
　　　　She keeps fit, and that might

be why. Dad is round. Mom
　　　　is straight and slim and wears

skinny jeans with all the aplomb
　　　　of a woman thirty years younger.

Shane is in earnest conversation
with Dad, but turns his attention

my way. *Whoa. What happened
to you, Mom? You look like a girl.*

That makes me laugh. "I still
clean up pretty nice, I guess."

I go over, give Dad and Mom
consecutive pecks on the cheek.

Not enough for Dad, who
reciprocates with a grizzly bear

hug. *That's how to say hello, little
girl. I've missed the hell out of you.*

Save the small talk, says Shane.
You and Gram get out of here.

"Let me just check on Shelby
first . . ." I start in her direction,

but Dad stops me. *Shane and I
will take it from here. We've got*

our own plans. You go on now.
He propels me gently toward the door.

JULY HEAT

Presses down hard. Mom and I
hurry to the car. And then I freeze
beneath the steering wheel. Maybe
this wasn't such a good idea.
"Uh, where do you want to go?"

Someplace close, I hope. Just
in case. *Andrea recommended*
Sierra Summit. Nice theater and
excellent shopping. In fact, we're
supposed to meet Andrea there.

Another setup? "Sounds good.
I've never been there." Haven't
been that far from home since
they built the place, and it's only
five or six miles. We head east in

silence, merge onto the southbound
freeway. Out of the corner of my eye,
I can see Mom giving me the once-
over. *You need to get some sun.*
Your vitamin D count is probably low.

No use arguing. Especially when
she's totally right. "I know. It's just
hard. Christian has been so busy at
work, and Shane's been escaping
lately too. I can't leave Shelby alone."

Pack her up and take her with you.
A little sunshine wouldn't hurt
her, either. She clucks her tongue—
a forever-annoying habit. *So, what's*
going on with you and Chris?

Straight for the jugular, that's my mom.
But where did the question come
from? "Who said anything was going
on?" Or did that someone say nothing
was going on? "We're doing okay."

Mom stares wordlessly out
the window. Finally, she says,
I heard Chris sleeps in the guest
room. That the two of you barely
speak, and when you do it's always

with anger. A marriage can survive
a lot of things, but not a total
dearth of communication. I know
it's really none of my business,
but if you want to talk about it . . .

She waits expectantly. But I'm in
no mood for confession. I could
ask about her own marriage's near-
death experience. Instead, I respond
simply, "Not much to talk about."

CONFESSION

The last place any wavering
Catholic wants to find himself
is behind an incense-woven
curtain, waiting to offer up

confession.

A priest might say it's a tonic,
but the confessor knows
it's a bitter brew, not sweetened
by the promise of absolution. He

wrings

his hands as he considers how
much time he has this week
for Hail Marys. Should he rattle
off each and every sin, or save

one

or two for next time? Would
God know—or care—if he left
a rotten little secret or five
stashed way down deep

inside

his heart? Would Lucifer
quit whispering to him if
he opened his mouth, let all
his nasty bad habits spill

out?

Andrea

NASTY BAD HABITS

If you needed a definition of "Steve,"
that's what the dictionary would
give you: nasty bad habits. He smokes

(tobacco hourly and pot when he can
afford it). He drinks (way more than
the two per day that are supposed

to be kind of okay for you). He's on
some sort of prescription feel-better
pills (allegedly to combat depression).

What's he got to be depressed about?
He's working part-time, contributing
not much to Cassie in exchange

for a place to live and three square
(okay, maybe triangular) meals a day.
And Harley can't wait to see him.

God, that pisses me off. It almost
makes me hope who she really wants
to see is Chad. Almost. Not sure

which of those two losers, with very
large *L*s, I'm most jealous of. Neither
will ever love her the way she deserves.

I'M TORN

About letting Harley visit her dad.
I know she's being exposed to
things she shouldn't be. But I worry
that if I throw a fit, keep her away,
all she'll do is rebel. Isn't that what
teenagers do anyway? I would have.

But I didn't need to. As I kid, I was
free to experiment with whatever
I wanted, however I pleased. My parents
were regular hippies. When I was
little, we lived a communal lifestyle.
Six hippie couples, their children,

and the odd stray, farming soggy
ground in Oregon. We had white
chickens. Mallards. Big hissing geese.
Cats to kill mice. Mutts to kill cats.
Guns that went hunting and came
back with rabbits. Squirrels. The choice

parts of deer because whitetail were so
plentiful that the rest of them was
left to rot in the woods. *Don't fret*
about it, Dad would say. *Something*
out there will eat the leftovers. I'm sure
he was right. But I fretted anyway. Still do.

NOT QUITE AS MUCH

As I'm fretting about my daughter
right now. She's with her dad—not
to mention Chad. At least Brianna
is with her. Can't believe it was so

easy to talk Holly into it. Then again,
lately Holly's head is anywhere but
where it should be. She called last
night. *Hey,* she said. *I need you to*

cover for me. I told Jace I was going
out with you. She hesitated, no doubt
wondering how much to give up. *I . . .*
um . . . am having drinks with Bryan.

Nothing kinky. He's having some
marriage problems. Like Holly's
the one who should be counseling
someone about their marital woes?

Whatever. God, if I worried about
Holly every time she did something
stupid, I'd be soot-gray and sea-hag-
wrinkled. It's not like Jace is going

to come to me, looking for Holly,
though. Right? Holy crap. Why did
I say okay? Great. Something else
so not my problem to worry about.

LATE SUNDAY MORNING

Sierra Summit is relatively quiet—
people still sleeping, or maybe at church.

I went to early services. Wouldn't Mom
and Missy be surprised? No one knows

I've gone looking for God. Not sure
I've found him yet, but there is this huge

emptied well in me that feels sort of half
full when I melt into the small congregation,

sit quietly, and open myself to the light.
Not looking to judge or be judged. Just

searching for possibilities. Which reminds
me of Holly. I can hear her now. *Possibilities?*

You mean, like, the kind with penises?
I wish I could quit thinking about her.

Maybe the movie will help. I drive
around the parking lot, looking for

Missy's van. It's easy enough to spot—
a hulking blue Ford, big enough to hold

Shelby's special equipment. Not that Miss
takes her out much anymore. The two

of them are cave dwellers. Glad Shane
talked her into venturing out into the real

world. The one she inhabits is where
nightmares germinate. I dial her cell.

She picks up too quickly. Waiting for it
to ring? "Hey, girl. I'm here. Where are you?"

Mom thought Thai sounded good
for lunch. You ready to Thai one on?

Oh my God. A joke? She must be hitting
the plum wine. "Sounds great. See you in a sec."

The restaurant is right next door to
the theater, which is much too far across

the blistering parking lot. It must be
pushing ninety-five already. I can see

Mom and Missy through the window. Wow.
The resemblance gets clearer every year.

Mom must have found the fountain of youth.
She could pass for Missy's sister. Considering

the way pain has notched itself into the skin
around Missy's eyes, her not-much-older sister.

NOT ONE WORD

Of which I say, of course, as I join
them at a simply appointed table.
Hope the food is spicier than the décor.

I slide into a stiff, straight-backed
chair. "Hello, girls." I look directly
at Missy. "Great to see you out

in broad daylight. I was beginning
to think you'd joined the living
dead." Missy's smile slips and, too

late, I consider what I just said.
Shit. Damage control. "What?
You don't read vampire novels?"

The corners of her mouth twitch,
but her eyes hold zero humor.
Not a big fan of the genre, no.

Mom attempts rescue. *I am. Just*
as long as the vampire doesn't
sparkle his victim into submission,

or come in through her window
to hang out and watch her sleep.
Can't stand boring bloodsuckers.

OKAY, THAT WAS FUNNY

Too bad I just took a big sip of water.
It comes snorting out my nose. That,
at least, makes Missy laugh, though
Mom looks horrified at the spray.

Andrea Dawn! You are disgusting.
If there was ever any doubt about
your paternity, this erases it. Uh . . .
Not that there ever was, of course.

Wait. What? The buoyant mood
sinks just a bit, but I can't quite
wrap my brain around the reason.
"Are you trying to tell me something?"

No, no. It was just a joke. But then
it didn't sound like one and I . . .
should probably just shut up now.
What looks good? She opens her menu.

Wow. Talk about planting a seed
of doubt. But he has to be my dad.
I inherited his skyscraper forehead,
steep cheekbones, aquiline nose.

My eyes are the same peculiar
speckled blue. *Robin's eggs,* Mom
has always called them. And always
she adds, *Just like your father's.*

Which should completely assuage
the disquiet sifting through me
right now. The waiter ambles over
to take our order. Mom requests

green curry with tofu—having
a vegetarian day, I guess. Missy asks
for pad Thai, obviously the only
dish she knows. Somehow I've lost

my taste for Thai. But, lucky me,
they also have limited Japanese.
"I'll have the tempura vegetables
and a California roll, please."

The waiter nods, heads toward
the kitchen. Mom waits until
he's out of earshot. *You have to
be really careful of sushi, you know.*

*One time your father got hold of
some badly prepared sashimi. Boy,
was he sick! I mean, geysering out
both ends. He never touched it again.*

Perfect. I'll probably never touch
it again, either. And it's long been
a favorite of mine. "Thanks, Mom.
Maybe I'll just stick to the tempura."

THE CALIFORNIA ROLL

Goes untouched. I must be losing
it. Mom and Missy chitchat around
bites but, as hard as I try to tune in,

my mind keeps sliding away from
now, into a slipstream of yesterday.
Black-and-white reruns of Oregon.

Missy and I, silent, outside the window
as Mom and Dad loudly "discussed"
the emotional toll of communal sex

and possible outcomes. One of them
being pregnancy and hazy genetic
markers. Holy shit. I am mired there

in the manure when my cell rings.
The conversation around me halts
as I reach for my phone. Harley.

In hysterics. *Mom? Come and*
pick me up right this minute, okay?
Please. I want to go home, and

you have to take Brianna home
too. I freaking hate her. I thought . . .
She shatters, and I'm not there.

"What did you think, honey?"

I thought she was my friend.

A FRIEND

Is a wellspring
of understanding.
A catch basin for grimy
little secrets that can
scarcely be voiced.

A friend

holds the tissue
box when you splinter.
Accepts confession, and yet

won't

demand details,
regardless of perceived
juiciness, too intimate to
confide. A friend is never too

cross

to commiserate.
Never too busy to
pull up a chair. Never so

certain

about an outcome
as to insist you've made
a mistake. A friend is never
so unclear about the definition
of friendship as to straddle its

boundaries.

NO RUN TODAY

Hangovers and jogging do not
mix well. Can't believe I got so
toasted last night. Can't believe
I did half the things I did last night.

Bryan and I were only supposed
to talk. But misery loves sympathy.
And I'm great at commiseration,
especially when fired up on rum.

We met up at a quiet little club.
Low light. Corner booth way in
back. He was already there when
I arrived, and the way his eyes

stopped scanning the room once
they found me made me feel
like the only woman in the place,
though that wasn't even close to true.

I don't think I've ever felt exactly
like that, and it only got better
when he stood and held out his
hand, coaxing mine into its warmth.

He tugged me close, put his mouth
against my ear. *Thanks for coming.*
His voice was a low growl, and my
body responded with animal interest.

I tried to ignore the hollow
longing, but by the time our first
round was drained and another
on its way, it had swollen into

something I couldn't ignore. Easy
banter was not enough distraction,
so I chose a direct route to distance.
"What's up with you and your wife?"

He was evasive at first. *How long
have you and your husband been
married?* The quick change of subject
surprised me. I wasn't there to talk

about myself, let alone Jace or our
relationship. I didn't want to think
about us at all. "Nineteen years, give
or take. I was . . ." I wished I could lie

about my age, but he knows how old
Mikayla is. I could have been pregnant
when I got married and all, but . . . oh,
hell. "I couldn't quite drink legally yet."

He smiled. *Hope you had champagne,
anyway.* Then he grew serious. *Tanya
and I have been married for twenty-six
years. Yeah, yeah, I'm older than I look,*

and so is she. She looks absolutely
great for her age, in fact. I've no
complaints there. But after so many
years together, things have gotten

a little stale. She goes to work. I go
to work. We both come home tired.
We have dinner. I grade papers. By
the time we go to bed, well . . .

My head bobbed up and down
as he talked. "I know the 'well'
intimately. Some of us get there
long before twenty-six years."

His turn to nod. *I think most couples*
get there eventually. The question is,
what next? For me, divorce was
unthinkable while our daughter

was with us. Now Rhiannon is in her last
year of college. Still, I've been looking
for ways to avoid out-and-out mutiny.
The writing is one, of course. If I

manage to publish a book, it will
satisfy at least one very big desire.
I'm not sure the cerebral can totally
replace the carnal, however.

CAUGHT UP COMPLETELY

In my own little set of fantasies,
I did not expect what he said next.

He lobbed the words like grenades,
and they fell around me: splat, splat,

kaboom! *Have you and your*
husband ever tried swinging?

Call me naïve, but my doofy brain
only went as far as the playground.

Maybe it was the second mojito, almost
finished. "Not since the kids were little."

Bryan tried not to laugh, without
success. *No. You know. Sex, with*

another couple. Or maybe a three-
way? Another woman, another man,

whatever. My jaw must have dropped.
Yeah, that's pretty much how my

wife reacted when I suggested we
should give it a try. He signaled

the waitress to bring another round.
Have you never even considered it?

I PLUMBED THE QUESTION

And how, exactly, to answer it. Hell,
he'd opened the door. "I've thought
about it. But Jace would never . . ."

Are you sure? Because, in my truly-
not-humble opinion, the guy always
thinks about stuff like that first.

Then my comment seemed to sink
in. His emerald eyes traveled over
me with pantherlike zeal. The hungry

cat in them only amplified the desire,
pulsing like a heartbeat just in front
of my pubic bone. Once again, I tried

to redirect myself. "If Jace even suspected
I've considered having sex with someone
else, he'd insist on marriage counseling."

Bryan smiled with feline intensity.
So you have *contemplated sex outside*
your marriage? With multiple partners?

Just then, the waitress delivered
our drinks. I waited for her to leave.
Looked him right in the eye. "Yes."

AND THAT LED

To an invitation I'd never imagined
when I agreed to meet Bryan for drinks.

One I never even knew was possible
in a Podunk little city like Reno.

But Bryan knew. *Would you want*
to give it a try? I've heard about

this place. You have to be a couple
to get in, so we'd have to become

one for a night. What say you?
Are you up for some fun, or . . .

"Or what?" I asked, half wondering
if he could hear the buzz in my head.

Or are you all talk? He reached
across the table, traced my lips

with one finger. It was almost
sexier than sex. Almost. He could

have taken me, right there in
that bar, with everyone watching.

At least, I think I would have
let him. Actually doing something

like that is probably daunting.
So without actually thinking

it through, I told him, "Sure,
I'll go with you. I'm a whole lot

more than talk, baby." Something
I'm discovering more and more

is true. *Really? Then I want details.*
Should we play Truth or Dare?

"Okay. I'll go first. Truth or Dare?"
He chose Truth, and I asked, "Have

you ever cheated on your wife?"
Lies come easily to men, so I was

surprised when he admitted, *Many*
times. But I've never had an affair.

Third mojito polished off, I sort of
sputtered, "What's the difference?"

Emotional attachment. My turn.
Have you cheated on your husband?

"Once." I would say it was a fib,
but Grant will never count. I did add,

"With a woman," omitting the part
about her being a mutual acquaintance.

But somehow he knew. *Another*
writer, perhaps? Oh, don't be shocked.

Sahara is a voracious woman—
an omnivore, if you know what

I mean. And yes, I speak from
experience. Be very careful of her.

That emotional Velcro I mentioned?
That's what she's hungry for, not that

I can blame her. She's been used
and abused, and if she was ever loved,

it must have been a very long time
ago. His last remark ignited a flicker

of guilt. I am loved. But there was zero
judgment in his observations, and that

realization extinguished the spark.
Drinks finished and Truth or Dare

enlightening us both, Bryan settled
the check and walked me to my car.

WHAT HAPPENED THERE

Goes into my journal now, not as
an *Essential Oil*, but simply as memory.

And beneath an indigo sky, beaded gold like Versace,
he cupped my jaw in plush-leather hands, lifting my chin
so our eyes connected. "You are stunning," he said.
Then he kissed my forehead, kissed my eyelids closed.
And when his mouth covered mine, there was nothing tentative
about the way his tongue parted my lips, reached inside.

Jace has never kissed me like that, not even when our love
was brand-new. That's how our kissing felt too. Young.
But Bryan's kiss was knowing. The kind of knowing
that made me wonder just when I'd revealed so much.
No one could assume to understand the part of me
I've worked so hard to keep hidden . . .

A door slams. *Mom!* Brianna's footsteps
slap the hallway tile. I shut the cover
of the journal, stash it away. *I hate her!*
It's not my fault. I didn't do anything.
I can't help it if he likes me. Mom!

Uh-oh. Boy problems? Since when?
I slip out of "temptress," downshift
into parent. Guilt grinds the gears.
Priorities. I can't ever forget about those.

PARENTAL PRIORITIES

Are generally unpopular,
all the way around. And yet,
they are integral to keeping
family peace. A

Top Five

list can be useful, if agreed
to by all parties, then posted
in a prominent place, lest
someone forget one or more

prohibitions.

Try organizing in order of
importance. For instance: No

sneaking out,

particularly if said activity
is meant to accommodate

unsupervised parties,

and most especially if said
partying will be enhanced
by the illicit use of

drugs and alcohol,

which invariably lead to
unsavory outcomes, perhaps
the very worst being

unprotected sex.

NOT THE WORST DAY

Not the very best either, although it
was mostly good, I guess. And, for once,
the bad wasn't in my ballpark.

It was a shame Andrea had to run out on
the party. But I understand. Your kids
must come first, no matter how much fun

you're having without them. Or maybe
she wasn't having fun. Maybe she
was relieved to get called away.

Mom's offhanded comment about
her murky paternity really seemed
to bother her. I thought she knew

or at least suspected that communal
hooking up meant everyone on the farm
belonged to everyone else, in some

fashion. I quit worrying about it years
ago. Pretty much, anyway. What good does
it do? But even without Andrea, I enjoyed

spending time with Mom. The movie
was a tearjerker. The shopping netted
three new outfits, like I have anywhere

special to wear them. Should something
come up, they're there. Oh, and I got
a makeover—new cosmetics to enhance

my natural "beauty." What a joke. But hey,
the just-barely-out-of-high-school
department store "expert" managed to sell

this "in need of advice" middle-aged hag
three hundred plus dollars' worth of lotions and
creams, which do make my skin feel plumped

and moisturized. Plus concealer, foundation,
blush, liner, shadow, and mascara, which
definitely highlight my cheekbones and bring

out my eyes. Not that I'll remember how to apply
them or find the need to. But Mom is content
now that she spent the requisite number

of hours with me to assuage her own guilt
about not being around more, or her possible
genetic input into Shelby's condition. But

considering the whole commune thing,
who can say where the mysterious factor
came from? And at this point, who cares?

STILL, AS WE MOTOR UP

The last hill toward home, I ask,
"So, Mom. Any regrets? I mean
as far as Oregon and the farm."

What good are regrets? she snaps.
The echo of my own sentiment,
in a voice so like mine, is

unnerving. Yet I persist. "If you
could change one thing about
those years, what would it be?"

You really want to know? Okay,
then, I wouldn't have stayed.
I would have left your father.

The momentous admission
is not what I expected at all.
"So . . . tell me, why did you stay?"

She hesitates, but not for long.
This will probably sound stupid,
but I stayed to spite my mother.

She told me things would not
work out. I was determined
to prove her wrong. Sheer

stubbornness kept me there
on the farm. That, and making
sure you and Andrea were safe.

I mull that over as I make the last
left to home. "But everything
worked out okay with you and

Dad, right? So why would
you do things differently now?
How would things be better?"

I can't say things would be
better. But I wouldn't have
invested my youth in someone

who didn't cherish me. Your
father loved me in his own
way, I guess. But it was selfish

love. I didn't see that for years.
And when it became clear, it was
too late to go looking for something

new. He's tried to make it up
to me, but only because he's
afraid of being old and alone.

"But if all that's true, how can
you stand living elbow to
elbow with him in an RV?"

She shrugs. *Once you've given*
up on filet mignon, chuck steak
isn't so hard to put up with.

HAVE I BEEN ASLEEP

All these years? Navigating coma?
So holed up in my own little surreal
world I never bothered to venture
beyond its nightmarish boundaries?

What else have I closed my eyes to?
"God, Mom, I am so sorry. I swear,
I never saw it. I mean, I know you
two used to argue . . ."

Oh yes, that we did. But don't
apologize. You weren't supposed
to be privy to the ugly details.
Anyway, we don't argue much

anymore. We finally found a way
to compromise our divergent points
of view. I hope you and Chris can
manage that too. But if you can't,

don't wait too long to change things.
After a while, you'll settle. And you
deserve better. She gives me the old
tongue cluck as the house rolls into view.

I pull into the driveway just as the sky
on the western horizon blazes tangerine
grandeur. If I believed in God, I might
think he was trying to tell me something.

I STEP OUT OF THE CAR

Into the breezeless evening.
The first thing that hits me

is the scent of hickory-tinged smoke,
and it's coming from my backyard.

Smells like the boys have dinner
started, comments Mom.

"I . . . uh . . . didn't even know
we still owned a barbecue. It's been

so long since . . ." Since lazy summer
cookouts, Christian and I sipping drinks

with friends, Shane and his buddies
doing laps in a low wading pool.

Shane wanted to surprise you.
He's a pretty great kid, you know.

"I do, actually." Even if he does piss
me off pretty regularly. I can hear him

laugh, and he isn't laughing alone.
For the first time in hours, I think

about Shelby. They haven't neglected
her, have they? I leave the shopping

bags in the car, hurry into the house,
start down the hall toward her room.

The door is open. The room is empty.
Unreasonably scared, I turn on one heel,

practically run toward the backyard
noise, on the far side of the living room

glass. But as soon as I reach the door,
I stop. I would say this is a scene

straight out of some television family
drama. Except it's more like a sitcom.

Dad is scraping the grill while Shane
and some strange boy push Shelby

in her stander back and forth between
them. I may not have ever seen her

look so happy. The barbecue puffs,
and I know the smoke isn't good

for her, but the boys seem to have her
upwind, and how can I possibly bring

her inside when she is enjoying
herself in such an elemental way?

> I think back to Christian. *She's failing.*
> Wish he were here to see her now.

BUT NO

Instead, he's in New Orleans,
schmoozing clients. Or maybe
he's on his way home. I'm pretty

much the last person to know
if he's coming, going, or touched
down somewhere for a layover.

Mom comes up behind me,
carrying a platter of marinated
rib-eye steaks. *Can you believe*

they got everything ready, all on
their own? Shane must be more
organized than his grandfather.

"Not usually. Guess we should
join the party?" I open the door
for her, and at the sound, everyone's

attention turns our way. Shelby
sees me and gives a little squeal,
approximating *Hi, Mama.*

I go over to give her a kiss
and, when I straighten, find
myself looking the unfamiliar

boy in the eye. He is tall but
narrow-boned. Handsome.
No . . . pretty, with emerald eyes

and Irish black hair and a killer
smile, which he flashes at me.
Hi. I'm Alex. Great to meet you.

Shane starts to stutter some
explanation, but it is Dad who
says, *Alex is Shane's boyfriend.*

Bam. Shane has never brought
anyone home before, and when
his eyes finally connect with mine,

I find something brand-new in his.
Pride. Still, the situation makes me
uncomfortable, and I might have

a harder time with it if not for
the way my parents act so accepting,
like it's just another day at the Trasks'.

Probably a good thing Christian isn't
here after all. "Uh, good to meet you
too, Alex. And thanks for helping

Shane entertain his sister." Kind
of a lot to ask of a new relationship,
come to think of it. Alex must be

a pretty good kid himself. God,
look how far I've come—light-
years, in the last fifteen minutes.

HOW FAR

We claim to have come—
accepting all men as created
equal. Gender being the requisite
qualifier, as women

are

not reviewed in the same fashion—
their fashion hopefully better
suited to the bedroom
than the boardroom. And,

you

know, homosexuals not
really being "men," cannot
be judged equivalent
to their stiffer-wristed brethren.
On religion, well, some Christians are

willing

to make room for a Jew or two
in their inner circles. But Mecca-
facing prayer must be met
with flaming crosses. Close your eyes

to

the details, the big picture
can still be viewed through
rose-colored glass. But

go

any distance beyond
the rhetoric, truth
becomes a shadowed lens.

Andrea

ALL RHETORIC ASIDE

I'm kind of happy that little prick
Chad tossed Harley's affection
to one side.

I hate seeing her hurt. And I hope
she'll find it in her heart to forgive
Brianna,

who I'm really quite sure did nothing
to encourage Chad's interest in her.
Well, except

to let him kiss her. Harley thinks Bri
led him on, but she is an innocent
thirteen.

Holly says she's mortified, and I believe
it. Just have to convince Harley to
believe it

too. Meanwhile, she's not dying to visit
Steve every day. Hooray. And it's all
because of

that little prick, Chad. Valuable lesson,
learned before love plunged her into
a sea of regret.

FIVE DAYS AFTER THE FACT

Harley is still fuming, however. That girl
knows how to hold a grudge. Hmm.
She might have gotten that from me.
But unlike me, who scarfs everything
in sight when I'm mad, Harley will

hardly eat a thing. I keep telling her
I'll have to take her in for intravenous
fluids and she keeps telling me not to
worry, and anyway, I'd probably pass
out at the sight of that big hollow needle,

poked into her skinny arm. When did
she get so wise? Even worse than not
eating is how she stays in her room,
only coming out to exercise, pee,
and once in a while argue with me.

Thank God Mom talked her into
going with her, Dad, and Shane to
Tahoe tonight. Harley's first rock
concert will be Bob Dylan. "Harley!
You almost ready? They'll be here

soon." Out of her dark dwelling
she comes. Too much of her legs—
summer-browned from the walking—
poke out from beneath a very short
denim skirt, and the skimpy tank

top grips her, tight as skin. Yowza!
"Uh, wow. Where did you learn to
put on makeup like that? And where
did you get it?" Pink eye shadow. Black
liner. Blue mascara. Cranberry gloss.

I actually know the answer before
she says, *Cassie bought them for
me, and she showed me how to
do my eyes. She says my skin
is flawless. I don't need foundation.*

I could tell her she, in fact, has
a small ribbon of freckles across
a face often pale, but now sun-tinted.
Instead I just say, "No, you don't
need foundation. You look great."

She looks like a child trying
too hard to look like an adult.
But had I said that, she wouldn't
have rewarded me with her beautiful
smile, the way she does now. *Thanks.*

A horn honks, outside and near.
"That must be Gramps and Gram.
You have fun. But be careful. You
never know what kind of . . ." Don't
finish it. "Never mind. Go on, now."

WHY DO I FEEL

Like she's headed off on her first date
or something? I watch her try to imitate

a slink, but seductress she isn't. Not yet.
Speaking of vamps, however, Holly

called and asked if I wanted to go
with her to Rumble from Down

Under tonight. Beefy guys, stripping
to thongs, have never seemed all

> that appealing. But Holly being Holly,
> she talked me into it. *It's free! Sahara,*
>
> *from my writing group, scored the tickets.*
> *And guess what. She pulled some*
>
> *strings and got us into the wrap*
> *party.* Holly didn't mention exactly

what kind of strings, but if anyone
could pull them, I'd expect it to be

her. This Sahara must be a real piece
of work. Whatever. I haven't been

out in a while. I'm game. I guess.
And only a smidgen worried.

WORRIED ABOUT WARDROBE

What does one wear to watch
overbuilt Australian men strip
down to their underwear? And
the bigger question. What does

one wear to party with those men
after they're finished stripping?
Maybe I should have asked my
daughter to help me pick my outfit.

Maybe I should call up Cassie
to come over and teach me how
to line my eyes much too heavily.
Maybe I should call Holly and tell

her to forget the whole freaking
thing. On the other hand, maybe
I should take a lesson from Harley
and throw all caution to the wind.

I'll never compete with Holly,
but I can take a page from her
handbook (*The Holly Handbook*—
ha!) and wriggle into the smallest

dress I possibly can—a size eight.
Whoa. Diet and exercise *do* work.
Have to thank Harley for that too.
Now, if I can just find shoes that go.

TEETERING

On heels that don't quite work
for me, in a dress I can't quite believe
fits again, I meet up with Holly

and Sahara at the Atlantis. I've always
liked this casino because it isn't all
the way downtown. Easy parking.

Easy-to-get-to restaurants. And now,
an easy-on-the-eyes revue for girls.
At least, that's what they promise.

I join the women—one friend,
one totally unfamiliar—at the bar.
Sahara assesses me like a real estate

appraiser looking at a piece of aging
property. *Holly has told me, like, every-*
thing about you. Hope none of it is true.

She laughs, but the joke is totally
lost on me. Because, was it a joke?
"Cool. Holly hasn't told me, like,

one little thing about you. Hope
it's all true." Wow. Did I just say that,
alcohol-free? Instant dislike between

us, bad chemistry Holly doesn't notice
at all. *I didn't know you wore makeup!*
Let alone, a dress like that one. Brilliant!

Pretty sure that was not the right
adjective, but whatever. I almost
order my usual beer, reconsider.

This is supposed to be a let-your-
hair-down kind of night. "Mai tai,"
I tell the bartender. We pay for our

drinks and head for the showroom,
Sahara in the lead. Casinos are crazy.
This one has a tropical theme, with

trees and waterfalls and palm fronds
representing grass huts, all surrounding
the usual flashing lights and coins

clunking into slot machine trays
and people whooping through cigarette
smog. At least the show will be smoke-

free. A long chain of cackling, crowing
women has already formed at the entrance.
Sahara opts for the invited guests line.

Apparently, we are that. She greets
the guy at the door like they're old pals,
and the next thing I know, we are whisked

down the aisle, all the way to the front
row. Figures. The seats fill and the room
throbs with noise until the lights go down.

NOW THE ROOM THROBS

With music. Exceptionally
loud country. The crowd
claps and a few *Yee-haw,* and
wouldn't you just die being
with someone who did that?
Even Holly does not do that.

I suck my mai tai—strong!
Watch as a lineup of men
rodeos onstage in jeans and
cowboy boots. They are all
very different—long hair.
Spiked hair. Dark. Ice blond.

Slender. Thick. The one
thing they have in common
becomes clear as soon as the
shirts come open—six-packs.
Scratch that. Twelve-packs,
maybe. I've never seen abs

so sculpted. Not even on
those stupid exercise shows
Harley has been watching.
Holy crunches! These guys
really have spectacular bods.
They must live in the gym.

Hey, says Holly as the opening
number ends. *How come their
pants are still on? I'm looking
for G-strings.* She slurps her
mojito and signals to a cocktail
waitress, who makes her way

over. *No worries, mate,* says
Sahara, imitating the [very hot]
host's thick Australian accent.
*Eventually, the pants do come
off.* And they do, with the very
next number, a solo by a guy

with not much hair anywhere
and piercings that look like
they hurt. I turn to Holly to
ask if she would ever wear
a ring through her nipple,
despite knowing the obvious

answer—of course she would.
I find her leaning toward
Sahara, saying something into
her ear. Maybe it's the mai tai,
or maybe it's just selfish friend
me, but jealousy pokes viciously.

JEALOUSY

Is a rockslide—one pebble
of suspicion initiates
an avalanche, leaves sanity
buried beneath the slag.

Few

emotions attack with such
intensity and yet, with rare
exception, accomplish so little.
It can be difficult to

circumvent

the little green monster
who loiters, jaws snapping,
never far from view.
Decide to swim with him,

the undertow

will capture you, drag you
to deep, drowning places.
A word to the wise: never
underestimate the power

of envy.

THE POWER

Of connections is free tickets.
Front-row seats at sold-out shows.
Being called up onstage by men

with ripped torsos, who jerk off
their pants two inches from your
face, encourage you to touch

the bulge in their Speedos
before returning you to your
up-close seat. Andrea is currently

up onstage, on her knees in
front of a thong-clad Australian
hunk, who rocks toward her as if . . .

She looks half horrified,
half fascinated. She'll either
kill me or kiss me when she gets

back. It was my idea to send
her up there, so I lied and told
the emcee that it's her birthday.

"Just play along with it," I told
her. Okay, practically begged
her. I have to admit I was a little

surprised when she said okay.
Then again, I'm pretty sure
it's been a while since she's had

anything quite like this guy
literally in her face. If ever.
I've never. But maybe that will

change later tonight. Only
for real. Only there is that
regular gossip about male dancers.

"So . . . ," I say, too loudly, but
how else will Sahara hear me?
"Is it true these guys are gay?"

Can't speak for all of them,
but I know for a fact that at
least a couple are pure hetero.

Mr. Hunk pulls Andrea to her
feet, sends her offstage with
a slap to the ass. As she goes,

tilting a bit from the booze
combined with skinny heels,
the music changes to *Happy Birthday*.

THE AUDIENCE SINGS ALONG

And by the time Andrea gets back
to her seat, I'm pretty sure her choice
will be "kill" rather than "kiss" me.
She has bloomed scarlet, cleavage

to scalp. She plops into her seat,
finishes half a watered-down drink
in one large swallow. *Thanks a lot!*
Oh my God. How embarrassing!

"Are you kidding? That was excellent!"
I signal to the cocktail waitress to
bring another round. "What I want
to know is . . . how big is his bulge?"

Andrea sputters, but Sahara answers,
Pretty damn big. Take it from me.
She returns her attention to the action,
now a chorus line of firemen.

These guys aren't the best dancers
in the world, but they're definitely
entertaining. Almost as much as
some of the people in the crowd.

In addition to the women, not all
of whom are what you'd call young,
there are a few single men who keep
yelling for the Aussies to *take it* all *off.*

No. She's still too pissed about Chad.
My parents took her to see Bob Dylan.

"That should be interesting. He's kind
of getting up there, isn't he?" I offer

the mojito and she accepts it. *Uh, yeah,*
he is. So, how does Sahara know these

guys? And is she the one who rented
this suite? Kind of pricey for a party.

Sahara comes back into the room,
all freshened up and lipstick reapplied.

I used to be a dancer. Sounds like she heard
Andrea's questions. *So I've known the show's*

producer for years. As for the suite, you'd
be surprised how reasonable it is. Her tone

is curt, and some uneasy current
flows between her and Andrea.

A loud knock interrupts, diverting
the strange energy. *Coming!* calls Sahara.

She goes to let in the food. Andrea
sips her drink in silence. Some party.

AS THE WAITER LEAVES

The real party arrives. Seven
Aussie dancers—two with girls,
two obviously with each other—

plus another guy, obviously not
a male stripper. He's kind of cute,
but built more like an accountant.

The suite shrinks as it fills with
mostly beautiful bodies and faces.
And it gets loud with voices.

Big voice: *Check out this spread!*

Deep voice: *You talking food or pussy?*

Squeaky voice: *Make me a drink, baby.*

Taunting voice: *You can drink this, darlin'.*

Gentle voice: *Look at the view, hon.*

Tandem voice: *I'd rather look at you.*

Too many people to bother
with introductions all around,
Sahara leaves it to us to connect.

One of the dancers corners her,
so I go over to keep Andrea company,
hoping a guy or two joins us.

It doesn't take long for Mitch—
the one who danced for dentures—
and the accountant to come over.

The latter directs his attention
to Andrea. *Hi. I'm Robin.* Turns
out he's Sahara's producer friend.

Andrea manages a smile. Good
sign. And now Mitch says to me,
You were sitting in front tonight.

He has long, sable hair and
black coffee eyes, and they're
scoping me out. "You noticed."

*I'd have to be blind not to notice
legs like those. You're a runner.*
And we're off. He's an actor,

of course. But he's making me
feel like a starlet. I realize he's had
lots of practice. But I don't let that

bother me. I glance over at Andrea,
who is enmeshed in conversation
with Robin. Wonder what about.

Oh well. I've got more important
things to worry about, like Mitch.
"Do you want to sit for a few?"

We do, on a small loveseat. He begins
a downstream flirtation—easy ride,
no demands. No real work. *I'm pretty*

good at massage, he says in a honeyed
Down Under accent. *Kick off your*
shoes and I'll show you. He pulls

my feet into his lap, works the high
arches with his thumbs. Oh, yeah.
"Ever do this for old ladies?"

He smiles. *Once or twice. Mostly*
the old birds just want company.
He adds a few matter-of-fact details.

I'm pretty sure I could go with him to
his room. But I won't. He is fine,
and no doubt well practiced in bed.

Too practiced. I want to feel special.
Andrea shoots me a disapproving
look. God, what would she say if

I told her about Sahara, and why
she seems so proprietary? But no,
Andrea would never understand that.

It comes to me that there are different
degrees of infidelity. And while an extramarital
foot rub isn't exactly right, it really isn't so wrong.

DEGREES OF INFIDELITY

Even lust isn't black
and white.
Would it be wrong
to scan an unfamiliar room, and

when

your lover's back is turned,
lock eyes
with a stranger? What if
you carried the rush home
to warm your tepid bed?

Is it

faithless to let someone new
kiss you,
soft as a drift of eiderdown,
knowing that kiss
is a solitary tick of

time,

never to be repeated?
Should you
bump into a once-upon-a-time
flame, still an ember,
would you call it betrayal

to say,

I will never stop loving you?
Would the gesture
hold deeper meaning
if you had already
decided to tell your lover

goodbye?

Marissa

SAYING GOODBYE

To Mom and Dad has never
been quite as difficult as it
was today. For one thing, I'd
always assumed their riding
off into the sunset together
was a mutually satisfying
experience. Learning their
relationship is like lukewarm
bathwater opened my eyes
to some things I had chosen
to ignore. Or to be honest,
I've been so mired in my own
personal pile of misery, every-
body else's problems seemed
insignificant. I hope Mom's
decision to stay with Dad was
the right one. Either way, it
was great spending time with
the two of them. Having them
here helped me realize how
much of a hermit I've become.
Not good for Shelby. Not good
for Shane. Not good for me.
It was really Dad who made me
see that, and Dad who made
damn sure to introduce Alex
into our midst, make him feel
accepted. Dad and Shane had
the heart-to-heart that Christian
refuses to have with him. Ever.

TO SAY

Christian has been unsupportive
of Shane would be an understatement.
He was hoping his boy would be

a quarterback, not queer. Pop Warner
was a disaster, especially since Christian
was coaching. Two years was all Shane

could take. Little League wasn't much
better. When it comes to sports, Shane
prefers boards—skateboards, snowboards,

wakeboards. Christian used to ski but doesn't
so much anymore. Too busy. Shane
boards with his buddies, not his dad,

who is not exactly homophobic, but
neither has he totally accepted the fact
that his only son is gay. Shane knew

in sixth grade but didn't find the courage
to tell us until his freshman year.
I suspected by then, and so I'd had

some time to process the idea. Christian,
though, looked like he'd been smacked across
the face. He didn't say a word. But beneath

his diamond-jawed exterior, one emotion
was clear—anger. He has tempered some.
But he still won't talk about it. To anyone.

HE BARELY TALKS

To Shane at all. So it surprises me
when, post Shelby's morning CPT,

I start toward the kitchen and overhear
the two of them, attempting communication.

But I've been old enough to get
my license for over a month . . .

Wait. His license? Shane's birthday.
Oh my God. I forgot all about it.

Why didn't he say anything?
How could I not remember?

I didn't say you couldn't have it.
Just not this week. I don't have time.

You never have time for me. For any
of us. You pretty much suck as a dad.

Yeah, well, you're not exactly
my idea of a noteworthy son, either.

Going downhill, and fast. Time
to interrupt. "Shane! I'm so sorry

I forgot your birthday. I must have . . .
I don't know. No excuse, really."

It's okay, Mom. Not like you don't
have enough stuff on your mind.

Oh, and I don't? Christian snaps.
You have no fucking idea—

"Stop it. Just stop it. Look, maybe
I can take you to the DMV this week.

Only problem is the van is not the best
vehicle for a driving test. It's huge."

I'd just need you to sign the papers.
Alex will let me use his car.

Alex. Perfect. Christian creaks out of
his chair, goes to the counter, pours

a cup of coffee. Then he opens a high
cupboard, reaches for a large bottle

that turns out to be Irish whiskey.
I glance at the clock. Not even ten.

Shane pounces. *No wonder you*
don't want to take me to the DMV.

You'd get busted for drunk driving.
Do you drink at work too, Dad?

VALID QUESTION

But probably not one Shane should
ask. Christian turns slowly, razor-eyed.
Do you screw your boyfriend at school?

Whoa. "Just wait a minute. This
conversation doesn't need to get
any uglier. Mellow out, Christian."

Me? You want me *to mellow out?*
I did not start this. He pokes the air
between him and Shane. *He did.*

All I did was ask for your help, but
obviously my sexuality precludes that.
What is it about "gay" that upsets you?

Christian sips his coffee. *I'm sure it*
doesn't concern you in the least,
but homosexuality is a sin.

A sin? *That's what you're worried*
about? My qualifying for heaven?
Since when has that concerned you?

Christian was raised Methodist and
attended church regularly when
we met. But as the years progressed

and life got busier, Sundays began
to blur into every other day
and he made time for services less

and less. He slammed the door
on religion completely when a hit-
and-run driver took out his mom

in a crosswalk, a few weeks before
Shelby was born. I haven't heard
him mention salvation since.

Now, he says, *I'll pray for you.*
Cinches tight the cloak of silence
I know so well. Shane recognizes

it too. *Well, Dad, if you really*
believe in God, you'll quit worrying
about me. Because if there is *a God,*

he wants me this way. This is the way
I was born. This is the way he made
me. You, on the other hand, weren't

born with a whiskey bottle. Maybe
drinking isn't technically a sin,
but the way it makes you treat

your family surely must be. Don't
bother praying for me. Pray for
yourself. He leaves before he can

see Christian's eyes fill with tears, to
overflow. He leans his head into
his hands. Could he be praying?

WHEN HE LOOKS UP

His eyes are dry. Mushroomed.
Tinted crimson. But totally dry,
tear quota used up for the day.

I want to hug him. Instead,
I settle for, "Maybe you should
go back. To church, I mean."

He flushes. *What are you*
saying? That I need saving?
Or God's forgiveness, maybe?

"I didn't say—or imply—any
of that. All I meant was, it used
to be important to you, a source

of comfort. I hate to see you
hurting this way. And I wish you
could reconcile with your son."

Fine. Sorry. Shouldn't have
snapped at you. But faith is
a personal thing. I don't even

know if I own faith anymore.
I think God has deserted me.
No, worse. He kicked me after

he knocked me down. Okay,
I haven't been perfect. But who
deserves what he's handed me?

"I think you mean us, right?
Last I looked, we were in this
together. That hasn't changed,

at least, not for me. You have
pulled away. That is obvious
to everyone, especially Shane.

Can't you see how he's hurting?
Is it really because he came out—
told the truth about such an integral

piece of who he is? I guess
you don't have to accept it.
But gay, straight, or ambiguous,

he is still your son. Would
you really push him out of
your life? For any reason at all?"

He stares at me silently for
a good long while. Pours
another coffee, plus. Finally,

he answers with three one-syllable
words, not the ones I want—or
expect—to hear. *I don't know.*

BY NATURE

I am Earth Mother.

Solid. Placid.
Caregiver.
Peacekeeper.

Sometimes, I'm told,
I become Wood.

Hard. Smooth.
Immovable.
Predictable.

I also have Water days.

Cool. No, cold.
Conflicting currents.
Eddy. Whirlpool.

But at this moment,
I am Fire.

Rash. Brash.
Indomitable.
Unstoppable.

Words rage up in me.

Flare. Burn.
Scalding.
Blistering.

Shoot from my mouth,
dragon flames.

"You bastard.
Shane is your son.
Like it or not, he always
will be. Damn it, you used to
love him so much. What the fuck
happened?" How can love disappear?

LOVE DISAPPEARS

Like raindrops pelting
lake water. Splash by splash,
spattering concentric rings,

small
reminders

left upon the storm-mirrored
plane. And in the geometry,
integral to the pattern,

a hint
of

immortality—the recurring
journey of the Genesis sea,
earth to sky, and back again,

what
was

and what will be, inextricably
married. The promise
of tomorrow, buried in

once
upon
a time.

Andrea

BURIED IN BOOKS

That's where Harley's been since
her blowup with Brianna. She even
quit exercising, and her moping
around is getting to me. Which is
why Holly and I planned a little

surprise for the girls. Hopefully,
it will lead to reconciliation, rather
than all-out war. I'm pretty sure
Harley will balk if I tell her where
we're going—even without

the information that her "former
BFF" is coming along. So I grab
her swimsuit, pack it with mine,
a couple of towels, and a healthy
lunch. Still liking how the size

eights are fitting. Think I'll leave
the hot dogs alone. I find Harley
where I figured I would—in the old
recliner, nose-deep in some dystopian
tale. I tap her shoulder. "Let's go."

The book falls back against
her face and her eyes roll up—
just barely—over the cover.
Where are we going? she mumbles
from behind the chunky sheaf of pages.

"Never mind. Just come on.
You can bring your book."
Harley follows me dutifully out
to the car. I start to throw the beach
bag in the back, and it hits me

that I forgot sunscreen. "Be right
back." I rush into the house—it's hot
in the car—and as I come inside,
the telephone is ringing. I let it go
to voicemail, run for the SPF 30.

But as I start toward the door,
I can hear the voice on the answering
machine. *Robin. From the Atlantis*
the other night . . . Like I wouldn't
recognize the accent . . . *enjoyed*

talking with you and wondered if
you'd like to go to brunch with me . . .
A familiar horn honks outside. Harley
is losing patience. I don't pick up
but do pause long enough to write

down the number he leaves.
Not one hundred percent certain
I'll call him back. Men are distractions.
Then again, he was a pleasant enough
distraction. Guess I'll think about it.

I START THE CAR

Head north, toward Reno.
Harley asks again, *Where*
are we going? Adds, *Mother?*

She saw the beach bag and
sunscreen. Might as well tell
her. "Wild Waters." But now

I detour off the main highway,
into Washoe Valley. *Why are*
we going this way, then? Mom?

Only one reason why we would.
She has to know. So, "We're picking
up Holly. And Trace. And Brianna."

No way! Why would you do
that to me? I'm not talking to
Bri, and you damn well know it.

"Excuse me? You did not just cuss
at me, did you?" She rarely even
raises her voice. "Unacceptable."

Sorry, she says. But she is fuming.
This is a dirty trick. We skirt
the serpentine edge of Washoe Lake,

little more than a shallow
silver waterhole this time
of year. Still, the landscape

is serene. As we maneuver the curves,
steeped in silence, I can feel Harley's anger
ease. "You and Bri have been friends

for a really long time. True friends
don't let other people come between
them, especially not guys. Face it.

You're miserable without her. I'm
betting she's miserable without you
too. Find a way to work things out."

Whatever is what she says, but
I know she's thinking it over.
When we get to Holly's, I give three

short honks before I open the door
and am sucked into a vacuum of early
August heat. Usually, the weather

tempers by now. But today, midmorning, no animal moves and no
bird flies. I leave the car running, air-

conditioning on. "We'll hurry,"
I promise. "If you wouldn't mind,
though, I'd appreciate you getting

in the backseat." I'm pretty sure
she *does* mind, and also relatively
certain she'll honor my request.

SHE DOES, OF COURSE

Holly and kids are ready to go,
so we return to the car in short

order. Harley is in the backseat,
scrunched up against the passenger

side door. She makes a point of
keeping her face against the window

while Brianna and Trace climb in
beside her. Bri pushes her brother

into the middle position. *Hey,*
he complains. *Chill, would you?*

You chill, says Brianna. *But first,*
move over. You're squashing me.

She gives another shove and Harley
snaps, *Both of you are squashing me.*

Please stop bickering! says Holly.
I've got a major headache.

I don't have one now, but if the day
progresses like this, I definitely will.

"Ibuprofen in my purse, water in back."
I turn onto the main drag, behind

an eightyish woman, snoozing along in
a big Pontiac. "What's up with Mikayla?

She didn't want to come?" And now
the guy behind me lays on his horn.

Mikki is grounded again, says Brianna.
Got caught sneaking out the window.

Yeah, says Trace. *She really ought to
get a life besides screwing Dylan.*

Must you air all our dirty laundry?
asks Holly, chasing Advil with Dasani.

*Not all. Only the stuff with used
condoms in the pocket,* jokes Trace.

That makes us all laugh, even Holly.
At least until the guy behind us honks

again. *Stupid noise!* Holly turns, flips
the guy the bird. *Big beep, little penis.*

Harley gasps. I wish I could see
the color of her face right about now.

Mom! exclaims Brianna. But she
is still laughing. Like the rest of us.

ICE BROKEN

I concentrate on driving
(thank God Old Woman
has turned off and Pickup
Dude passed me, even if
it *was* on a blind curve.)

Holly reclines her seat,
much to Harley's chagrin
(she doesn't comment,
but the huff is audible),
closes her eyes to the light.

I can't help but listen in
to the conversation behind
me (as opposed to an actual
argument, though it moves in
that direction), in snippets:

Brianna: *I don't want to*
fight anymore, okay?

Harley: *What would you say*
if I kissed your brother?

Trace: *Hey, wait just a sec.*

Bri: *I'd ask why you didn't*
have better taste in guys.

Trace: *Hey, wait just a sec.*

Brianna: *I'm really sorry. I swear,*
I only like Chad as a friend.

Harley: *I like Trace as a friend.*
Doesn't mean I'd kiss him.

Brianna: *I only let Chad kiss me*
to know what it's like. I figured
since he's older, he'd be good.

Trace: *Kinda too much info.*

Harley: *So . . . was he good?*

Brianna: *I'm not sure what*
good is, but if that was it,
I'd hate to know what bad is.

Trace: *I know what bad is.*

Harley: *What wasn't good?*
Did he have yucky breath?

Brianna: *No. It was just kind of*
icky wet, and we crashed teeth
together. And then, his tongue . . .

Trace: *Enough. Holy crow! Way*
TMI. Are you guys made up now?

I think the answer is obvious.

WILD WATERS IS PACKED

Hot weather and water parks pair
nicely, unless the desert works her
mischief, lifting thunderclouds overhead

to zap lightning down toward tall, wet
structures like slides. Right now, the sky
is clear. "I have to change," I tell Holly.

"Can you try to find some lounge
chairs, maybe over by the snack
bar?" Harley and I go slip into

our suits. She is quicker than I.
Bri's waiting for me by Viper.
I'll see you a little later, okay?

"Whenever you get hungry.
I packed a healthy lunch."
I brought my size-eight suit—

a floral one-piece, with a cute
little skirt to hide the dappled thigh
flab. When I exit the bathroom,

the sun makes me squint, but
I locate Holly easily. How could
I miss her? Every guy here is

ogling the buff bronzed woman in
a pink crocheted bikini that leaves
absolutely zero to the imagination.

IMAGINATION

Is a fallow field,
rich sleeping loam
awaiting seeds
of fantasy. It is

where

you play dress-up,
don tiara and chinchilla.
It is where you strip
it all away, right down to

perfect

nut-butter skin,
invite a certain someone
for afternoon gin,
and nothing you request

is

beyond the reach of yes.
Imagination is a meadow
of wildflower dreams,
pastureland sown with

possible.

Holly

POSSIBLY THE BEST DAY

I've ever spent at Wild Waters.
Last time I went, I looked about
like a beached manatee. No way
would I have worn a two-piece,

let alone a teeny bikini that makes
me feel every bit as appealing as
girls here half my age. Andrea,
of course, does not approve.

Every time a guy meanders by,
copping a feel with his eyes,
she gives him a dirty look. Who
does she think she is? My mother?

Ha. Mama would have grabbed
me up by one ear and given me
total hell for wearing this. Are you
up there, Ma? Whaddaya think?

I adjust my sunglasses, settle
back into the lounge chair,
notice a dark froth creeping
up over the Sierra's lip. "Storm."

Andrea assesses. *Maybe. But not*
for a couple of hours. The kids
will be worn out by then. And
if it comes, rain will be a blessing.

True enough. The heat has been
relentless, barely a breeze to cool
the evenings. The wind kicks up
a little now, though, carrying

the scent of cooking hamburgers.
"Doesn't that greasy grill smell
delish? I didn't eat breakfast
and I think I'm starving to death."

I packed a couple of salads
and some watermelon. Organic.
Help yourself. I can always buy
Harley a hot dog or something.

"No way. I want french fries!"
As I dig for money, a low *varoom*
rattles the sky. "Thunder. Not sure
your weather prediction was accurate."

We'll see. She watches me get
up and start toward the concession
stand. *Hey, when was the last time*
you even looked at a french fry?

Pretty sure it was a rhetorical
question, so I don't bother to answer.
Nor am I insulted. Andrea will be
Andrea, as Mama would have said.

THAT'S THE SECOND TIME

Today I've thought about Mama.
        Weird. Maybe she's the one stirring

up the storm clouds. A little
        girl runs screaming by, chased

by her own mother. I would
        never have made so much noise

when my parents were close.
        Quiet as a sigh kept me out of mind.

I queue up for fries, salivating
        just a tad. Andrea was right, actually.

I haven't given in to temptation—
        food temptation, that is—in a very

long time. But all that running
        has to allow giving in to temptation

once in a while, right? At last,
        my fries come up, sizzling oil, and

I know every calorie invested will be
        worth the extra distance run tomorrow.

Andrea is munching salad when
        I get back, but her eyes glom on to

the cardboard container, piled
high with crispy shoestrings. No way

could a person resist. "Have some,"
I offer. At her hesitation, I add, "Please."

There is something intimate about
sharing food, which I suppose is why

you only do it with a partner,
a child, or a very good friend. People

worth the threat of germs. People
who, in the most basic sense, you want

to survive. Thrive. For Andrea
and me, this is a bonding moment.

Or, more accurately, a rebonding
moment. Between our daughters' falling-

out and our lately disparate goals,
a wedge has formed between us. Grown.

Probably more my fault than hers,
and so when she puts down her fork,

forgoes lettuce in favor of sharing
fries, the gesture is not insignificant.

WE ARE ALLOWED

A solid four hours of Wild Waters
before the sky bubbles ebony clouds
and the rumbled threat of thunder

becomes the promise of lightning.
The kids might stay anyway, but park
officials let us know we have no choice.

We jam our stuff into canvas bags,
sprint for the car, and reach it just as
warm, fat raindrops splatter the parking

lot, raising a hot, wet asphalt smell
and smearing the dirt on Andrea's
windshield. When I glance into

the backseat, Harley and Bri are side
by side, wearing a sun-toasted glow
and heavy-lidded eyes. They'll be asleep

before we hit the freeway. The rain
begins to fall harder, in solid sheets,
and suddenly the windows ignite.

Holy crap! says Trace, exercising
his adolescent First Amendment
rights. *Did you see that lightning?*

Harley snorts. *Jeez, dude, we're not
blind.* Thunder punctuates her
sentence. *That one was close too.*

Andrea is a cautious driver.
It's a slow, slippery drive home.
As predicted, the kids zonk out

before too very long. When it gets
quiet, she says, *Hey, I almost forgot.*
Guess who called and asked me out.

I scan my memory banks but
can't come up with a single name,
except her ex's and . . . "Geoff?"

No, although I did bump into him
and got the impression he might.
Robin. You know, the Aussie?

"Really? He was totally cute.
You did say yes, right?" She hasn't
gone out with a guy in ages.

Not yet. He called just as we were
leaving. And I wanted to think it over.
We don't have much in common.

"It's just a date, Andrea, not a commitment.
He's got a penis and you've got a vagina.
What more do you need in common?"

God, Mom. I can't believe you
said that. Trace's complaint drifts
over the headrest. *You are disgusting!*

MY FACE FLOWERS HEAT

Way to talk in front of my son,
who is not quite a man, but old

enough to understand I just told
my friend she should go get laid.

"Sorry. But call him and tell him
okay. Okay?" I'm more excited

for her than she is for herself.
Still, she sort of promises, *Okay.*

"And don't be so lukewarm
about it when you talk to him.

A guy likes to believe he's alluring,
you know?" I have to quit talking

about it because Trace comments,
Like you're such an expert, Mom?

"I . . . well, I used to . . . uh,
I read a lot of novels, remember?"

Trace laughs, and that makes Andrea
laugh, and now the girls are stirring.

I force myself into silent mode
so I don't make a total fool of myself.

WE PRACTICALLY SURF

Up the driveway, water rushing
down in wide rivulets. Brianna
begs to let Harley stay the night.
Neither Andrea nor I dare say no.
The kids grab their stuff, rush inside,

ducking. As if that could keep them
dry. I gather my things. "Thanks
for thinking of this. It was a great day.
Now go call Robin. A little male
distraction would do you good."

She tells me again that she will.
I slog through the door, dripping,
take the wet towels to the laundry
room. When I turn back toward
the kitchen, Mikayla is standing

> there. *Hey, Mom.* Her expression
> is dour. *Um, I heard back from*
> *Leon Driscoll today. Come on.*
> *I want you to read the email.*
> Her posture tells me the news

isn't what she hoped it would
be. "You know, whatever he said,
it's okay, honey. I'm pretty much
resigned to not finding them.
I'm still grateful to you for trying."

She turns. *You don't get it, Mom.*
I think we did find them. It's just . . .
Well, look and see. She leads me
to her computer, where there's
an open email from Leon Driscoll.

It says: HELLO, MIKAYLA. IT WAS A SURPRISE
TO HEAR FROM YOU. MY EX SHOULDN'T HAVE
GIVEN YOU MY NAME. BUT I'VE ALWAYS
BELIEVED MY BROTHER, PAUL, SHOULD

HAVE MADE HIMSELF AVAILABLE TO HIS CHILD,
SO I FORWARDED YOUR EMAIL TO HIM. IT IS
MY OPINION THAT HE IS, IN FACT, YOUR GRAND-
FATHER. HOWEVER, THIS IS HIS RESPONSE:

"PLEASE INFORM HER THAT I HAVE NEVER
HAD SEX WITH ANYONE OTHER THAN
MY WIFE, SO I CAN'T POSSIBLY BE RELATED
TO HER." I'M SORRY HE SEEMS UNABLE

TO COWBOY UP AND TAKE RESPONSIBILITY
FOR SOMETHING THAT HAPPENED
FORTY YEARS AGO. VERY SORRY. BEST
I CAN DO IS GIVE YOU TWO THINGS.

The first is an attached photo of the man,
who doesn't look a lot like me, except
maybe for the slope of his cheekbones.
The second is, perhaps, the bigger gift.
It is a name. Sarah Hill. Likely, my mother.

COWBOY UP

It's a phrase delegated
to a certain culture,
but one that speaks
boldly, should you care
to listen. It means to

live by

embracing the cowboy
spirit—a love of the planet,
nature, and your fellow man,
regardless of his belief or
homeland. It is adhering to

the code

of courage—fearing none
but the Maker. Protecting
the helpless. Owning up to
doing wrong, always keeping
in mind the highest badge

of

honor one can wear is honesty.
As the Lone Ranger said, *All*
things change but the truth,
and the truth alone lives
on forever. The ethos of

the west

is straight-shooting living
and hard forward riding across
the ever-varying landscape.

THE WEST

Has had its fair share of unusual
weather this summer. Yesterday's
downpour was unexpected,

but also appreciated. It scrubbed
the air, scented it heavily with damp
sage and sand. Cleaned it enough,

in fact, that I made a momentous
decision. Why do I do that more
and more? The answer, of course,

is easy. I've grown tired of having
every decision made *for* me. Tired
of being a bystander to life, not even

an observer because I've locked
myself away in self-imposed asylum
for almost five years. Out of the blue,

as if waking from a nightmare and
choosing to beat back the fear,
I've decided to reimmerse myself in

living. To expose myself and my broken
child to the throb of the city, the song
of August wind, the smell of wet sage.

LITTLE STEPS

Forward—a shopping trip, fireworks
on the patio—have given me the impetus
to lengthen my stride. So when Drew
called to let me know our once-favorite

band, Grit, is giving a free concert
in the park today, I figured why not
give Shelby a little taste of grunge?
But I don't want to go alone. Drew has

to work but said he might try to
meet up later. Andrea is busy. Some
big date or something. And Shane,
who is more the rap type, would rather

hang out here with Alex. Not that
I can really blame him. Only one other
person came to mind—Claire, whose
husband, Tyler, was one of Christian's

college friends. His best friend, in
fact. We used to spend time together—
played some tennis pairs, drank a little
wine. But Shelby wedged us apart.

Claire is two weeks away from having
her baby—a girl. Camille Emily looks to
be perfectly healthy, which, I think,
makes Claire uncomfortable around me.

WHEN I INVITED CLAIRE

To come today, her hesitation hung, thick
as a swarm of honeybees. When I twice added

"please," she agreed. I dress Shelby in a pretty
summer frock. "Look, baby girl, your outfit

matches Mama's." I picked them up on
a whim on my recent shopping spree, not

sure we'd ever get the chance to wear them.
Mom told me then, *Create an opportunity.*

It's fractionally cooler today. Around eighty
right now. Shelby does not often see the brightest

light of day, so I'm careful to sunscreen every
exposed millimeter, though Wingfield Park is shady.

"Look what else I've got for you." The sunglasses
have pink frames, studded with rhinestones.

I slip them over her eyes. "Beeee-yooo-tee-ful!
Just like a rock star!" Her face illuminates

with the spread of her lopsided grin.
. . . ma . . . na . . . shun Moo, she tries.

"That's right. Just like Imagination Movers."
A much-loved Disney Channel invention.

"Want to see how pretty you are, cupcake?"
I wheel her over to the full-length mirror

hanging on her door. "You'll be the queen
of the concert, and Mama will be your lady-

in-waiting." A worn lady-in-waiting, but
it's all good. Shane is in his room with

Alex. "We're leaving," I call, pushing
the stander down the hall. The door to

Shane's bedroom opens. *Let me help*
you get her in the van, volunteers Alex.

Shane follows, and I ask, "Sure you
won't change your mind and come along?"

He smiles at Alex. *Yeah, right, Mom.*
A has-been grunge band? No thanks.

Alex gives the stander a playful spin.
Anyway, we need a little alone time.

He blows Shane a kiss and I shudder
to think what they've got planned.

I file that somewhere beyond worry,
help Alex strap Shelby in her special

bed in the back of the van. "Ready, Queen
Shelby? Wave goodbye." She does her best.

CLAIRE AND TYLER LIVE

In the same tidy brick bungalow
they've shared practically forever.
They'll probably need a bigger
place once the baby grows out

of her bassinet. Three short, staccato
bursts of the horn and Claire
comes waddling out. Wow.
She's huge. Camille is a whopper.

With a bit of effort, Claire climbs
into the passenger seat. I reach
over for a quick hug. "So good to
to see you again. You look great."

> *You too.* She smiles and then, at
> Shelby's welcoming coo, pokes
> her head over the seat. *Oh, my God.*
> *I can't believe how big she's grown.*

"Kids have a way of doing that.
You'll see before too long."
We take off for the park, chit-
chatting catch-up. She tells me

Tyler got laid off from work and
is driving her pretty much bonkers.
I tell her all Christian does is work,
which drives me totally crazy too.

I ALMOST CHOKE

At her response. *Tyler told*
me about Chris's new project.
Sounds like it keeps him busy.

"What? How does Tyler
know? I wasn't even aware
of it myself until recently."

Really? She sounds totally
surprised. *Chris discussed*
it with Tyler months ago.

I had no idea they were
talking at all. Then again, why
wouldn't they be? "Guess I didn't

realize Christian and Tyler
had kept in contact. Shows
how much I know, doesn't it?"

Claire reaches over, pats
my knee. *Sorry I haven't*
stayed in better touch. It's

just, between the baby and
Tyler's job and trying to
keep afloat of the bills . . .

But I understand the real reason.
It's hard to stay close to
a friend whose kid is dying.

BUT SHE WON'T DIE TODAY

Today, she'll listen to grunge
beside the Truckee River,
beneath ancient cottonwoods.

I luck into a handicapped
parking place along the river
walk. "Here we are. You ready,

Queen Bee?" Shelby shivers
excitement as I unbuckle her
from her seat restraints. Claire

looks the other way as I strap
Shelby into her stander, tuck
the necessary bags and tubes

into covert cubbyholes. Then
I reach into the van for the wide
straw hat I brought to protect her

head from any errant sun ray.
"I figured we could pick up
a couple of sandwiches. I don't

know if it's still there, but there
used to be a great little deli
a couple of blocks from here.

Christian and I used to eat
there a lot." It was one of our
favorite places, with big windows

overlooking the river walk.
We would drink wine and
people-watch. Back in the day.

With the concert as a draw,
there are plenty of people
to watch today. The sidewalk

is crowded. A pleasant hum
enfolds us as we make our
way toward where I hope

the deli is still in business.
It is. And for some ridiculous
reason, it makes me really happy.

We push through the door,
and just as I turn to tell Claire
how great the chicken salad is,

she says, *Well, look who's here.*
It's Christian, sitting at a table
in the very back, with a stunning

brunette. I recognize her from
the newsletter photo. Skye Sheridan.
Her hand rests lightly on his forearm,

and her tight-lipped expression
tells me their conversation isn't
exactly going the way she wants it to.

AWKWARD

I'm not sure what to do, but then
the choice is taken from me as
Christian glances in our direction.

Claire and I both wave. What can
he do but shake off Skye's hand and
leave her sitting there while he comes

over to say hello? *Good to see you,*
Claire. He bends to give Shelby a kiss.
Straightens. *What are you doing here?*

"Getting lunch. Then we're going
to the Grit concert in Wingfield."
I don't ask what he's doing there.

But I can't help but notice the way
Skye stares with gold, lupine eyes.
"Well, I guess you should get back to . . ."

Skye. She's ITV's hotshot lobbyist.
He finally lets himself look at her.
Okay, then, I'll see you at home.

He pivots, returns to his table.
Settles in across from hotshot Skye
Sheridan, who does not return her hand

to his arm. I order chicken salad.
Take Shelby to the park for grunge.
Sit for an hour, not listening at all.

HOME

Is haven. A place
with familiar corners
to tuck yourself into
when you need
a bottomless cry
or to let loose a

bitter

scream, sans a single
judgmental eye.
It is where you know
you're safe, alone.
And where you
can listen to the

sweet

song of family,
a melody to allay
all manner of heartache,
moored behind
the breakwater
in the harbor that is

home.

Andrea

MOORED

To buoys fringing the deepwater
drop-off, catamarans, fishing boats,
and a handful of yachts bob and
dance in Tahoe's sapphire sway.

I haven't been to Camp Richardson
since Harley was a little girl.
One of the kids, running along
the edge of the beach, reminds

me of her—gold-streaked wheat-
colored hair, a cascade over copper
skin. The breeze carries the sound
of the child's delight as she dodges

the reach of cool shore-drawn
ripples. I wish Harley could laugh
so easily. Why must adolescence
substitute angst for joy?

> *Nickel for your thoughts.*
> Robin sits close beside me
> at the windowsill countertop.
> *Ah, hell. I'll give you a dollar.*

"Cheap at half the price." I smile.
"I was just thinking about my daughter
and wondering what happens to
that great, pure childhood bliss."

I'm sure I don't know. I barely
even remember being a kid.
My father, using the term loosely,
buggered off before I was born.

I spent my childhood, such as it was,
trying to avoid Mum's interchangeable
men. Most of them weren't very nice.
I was on my own more than not.

Wow. Makes me almost nostalgic
for the "good old days" on the farm.
I'm not sure what more I can say
except, "Sorry." Robin's smile

is wistful. *No worries. I came*
to terms with it a very long time
ago. How about you? Did you
have a nice, normal upbringing?

I almost snort my mimosa.
"Guess that depends on how you
define 'normal.' My parents stayed
together somehow. Who knows

if that was what they should have
done." I offer a brief history of life
on the commune. "I grew up thinking
'naked' was how people dressed."

Robin laughs. *Mostly, in the outback.*
Too bloody hot to wear anything
but skin. Unless . . . he watches
a sculpted woman walk by,

wearing a thong bikini, totally
inappropriate for a family beach
like this one. *Unless you're*
wearing something like that.

"Reminds me of my friend,
Holly. The one I was with at
the party the other night? We
went to Wild Waters yesterday.

Her swimsuit was, like, a couple
of triangles held together by string.
Of course, she's got a figure that
can wear something like that."

He reaches over, puts his hand
on top of mine. *So do you. Not all*
of us men like twigs, you know.
Some of us appreciate curves.

THANKFULLY

Brunch arrives, distracting Robin's
attention from the, no doubt, horrid

shade my face has turned. It burns.
Hopefully, the sauce on my huevos

rancheros will provide a decent excuse.
I take a quick bite. "Whoa. Way spicy."

Robin is not fooled. *Looks like it.*
Would you like a taste of my crab

Benedict? It's delicious. I'll trade
you for a nibble of heat. He offers

a forkful, and we make the exchange,
the gesture surprisingly intimate.

Robin's eyes snap theatrically wide.
Okay, yeah, that's hot, all right. Mimosa!

God, he's cute. "So, have you ever
been married?" The question dropkicks

me right back to Geoff. "Wait. You don't
happen to be currently married, do you?"

His look is more confused than amused.
Never been, so I'm not now. Why ask?

"Long story, involving the last guy
I went out with having a secret wife.

Which is why he and I are not dating
any longer, although he didn't think

being married to someone else should
interfere with our relationship."

Ah, and he never mentioned his spouse
before developing a liaison with you.

"Bingo. Or as they say Down Under,
aye, mate." Like I'm suddenly an expert

on all things Australian. S*ome blokes*
are dingoes. Another mimosa?

"Absolutely." Something to tease the egg
and salsa out from between my teeth.

Tell me about your daughter.
How is it, being a single mom?

"Better than being married to her father,
and that's a fact." I give him a short

rundown on Harley—a basic primer
on living with a thirteen-year-old girl.

Robin takes it in. Offers a wry grin.
And to think I've missed out on all that!

IT'S BEEN A VERY LONG TIME

Since I've gone out with a man
who even pretended this much
interest in me as a woman.

Me as a mother. Me as a sister.
Me as a human being. Robin listens
more than he talks about himself.

Asks all the right questions. Laughs
at all the appropriate times. Gives
compliments freely. He's handsome,

in a down-home sort of way. Has
a career he loves, not just a job he puts
up with, and he's not afraid to spend

a decent chunk of his hard-earned cash
on a pricey Sunday brunch for two
at one of my all-time favorite places.

He's in relatively good shape. Has
a really great smile. Most likely
isn't married. And all that makes me

wonder, one: what's wrong with
him? And, two: if there's nothing
at all wrong with him, why me?

THOSE QUESTIONS

Simmer at the back of my brain
while we finish our mimosas.
The bill comes, and he puts down
a card, then excuses himself to
use the restroom. I watch him go,

designer shorts and polo shirt
revealing lean muscles and tanned
skin. Not bad. In fact, very, very
nice. So what *is* wrong with him?
When he returns, he has a back-

pack slung over one shoulder.
He offers a hand. *You don't have to*
get back right away, do you? I thought
we might take a walk. How could
I refuse, either the walk or his hand?

It has also been quite a while
since I've strolled, holding hands
with a man. Any man, let alone
one like this. Now question two
starts nagging again: why me?

We head up the beach, along
the softly slapping water. "Hang
on a sec." I slip off my sandals,
let my bare feet squish into
lake-licked sand. "Much better."

Great idea. Robin follows suit.
Here, let me take those for you.
Both pairs of shoes disappear
into his pack and we continue
for quite a distance, leaving

Camp Rich and its bustle behind.
Eventually, we come to Pope Beach,
with its thick stands of evergreen
and shrub-curtained nooks of sand.
It is much quieter here. A few people

picnic in scattered groups, but
when Robin draws me into a private
alcove, it feels like we're all alone
on the planet. From his backpack, almost
like magic, he produces a terry cloth

blanket, a bottle of champagne
and two glasses. "You've got to be
kidding! If I drink anymore, you'll
have to carry me back to your car."
He hands me the bottle—Perrier-Jouët—

which, unreasonably, feels cold.
No worries. We can always nap.
He spreads the blanket, sits, and
reaches for the wine. It opens
with an inviting *pop!* Oh, why not?

PERRIER-JOUËT

Is like liquid diamonds—brilliant.
A tiny bit sharp. Cost, relative to taste.
Robin and I sit, just touching, beneath

a cascade of light. I can smell sun on
his skin, the scent distinctly masculine.
By the time we finish the wine, my heart

rate has escalated, and when Robin
coaxes me to lie back, I think it might
implode. He settles beside me, one hand

stroking my thigh, the other fiddling
with my hair. *I love that you keep it*
long, he says. I should stop this now

with my usual no-first-date-kiss rule,
except we're already kissing, and it's been
so long, and I don't want to stop. This kiss

is spectacular. And maybe it's the Perrier,
or maybe Holly is rubbing off on me, but
when his hand slides up under my dress,

I don't stop that, either. I look into
his eyes, find desire more intense
than my own. Yet he asks, *Is it okay?*

I reach for his zipper. Mouth. Tongue.
Skin. Serious skin. Red champagne haze.
Over me. Under me. G-spot deep inside me.

THE G-SPOT

Arguably a woman's favorite
trigger, yet few have any idea
what the *G* stands for.

Some say

it must be "gynecologist."
Completely inaccurate,
although Ernst Grafenberg
happened to be one.

There's

a clue. Still confused?
consider the first letter
of his name. Ah yes. The *G.*
Back in the forties, when

no

medical professional worth
his new sulfa drugs believed
women had orgasms,
good ol' Doc G begged to disagree.

Such

an argument (not to mention
eyebrows) he raised when he said
a girl could ejaculate! Today,
the debate continues, and the best

thing

about it, for all concerned,
seems to be the research.

RESEARCH

I kept telling myself (not to mention
my best friend) that my forays into
the extramarital underworld were
all about research. Looking back, not

that I'm looking all that far behind me,
maybe I believed that's what they were.

I don't think I believe that now. Nor
do I believe I've finished exploring
the sexual underbelly. That night,
talking with Bryan about possibilities

like clubs where couples play openly
with other couples or singles or even
just with each other in front of a crowd
left my mouth watering for a taste of it.

Problem is, it also left me hungry for
less time with Jace and more with Bryan.

I have to wonder what it's like to be
together with someone equally intent
on no-boundary experimentation.
Bryan and I married the wrong kind

of people. Which means, essentially,
we married the wrong people. Period.

CASE IN POINT

After the fairly huge rejection
by my probable birth father
a couple of days ago, I've been
distraught. Okay, I was totally
stung, not only by his refusal

to develop a connection, but much
more so by his refusal to even
acknowledge that he ever had
an out-of-wedlock relationship
that resulted in a baby. Me.

He's a bigger bastard than he
made me, not to mention a
coward. All of which I wanted
to say in a return email. But Jace
counseled against it. Said it might

be construed as harassment.
And then he launched a not
totally unexpected attack.
I told you to leave it alone,
didn't I? Will you listen now?

Okay, yeah, he did give me
those exact instructions.
And yeah, the outcome was
what he thought it would be.
But how can he ice so solidly?

After two days, I have to
talk to someone. I try
Andrea first. But when
I call, she launches her
own story—Aussie Robin

and champagne brunch
and sex on the beach.
Okay, that part is pretty
good. But by the time
she finishes, all heady and

over-the-top happy with
the recollection, I don't
want to rain on her three-
ring circus. After I hang
up with her, I text Bryan.

SORRY TO BOTHER YOU.
BUT ANY WAY YOU CAN
SNEAK OUT FOR A DRINK?
I COULD REALLY USE
AN EAR RIGHT NOW.

It only takes a few minutes
for his response to come.

YOU'RE RESCUING ME FROM
WRITING LESSON PLANS.
GIVE ME AN HOUR, OKAY?

SIXTY-THREE MINUTES LATER

Bryan and I are sitting in Wine off
the Vine, my new favorite wine bar.
It's almost enough just to be here
with him. But a couple of glasses
of good cabernet make me open

my mouth. I start with Mama and Papa.
How they adopted me and why. Move
all the way through Mikayla's search
and to the results. "I guess it was stupid
to have any real expectation that

I would find my birth parents, let alone
hook up with them. But the closer
we came, the more I found myself
wanting that connection. Jace says
I'm being ridiculous . . ."

Why? I don't think so at all.
To be that close to realizing
a lifelong dream, only to
have cold water thrown in your
face? Your feelings are valid.

I realize my eyes have been
fixed on the table. I bring them
level with Bryan's, which hold
nothing but sympathy. Well, maybe
mixed with a little lust. "Thank you."

For what? Telling you the truth?
He slides his leg over, hooks mine,
draws it closer. *Where does Jace*
think you are right now? His hand
begins to circle my kneecap. Slowly.

Maddeningly. The shush of his
fingers against my nylons is giving
me goose bumps. "I told him I was
going out with some friends from
my writers' group." Not quite a lie.

His hand stops circling and he
spears me with those pippin
eyes. *Look. I keep thinking about*
the last time we were together.
Not so much our little game of

confession, although picturing you
with Sahara was, frankly, quite
the turn-on. I thought our flirtation
was only good fun. But the truth is,
I can't get you out of my head. I'm not

sure what that means, or where we can
go from here. I only know I want
to be with you as often as possible.
Right now, I want to kiss you
more than just about anything.

SOMETHING SHIFTS

Inside of me, like
stepping to one side
and suddenly I can see.
I know I shouldn't
do this here, but find
no way to stop myself.
Brash as lightning,
I bring my face into
his, trace his lips with
the tip of my tongue
before covering his
mouth with my own.
The kissing we did
the last time
I saw him was hot.
But this kiss is steeped
with intimacy. I keep
it relatively short, and yet
when I pull away I can
barely catch enough
breath to power words.
"Something sort of
like that?" I manage.
Bryan's smile is half
amused, half predatory.
Not quite, he says. *But*
practice makes perfect.

WE DECIDE TO PRACTICE

Midweek, casino hotel rooms go for
next to nothing, and there just happens
to be a casino right down the block

from Wine off the Vine. The room
isn't the fanciest, but it's clean and the bed
is decent, something we barely

discern before we're kissing again.
Kissing longer. Deeper. With intent. Passion.
So much passion, fear flickers in tiny

surges, fueling the electricity traveling
my veins as if they were high power lines.
Fear of falling? Fear of flying? Not

sure, but it's a spectacular aphrodisiac.
Bryan takes complete control, something
very different for me. But I like it.

> Love it. Give myself up to it, and
> that is the biggest turn-on of all. He stops
> kissing me. *Take off your clothes.*

He stands back away from the bed,
watching me shed my dress. When I am
down to lingerie and stockings,

> he says, *Come over here.* He sits in
> the overstuffed chair. *I want a lap dance.*
> I have no idea how to do a lap dance,

but what the hell? I stand in front of
him, moving my body to imagined music.
Blues. Billie Holiday. He reaches for

me, tugs me so I'm straddling his legs.
That's it. Beautiful. He gentles his hands behind
my shoulder blades, coaxes me forward

and unhooks my bra. Lets it fall. Slips
a hand under each breast, lifting them gently
and framing my nipples with the Vs

of his fingers, the motion unexpectedly
ingenuous, as if he's touching a woman for
the first time. And now his tongue

teases into the folds, circling the marble
tips. I bite my bottom lip against the moan trying
to escape—too much a cliché for this

moment. And the thing that shifted,
whatever it was, slithers sideways again, reveals
an emotion closer to love than lust.

His hands fall away, to my thighs. They
push me down, into his lap, only his jeans and
my panties between the thing I want

most right now, stiff and pulsing.
He kisses me again, and my body screams
to have him inside me, but he says . . .

HAVE YOU EVER BEEN TIED UP?

It is the most intense experience of my life, and when I get home I'm glad the house is fast asleep, so it can go into my journal.

Oil of Cloves

To offer up every slender thread of control is frightening. Exhilarating. I am naked when he lays me, trembling, on the bed. "I won't hurt you. Not if you're very good." He uses my stockings. One for my hands, which he crosses at the wrists, stretching them over my head. The other he wraps around my eyes. I'm swimming in a dark sea, where something unseen waits for me. "Don't move."

It's hard to comply when his teeth rake my neck in a vampire-style kiss, lower to my nipples. His bite is half brilliant hurt, half surreal pleasure. The scent, lifting from his hair, is spice. Cloves, I think. It's sharp, sexy as hell.

"Open your legs." His face dives between them, and his mouth claims what he finds there. And when he says, "You can come now," I am beyond ready. "Now that you're wet, I'm going to do something I've always wanted to." He slips one finger inside me. Two. Three. At four, the pressure becomes terrific. But when I squirm, he gives my arms a warning tug. "No. Hold still."

I do and he works his entire hand into that narrow place. And, over the flashing silver pain, I shudder orgasm. "That's my girl." I wish I could see his rigid cock, fevered and poised to push inside me. One wicked thrust and I come again. And again. And now, so does he.

ORGASM

Few things represent
so well the inequality
of the sexes. Picture

Adam,

running around the garden
with a nice breeze-induced
stiffy, meaningless until
that lecherous serpent

got

involved. Before it became
about intent, erection felt
good, and that was all. Then
his companion found some

off-

the-wall forbidden fruit.
One little nibble and

Eve

became the object of Adam's
no-longer-innocent stiffy's
desire. And here's the rub
(so to speak). He—man—

got

off pretty much by whim.
She—woman—discovered
hunger, difficult to satiate.
And when she tried, she was

censured.

Marissa

I'VE TRIED

To put the scene in the deli
out of my mind. Tried, with
no success. Hindsight sucks.

I should have marched over
to Christian's table, stood
there until he had no choice

but to introduce his hotshot
lunch date to his tongue-tied
wife. Instead, I didn't even look

his way, afraid her hand would
be back on his arm. I ate chicken
salad in the park, pretending to

listen to my friend Claire talk
about Braxton Hicks contractions.
When the music started, all I could

think about was how Grit
sounded more like the Grateful
Dead. And when Drew called

to let me know he was on his
way, I told him I felt sick.
"Think it was the chicken salad."

SO INSTEAD OF DREW AND GRIT

I dropped Claire off. Took Shelby
home, which proved completely
embarrassing for her brother, who
was in the kitchen, totally naked,
when we came through the door.

Shelby probably didn't care, if she
noticed at all. I, however, freaked.
"Shane Michael Trask! What the hell?
Go put some clothes on, would you?"
I've never seen a face quite so red,

> or a butt quite so pale as he made
> a dash for his room, trailing a weak,
> *Sorry. Didn't think you'd be back*
> *so soon.* Neither did I. Still, propriety
> seems in short supply around here.

At least a birthday-suited Alex wasn't
standing there with him. And I'm even
more grateful that I didn't catch them in
the act. Not sure if I caught them
post- or pre-, or that it really matters.

Obviously, they *do*. But it's one thing
to know your son is gay, and quite
another to be presented, up close, with
specifics. At least he can't get pregnant.
Thank God for small favors and all.

NOT THAT I BELIEVE IN GOD

Growing up, Andrea and I were given no
clear understanding of a possible Creator.
Dad was raised in a strong Jewish home.

But that teen questioning thing weakened
Ira Snyder's religious resolve. He never
thought twice about marrying Mom,

a lukewarm Lutheran. Both went through
a pagan phase, a Wiccan thing, and even
had a Buddhism fling, searching for deeper

meaning and ending up more confused
than anything. And that's the belief system
Andrea and I inherited—confusion.

When I met Christian, I attended
his church, mostly because he wanted
me to. But I also had an itching curiosity.

Was there anything to the hype?
I have to admit, I felt *something* there,
beneath the crucifix, in the midst

of believers. Maybe it was universal love.
Maybe a sliver of hope, a hint of reason
beyond the chaos. Then Christian's mom died.

Then Shelby came along. And in Christian's
own crisis of faith, any small sense of God
I had dissolved. Dissipated. Disappeared.

A RATHER AMAZING THING

Is that somehow, Shane held on to
whatever faith he found in Sunday

school. He clings to it, and to the idea
of an omnipotent Creator who cares

for the earth and its inhabitants—two-
legged or four-; winged, finned, or furred.

This, despite his father's insistence
that Shane's sexuality denies him access.

This, despite my agnostic outlook. This,
despite the hurt he will probably always

experience because of being "the way
God made him." It's fascinating, really.

And to be honest, I'm more than a little
envious. I could use a major infusion

of comfort on pretty much any given day.
Unfortunately, I don't think I'll find it

hovering in the clouds, or rising, orange,
at the break of morning. But if Shane can,

more power to him. And if that power
does, in fact, come from God, hallelujah!

I PONDER SUCH THINGS

When silence bloats the empty
rooms of this behemoth house.
Today, as most days, I have only
Shelby for company, and right

now, she's napping. Her door
opens like a whisper, and I
peek around it to check
on her. Small whimpers

escape her mouth, and her
legs move as if they know
things when she sleeps
that they cannot remember

when she's awake, and I
wonder for the thousandth
time where she wanders
when she dreams. What

does she see? Who does
she meet? Is she perfect?
And for the millionth
time, a tsunami of sadness

crashes into me, drags me
down into an undertow
of what will never be,
strands me, floundering.

RATHER THAN DROWN

I back out of her room,
close the door, leave Shelby
to whatever dreams she is allowed.
I need to do something mindless.
Routine. Laundry. I'll do laundry.

Sort.
Wash.
Dry.
Fold.
Put away,

leaving detergent scent to
perfume the stale summer air.
The first door I come to is Shane's.
I knock, though I know he's out.
Habit. His room is cluttered.

Books.
Plates.
Wrappers.
Dirty socks.
Ditto underwear.

Does the boy never throw away
anything? Does he never pick
up his clothes? I toss carelessly
discarded clothing into a laundry
basket. Wander over to his desk.

Lighters.
Rolling papers.
Marijuana crumbs.
Good china saucer.
Prescription bottle.

WHICH IS ODD

Because, at least as far as I know,
Shane isn't taking any prescribed
medications. What's even odder
is the bottle has no label. Inside

are blue tablets, stamped with
the brand name *Gilead.* I take one,
put the bottle back, and leaving
the basket of dirty clothes right

where it is, go to my computer.
Ten seconds' worth of research
tells me something I do not want
to be informed of. Cannot possibly

face. Gilead is a pharmaceutical
company that specializes in
HIV treatments. No! It's not
possible. Is it? I'm pretty sure

Alex is the first guy Shane has
actually slept with. I mean,
I could be wrong. But even if
I am, he's only sixteen.

No way can he be infected.
Right? He would tell me, yes?
Oh my God. I think I'm going
to be sick. My hands start to shake

and sweat erupts on my forehead.
Stop. Think. Okay, call him. I have
to know for sure. But, of course,
his cell goes straight to voicemail.

I leave a message there, and just
to be sure, I text the same request:
CALL ME RIGHT AWAY. VERY IMPORTANT!
Now what? First, calm down.

Second, there's nothing to do.
I can't call anyone. There's no one
to call. Not even Christian. Especially
not Christian. Not till I have some

definite information. I start to pace.
Highly ineffective. All it does is make
me more nervous. So I go into Shane's
room, put the blue tablet stamped

Gilead back into the bottle. Gather
up the rest of his dirty clothes.
Take them to the laundry room.
Sort them. Put light-colored tee shirts,

underwear, and socks into the washer.
Set it to cottons. Measure laundry soap.
Hit the start button, inhaling the only
semi-comforting scent of detergent.

IT'S A VERY LONG TWO HOURS

Until I hear his key turn
in the door. It's barely open,

his foot hardly through, when
I demand, "Why didn't you call?"

I'm halfway to hysterical, and
sound it. His jaw drops, his

expression goes from blank
to concerned. *What's wrong?*

I grab his hand, pull him
down the hall, into his room

and over to his desk. I pick
up the bottle. "Do you have

something to tell me? About
these, maybe? God, Shane . . ."

My eyes sting, but I blink away
the tears. "Tell me you're not HIV

positive!" He draws back
his shoulders. Toughens.

No, Mom. I'm not. Alex is. But
don't worry. It's under control.

IT'S UNDER CONTROL

Now there's a phrase
that should inject fear
into even the stoutest heart.
Not a lot of things in

life

are certain, except death.
Taxes. The need for
sustenance and the
inevitable results that

presents,

with luck, daily. But when
it comes to promises
spurring hope, it's wise
to remember there are

too

few reasons to follow
through, when hope is,
truthfully, the most tangible
goal. Far too

many

people believe in the intrinsic
commonality of their brethren,
and that good shall prevail,
disregarding completely the

variables

that allow evil to take root,
sprout. Branch out. Flower.

Andrea

FLOWERING

In a protected alcove just outside
my front door is a magnolia tree.
Everyone said it was impossible

to keep my tree alive. That one
hard-frosting winter would take
it out, right down to the roots.

That it would never grow. Never
flourish. Never, ever gift me with
its luscious fragrance. But we—

that tree and I—have proved 'em
wrong. It takes a lot of work: piling
compost around its slender trunk

as autumn claims its leaves.
Blanketing its naked head when ice
and snow threaten. Uncovering it

when faux spring days deny winter's
embrace, and when late-season clouds
march toward us, covering it again.

Maybe it's the super-tree strength
of one special magnolia. Maybe it's all
on me. But yes, we proved 'em wrong.

SYNERGY

That's what we have, my magnolia
and me, and when I think about it,

I have to wonder if all relationships
can be maintained and, more, made

to flourish, with the right combination
of synergy and energy. All around me,

I see them in various stages of meltdown:
My parents'. My sister's. My best friend's.

Can they be salvaged with enough energy?
Lacking proper synergy, should they be?

When I consider how many years and
tears I invested in my own failing marriage,

only to have it crumble because Steve
and I had zero synergy except hormonal,

the weight is suffocating. So why would
I dare take a chance on believing there might

be a future for Robin and me, totally on
the strength of three days of great synergy,

most of it involving food, wine, and sex?
Call me an optimist. Or just call me crazy.

CRAZY

Because as of tomorrow, Rumble
from Down Under, with Robin
firmly at their helm, return to
Las Vegas, their home ground.

You might think that would be Sydney
or Melbourne, but apparently American
women are more into male strippers
than Aussie women are. Or at least

they tip better. And one of the major
Vegas casinos is happy to ante up
regular male-stripper salaries to keep
those women coming in to eat, drink,

and play slot machines on their way
to the showroom. From the start,
Robin made it clear that Reno was
a temporary gig. But, hey, Tahoe

was just a date. One that turned
into delectable sex. So when he asked
to see me again, uh, was I going
to say no? The third time was

the talisman that made me want
to believe in magic again. So, yeah.
I know I'm crazy. But Vegas isn't so
far away. A lot closer than Sydney.

SO TONIGHT

I'm cooking him dinner—the way
to a man's heart and all. And he will
meet Harley, a very big step for both
of them. I have never introduced her
to one of my post-Steve relationships.
They have never felt permanent enough.

This one doesn't exactly feel that way,
either. But it's the closest I've come,
and maybe it's good for her to realize
my life isn't over because her father and I
split up. He has moved on. Why shouldn't
I? "Thanks for helping with the apples."

> She peels them carefully, trying not
> to take too much fruit along with
> the skin. *No problem.* It's the most
> she's said since I invited her participation.
> I think she wants to talk about Robin
> but isn't sure how. Guess I'll have to

start. "You'll like Robin. He's from
Australia, so he has a really brilliant
accent. Plus, he's cute. And funny . . ."
Her knife action speeds up, then slows.
She starts to say something. Shakes
her head. "What? Talk to me, Harl."

IT'S A VERY LONG FEW SECONDS

Before she finds her voice.

Finally, she spits it out, *I just never*
thought about you falling in love.

"Whoa, now, wait a minute.
I never said anything about love."

I know. But since you met him,
you're . . . different. Happier, I guess.

"And that's a bad thing . . . how?
You don't want me to be happy?"

I want you to be happy because
of me. Not him. Not anyone else.

The knife begins to tremble. I go
to her, steady her hand with mine.

"Harley, you totally make me happy.
Well, except when I see you crushing

on Chad . . . ," I try. But the joke fails
to make her smile. "Look, you know

how you feel when Chad smiles at
you? Every woman wants to feel that

way. Being a mom doesn't change
that, not even when you're the mom

of the best kid in the universe.
Anyway, I'm just having fun with

Robin. We're not getting married
or anything like that. You know?"

Still, the smile eludes her. *Not now,*
you're not. But that might change.

Irritation prickles. This is just dinner.
We're not moving in together. "Harley,

how come it doesn't piss you off that
your dad found someone new?"

I never expected anything different
from Dad. He's got personality flaws.

Total crackup! "Ha!" I spit. "Ain't
it the truth? Ain't it the truth?"

She's laughing too, thank God.
"Honey, don't worry, okay? Robin

and I have only gone out a few times.
He's leaving for Vegas tomorrow.

It's a friendship, not a commitment.
I just wanted him to meet the girl

who will always be my top priority.
Let him see why I love you, okay?"

THE APPLES

Are peeled, sliced, and simmering
toward sauce before Harley asks,
*Did you ever love Dad? I mean,
were the two of you really in love?*

I expected the question long before
this and have dreaded the discussion.
"I definitely thought so once. But
young love doesn't always last."

*But it does sometimes, right? I mean,
look at Brianna's mom and dad.
They've been together, like, forever,
and . . .* Anxiety edges her voice.

This narrow splinter of me wants
to pop her bubble. But for what
purpose? It will happen soon
enough. "Sometimes, it does."

*Have you ever been in love with
anyone besides Dad?* When I
tell her not really, she nails me.
Then why did you get divorced?

I've answered this question one
hundred different ways. But
ultimately, it came down to,
"Sometimes love isn't enough."

THE EVENING

Goes better than I hoped for.
Harley is completely charming.
Ditto Robin. The two joke and
discuss current events. At one

point, Robin looks at me.
Bright kid you've got here.
Then he winks at Harley.
Your mom takes after you.
The pork roast is juicy, hints
at the sage and garlic rub.
And when I tell Robin
he can thank Harley for

the applesauce, he smiles at
her. *Beauty, brains, and*
a fabulous chef too? Where
have you been all my life?
After dessert, Harley vanishes
into her room. Robin glances
at me, but I cannot see a way
to engage in a lust-soaked

goodbye, so we settle for
several desire-laced kisses.
God, he says, *I'm really*
going to miss you. But
we'll see each other again
before too very long. When
I ask him if he promises,
he crosses his heart. *Promise.*

MEANWHILE

It's back to
the same ol' grind.
The routine I have no choice but to adhere to.

Up early.
(Mostly) organic breakfast.
Dropping Harley at her summer program.

Work.
(Diverting) Vern's flirtation.
Fixing other people's problems, and lots of them.

Home.
(When possible) avoiding Steve.
Striving to be a good friend and better mom.

Dinner.
(Necessarily) watching TV with Harley
before making her shower, scrub teeth, go to bed.

Nothing new.
It's all the same as it was before, with
one big exception. I can't stop obsessing about Robin.

On a whim,
I call him. Just to say hello, that I miss
him. His phone rings. Rings again. I'm about to hang

up when I hear,
Hello? A woman. Not quite awake.
I ask for Robin. *Sorry, love,* she says. *He's sleeping.*

NOT QUITE AWAKE

That perfect state of being:
not here, exactly; not there,
completely. The beautiful,
horrible, lovely, awful place

where

what is and what might be
collide, merge. Create
alternative realities where
nothing is believable and

anything

locked inside imagination
is well within your grasp if only
you stretch a little taller. Shrink
a little smaller. The key

is

on the table. At the bottom
of the rabbit hole, behind
the looking glass, whatever
your obsession is

possible.

Holly

YOU CAN'T OUTRUN OBSESSION

For quite some time, running
was my obsession—my major
fixation, anyway. It was a way
to gain control. Claim power.

The problem with power is
knowing what to do with it
once you finally get it. Some
people go a little crazy. Count

me one of them. Today, I'm
running along the Truckee River
bike path. I needed new scenery.
Something to make me forget

about the bog I've totally been
sucked into. Namely, falling—no,
smashing myself face-first—in
love with Bryan. It was supposed

to be fun. Innocent flirtation.
A little sex on the side, maybe.
It was *never* supposed to turn
into this all-encompassing need

to be with him. To hear his voice.
Return his kiss. Feel the heat
of him on me. Around me. Over
me. Inside me, where I absorb him.

I KNOW

Loving him is more than wrong.
It's impossible. But I am snared.

We both have "others" who need
us. Others whom we are committed

to. And yet, we look to escape
our others. Search for hours away

from them, holding tight to what's
right about us, midst the sin of us.

Early morning on the river, the air
lifts, cool, though it will be ungodly

warm come noon. I am surprised
to find myself approaching a couple,

standing at the railing overlooking
the rapids. They are younger—maybe

in their late twenties—and even from
fifty yards away, everything about

the way they touch tells me they are
insanely in love. I don't want to look

like a voyeur, but I slow, savoring
the interaction—connection oblivious

to outside observation. Lost in each
other, neither takes the slightest note

of me. But I'm watching them—how
his hands never leave her sinewy body.

How her eyes never leave his striking
face. Such beauty in youth! I will never

be that young again, and while
I may be as beautiful as she, every day

brings me closer to old, and what
that means. Cracked leather skin.

Pitted thighs. Watery memory.
Passing men without their noticing.

Envy sizzles, though I don't care
about *her*. Don't care about *him*.

It is the *they* of them that plucks
the jealous chord. They are what I want

to be half of, and the half that I strive
to be is why I run. And as I pass, I wonder

if they, one or both, have others,
waiting for half of them to come home.

EXACERBATING EVERY DOUBT

Is the day—my fortieth birthday.
Forty. Likely halfway to death,
and what do I have to show for it?

River rushing by repeats:
halfway, halfway, halfway.

A tidy little life. Decent husband.
Privileged kids. Showcase house.
Enviable lifestyle, looking in.

Distant traffic echoes:
tidy life, tidy life, tidy life.

But spend some time behind my
walls, you come to understand
the truth of living a cliché.

Crow on the high wire caws:
cliché, cliché, cliché, cliché.

I have no dreams that belong to
me. Not one personal goal to aspire
to. No obstacles to conquer.

Breeze through the willows:
no dreams, no dreams, no . . .

What happened to the girl who
believed her touch could demolish
the conventions choking the world?

THAT WAS ME, ONCE

I didn't know exactly how I was going to do it,
but I believed that I could. And that I would.

All I had to do was escape the straitjacket
hold Mama and Papa had on me. Find my way

beyond small-town rules and expectation to
the freedoms a university afforded. Against heavy

odds, I succeeded in that, and though I was still
breaking trail, the journey had begun. And then

I had to go and fall, butt over brains, in love.
Yes, I could have done worse than to tumble

for Jace. But what I was too naïve to understand
was the importance of self-discovery. Sucked up

by the vacuum of filling him, I lost the essence
of me. I should have known, having witnessed

Papa unweave the tapestry of Mama's dreams.
Filament by filament, it tattered into rags

until she was eager enough for death to take
her. What good is a tomorrow void of hope?

I'M NOT READY TO DIE

Not even close, but if I am halfway
there, I'm damn sure going to do
some things first. I turn back toward
where I parked my car, pick up my pace,
composing my bucket list as I run:

One. Compete in and finish a marathon.
I don't have to come in first or even
in the top twenty, but I will not cross
the line in the very back of the pack.
And so, I will train even harder.

Two. Experience things other people
are afraid of. Skydiving. Bungee
jumping. Rafting class-four river
rapids. Maybe a taste of the S & M
scene. Maybe even more than a nibble.

Three. I will find Sarah Hill and demand
to know if she is my mother. And if she is,
I'll ask her what she ever saw in a son of
a bitch like Paul Driscoll, who won't
admit to sex with anyone but his wife.

Four. Remain open to possibilities,
while doing my best not to damage
current relationships. But should it
come down to a choice between love
and responsibility, love will prevail.

BUCKET LIST COMPLETED

And run accomplished, I towel
off, head for home. When I get
there, I push loudly through
the door. The kids are planning

a surprise party for me. I, of course,
know nothing about it, nor about
how tonight's fancy birthday dinner
with Jace is a total setup. Wink-wink.

I haven't let anything on, not even
to Jace. When I come in, the sneaks
are in the kitchen, and when they hear
me, their harried conversation quiets

beneath a blanket of *Shshshshs.*
"Hey, guys," I call loudly. "Where
is everyone? Did you fix your
old mom a birthday breakfast?"

Uh, yeah, Trace shouts back.
Special K, with a candle. I
can make you some toast with
ice cream too, if you want.

By the time I reach the coffeepot,
my children have attained covert
status. *Thanks for reminding us*
it's your birthday, says Brianna.

Yeah, agrees Mikki. *We probably*
would have forgotten all about
it. That would suck. How old
are you again? Oh, yeah, forty.

I give my sweet daughter a scathing
look, pour a deep, black mug of coffee.
"Thanks for reminding me of *that.*
It had almost slipped my mind."

Trace comes over, gives me a bear
hug. *No worries, old woman. You*
don't look a day past thirty-nine
and three-quarters. When did he grow

into such a smart-ass, emphasis
on the "smart"? Takes after me
in that way, I suppose. "Keep
talking, and I'll keep thinking up

ways to spend your inheritance
before I kick the bucket. Which
means, I guess, that I'll have to hurry
and spend it, since I'm getting so close."

Mik and Trace laugh, but Brianna
is her usual serious self. *Do not say*
stuff like that! Oh, and you stink.
Why don't you take a nice bath?

SEMI-REBUKED

And totally amused, I agree to go
destink myself. First, I refill my mug,

then head upstairs to my bedroom,
leaving the kids to their plotting.

Brianna was right. The scent of dried
perspiration follows me, though I kind

of like how it smells—like triumph.
I check my cell for messages. There are four.

From Jace: *I made six p.m. reservations*
at Glen Eagles. Can we meet there?

How romantic. Maybe we should
go Dutch. The second is from Sahara:

Hey, girl. Call me. I want to shoot
something past you. What's up

with her? Don't need to know right
now. Next, a very subdued Andrea:

Can we talk? I need your advice.
Can't remember the last time she

asked for that! Finally, the person
I wanted most to hear from. Bryan:

Can you get away Saturday night?

SATURDAY NIGHT

As the days go, one hovers above
the others when it comes to fun.
Sunday may run a close second,
being the favored day for resting,
but it's really just a breather after

Saturday
night

blazing. Those who value toil
above all else forget their shine
requires a weekly polish with
a healthy dose of play and Saturday

is
when,

by and large, the most options
present themselves. Sidestep
every boundary, toss logic out
beyond the threshold, and

the
world

is just a marble spinning
on a plate of possibilities.
Little wonder, really, that
the man hell-bent on
making sense of it all often

goes
a little
crazy.

Marissa

CALL ME CRAZY

Or, like Shane, call me ignorant
and self-absorbed, but I can't help
but wonder if his hooking up
with Alex, knowing the boy

is HIV positive, wasn't just a way
to get back at Christian and me.
Or, at the very least, a way to
shake us up and seize our attention.

Shane says my concern is fake,
And anyway, he claims, HIV
is no longer an automatic death
warrant, but even if it was, he

never fails to use protection.
Condoms. Hardly infallible.
Why must he present me with
this kind of anxiety? Worry

has been a daily staple for four
years, and now the measure
has been doubled. Thanks, if
the boys are to be believed,

to love. Young love. Young gay
love. My son's young gay love.
Why is it harder to accept that
than to accept just plain "gay"?

GOD, I'M JUST SO SICK

Of digesting and redigesting
the facts of my life. Invariable facts
that will not change, no matter how
many times I regurgitate them.

I'm a one-trick camel.

I wish I could go back to flying.
Except, if I were wishing, and wishes did
come true, I'd wish I could go back
and become an airline pilot.

Not an aerial waitress.

And if I could take stuff back,
some other purser would have been
working first class that day, serving
drinks and flashing cleavage.

I'd have been at the controls.

Only, there's this. Changing
even the smallest moment means
every single thing about my life would
no doubt be different. Everything.

Different isn't necessarily better.

WHO KNOWS

Where I'd be without Shelby?
She keeps me grounded,
roots me firmly in
the "what is," rather
than meandering
some "what could be."
And every precious day
with her is a reminder
of the tenuous foothold
each of us has on this planet.

Who knows

what I'd be without Shane?
For every challenge
he tosses my way, the trade-off
is his indomitable spirit.
How he surrounds me
with it. The way it infiltrates
my pores. My cells.
I gave him birth, and yet,
he breathes life into me.

Who knows

who I'd be without Christian?
Would I be as strong?
If I consider the breadth of our mutual
years, must I not admit
that for every pain-infused minute,
we shared twenty saturated with joy?

PHILOSOPHICAL MUSING

Is easy enough when the domestic
drama dies down and everyone
withdraws to their private corners.

An hour ago, everything blew to high
heaven, the napalm being the news
about Alex's HIV. I tried to keep it from

Christian. But he happened to walk in on
me, working at my computer. And up
on the screen was an HIV informational

website. He thought the worst at first.
Of course, so did I. But while I reacted
with fear, concern—anger, even—Christian,

who was already well on his way to
drunk, detoured all the way to righteous.
A half-full tumbler of scotch in one hand,

he marched straight to Shane's room.
It was, of course, locked. *Open up!*
he yelled at the wood. Shane, who was

still sleeping off Friday night, took too
much time. *Goddamn it, you little shit.*
Open this fucking door. By the time

Shane dragged himself out of bed and
complied, Christian was agitated. He grabbed
Shane by his tee shirt. *Are you plain stupid?*

Shane fell straight into smart-ass. *Is*
there another kind of stupid? Like,
uh, fancy stupid? Or beautiful stupid?

Christian gave the shirt a yank. The motion
sloshed whiskey out of the glass and down
the front of him, but he didn't seem to notice.

Shut up. What the hell are you doing?
Trying to die? You can't mess around
with HIV. The husky-voiced sentences

blurred around the edges. *AIDS is*
God's way of saying "gay" is a very bad
choice. Emphasis on the last word.

Shane remained unmoved. *Do you*
know how Alex contracted HIV, Dad?
He was raped. Held down, choked,

and sodomized by his stepfather's
brother. Good ol' Uncle Stu. No
choice in that, Dad. None at all.

Christian turned a dozen shades of red.
But he didn't back down or apologize,
though he did let go of Shane's shirt.

He stalked to his room, changed his
clothes, and slammed out the door with
a parting *I've got some work to finish up.*

THAT INEBRIATED

I'm pretty sure he won't get much
work done. What he really needs,

I think, is some private room to
process today's information slam.

He shouldn't drive in that condition,
of course, though I suspect he's had

a lot of practice. And what's a wife
to do? Try to wrestle the car keys

from his hand? I could worry. Should.
But what good would it do to shovel

shit on top of manure? Shane remains
sequestered in his room. I knock.

"Want some lunch?" His negative reply
is anticipated. Oh well. At least I offered.

I'm not hungry either, but a cup of tea
sounds pretty good. I put on the kettle,

and I'm choosing my tea when the phone
rings. It's Christian's work number. He made it.

> *Hey.* His voice is surprisingly clear.
> *Sorry about what happened.* An apology?

Uh . . . I don't know if you planned
on washing or not, but don't bother

with the stuff on the floor in my room.
I'll pick them up when I get home.

I shouldn't have left them there.
That was a slovenly thing to do.

I'm not even sure how to respond
except to say, "No problem. Be safe."

The kettle whistles and I pour my
tea—blackberry green—and while

it steeps, Christian's words percolate.
Something's wrong about the call.

First of all, he never says he's sorry.
And second, he leaves clothes

heaped on the floor all the time.
A little voice nags, *Better go see*

what he doesn't want you to see.
That's it, isn't it? There's something . . .

I don't hurry to look, because now
that tiny voice says, *You don't want*

to know. Wish it would make up its
mind. Do I want to know or don't I?

IT'S A SMALL PILE

At the foot of the bed. One chambray
shirt. One pair of boxers. One pair
of jeans, all smelling of scotch. I pick
up the shirt. Nothing unusual but
the spreading stain. Ditto the underwear.

Ah, but in the front pocket of the jeans,
there is an unfamiliar cell phone. Christian's?
I hold it in one hand, stare at the dark
screen while the minuscule voice whispers
fiercely, *Turn it on. Why are you waiting?*

If I were the type to talk to myself, I'd say,
"I'm waiting because I'm afraid if I look,
what's left standing will collapse
completely, crushing me beneath it."
But I really have no choice, do I?

I push the button. Slide the arrow
to unlock. Look at the apps lined up
on the screen. Messages. Calendar.
Games. Notes. Utilities. Camera.
Photos. My eyes stop there. Photos.

I tap and up comes the Albums screen.
Las Vegas. New Orleans. Atlantic City.
Paris. Rome. Venice. London. Istanbul.
Hawaii. St. Thomas. Puerto Rico. Trips
Christian has taken over the past five years.

TRIPS

Ostensibly for business.
Trips when I was pregnant.
Trips when I had a new baby.
Trips when there was no choice
but to leave me home, caring
for our chronically ill daughter
and sexuality-searching son.
Trips without me.
Trips with her.
Skye Sheridan, a rising star
at ITV. But whether her sun
began to climb before or after
she started sleeping with Christian,
I don't know. That she is sleeping
with him is clear in the photos.

Photos that show a couple in love.
A couple posing for the camera.
A couple kissing. Laughing.
Eating. Drinking. Being way too merry
across the country, around the globe.
A couple, doing those things
while I was home, pregnant.
Home, caring for Shelby and Shane.

Home, while my husband,
Christian Trask, took his heart away
from me and gave it to Skye Sheridan,
"just a coworker," who also happened to be
a rising star in the falling night
of his life.

A STAR RISES

Pale. Frail. A stitch
of embroidered light
upon the dark forever
fabric of space. And

somewhere

beneath the spreading
embellishment, night
creatures begin their opera
of croaks and hoots and
humming, unaware
that elsewhere

a sun

has risen into a parallel
plane. And what sound
mind could possibly claim
such precision is random?
As every alpha wave

begins

its forward flow,
an equivalent tide starts
its omega journey, fated

to die.

Andrea

FATE HAS DECREED

I am to remain single. I knew
that years ago. So why the hell
did I think Fate had changed
her mind? I am an idiot. Men lie.

I know that. Men cheat. I know
that too. They cheat *on* me.
They cheat *with* me. And what's
messed up is that it isn't any better

to be the cheated-with than it is
to be the cheated-on, because
the outcome is the same. I am
at home, alone, on Saturday.

No date. No dinner out. No sex
to come. No daughter, even. She's still
at Brianna's. Holly's surprise party
included a sleepover. Surprise!

Holly knew all about it, of course,
though she faked surprise pretty
well. I think what shocked her
the most was that her in-laws

were there. Jace's mom even gave
her a present—a live orchid. Uh,
okay. Holly is to plants what Raid
is to ants. A thing of beauty, doomed.

MORE THAN SURPRISED

Holly seemed majorly distracted
pretty much all evening. She picked

at her cake—a fabulously lopsided
chocolate-on-chocolate affair, baked

by Brianna and Harley. I tried to help,
but they wanted to do it all themselves.

The kids insisted on karaoke, and Holly
did do a pretty good rendition of *Material*

Girl before retreating into her obvious
desire to be engaged somewhere else.

As the evening progressed, I pulled her
off to one side, hoping to talk about Robin.

She allowed me a few minutes of
complaint before offering weak advice.

> *First of all, you don't even know who*
> *that was. Why don't you call back and*
>
> *talk to him? Maybe it was his sister*
> *or something. And if it wasn't, forget him.*
>
> *You deserve someone better.* That's right.
> Because they're lining up on my doorstep.

SHE MIGHT BE RIGHT

About calling Robin back.
Ascertaining whether or not
the sleepy-voiced woman
with access to his cell phone
while he was snoring nearby
was, in fact, his sister.

But logic rarely lies.

The real problem, of course,
is I am a coward. I hate
confrontation and validation
of my logical suspicions
would most certainly lead
to that. I'm tired of fighting.

My dukes are dropped.

I don't have much vested
in the relationship. I'm not
freaked-out in love with him.
All that breathless anticipation
was, realistically, a lot more
like adolescent crushing.

Like, totally doomed to fail.

MY CEREBRAL MEANDERINGS

Are interrupted by the telephone.
Robin?

Ah, come on, Andrea.
Just look at you.

No, not Robin. Marissa.

Leave it. She hardly ever
calls unless there's a problem.

I seriously consider leaving
it, and it goes to voicemail.

Hi. It's me . . . wavering.
Can you come over . . . ?

Damn it. Not today. Too busy
feeling sorry for myself to—

I really need someone
to talk to.

Someone to talk to? Me? Like,
sister to sister or something?

Wow. That's different, isn't it?
Probably shouldn't leave it.

I probably shouldn't. Whatever
it is sounds important.

Anyway, talking to her has to be
better than talking to yourself.

THEN AGAIN, MAYBE NOT

When I call to let her know
I'm on my way, her single-word
acknowledgment sounds shaky.

By the time I get there, she is
trembling. Pacing like a caged
panther. I imagine the worst.

But Shelby is not the source
of her distress. And what I see
on the cell phone screen makes

me ashamed of myself for moping
around about Robin. Holy, as some
people might say, fucking crapola!

When Marissa first hooked up
with Christian, I liked him well
enough, though I found him cool.

As the years progressed, and their
shared difficulties pushed him ever
further away from Missy, my opinion

of him retreated to the remotest
reaches of family connection. But I
wouldn't have called it active dislike.

At this moment, I despise him.
Infidelity is never a good thing.
But what I see here is adoration.

MARISSA AND I

Haven't been very close lately,
but a fierce swell of sisterly love
makes me wrap my arms around
her. Her first reaction is to tense,
but when I say, "Oh, Miss, I'm so
sorry," every muscle seems to liquefy.

I've rarely seen her cry, and she
fights it now. *I knew something*
was wrong. Maybe even suspected
he was sleeping around. But I never
expected anything like . . . this.
They're completely in love. Aren't they?

Rage jerks her from my arms, fires
up her tears, and suddenly I become
an impotent bystander. I want to
help. Have no clue how to. Guess
I'll just ask a ridiculous question.
"Who is she? Do you have any idea?"

Yes, I do. The words seethe from
between taut lips. *She works with him.*
Travels with him, as you can see.
According to the company newsletter,
"Skye Sheridan is a rising star at ITV."
Wonder who else there knows why.

SURELY NOBODY ELSE KNOWS

But when I suggest that, she tells me
about seeing Chris and this Skye person,
sitting across a table, looking into
each other's eyes as lovers do,

in unencumbered view by the window.
How he saw Missy, Claire, and Shelby.
How he jumped up to say hello, but returned
to his window-side seat unapologetically.

If he's that open about their relationship,
it is most probably assumed at work,
if not admitted to. Men are such dogs.
"Does Chris know you know?"

She shakes her head. *Not yet.* Now
she tells me about his argument
with Shane. How he left for work.
Phoned to divert her from his booze-

soaked clothes. *It's not his regular*
cell phone. I've never seen it before.
God, why would . . . how could . . .
I just can't believe all the lies!

I can but don't say so. Cheating
prick! A bloat of indignation
escapes in the belch of a single
question, "What are you going to do?"

THE OBVIOUS ANSWER

Would be to head straight to divorce
court. Take the bastard for all he's got.

Offer up the evidence, ask a judge
for alimony and child support. Make

Chris's bank account suffer so at
the very least he can't afford luxury

trips for himself and Ms. Sheridan.
Of course, that would free them to

get married. But who knows? Minus
the money, he might be less attractive.

Missy says none of that, however.
I'm not sure yet. And until I am,

please don't tell anyone. Not Mom
and Dad. And especially not Shane.

"Why not? Don't you think Shane
needs to know that his father is a—"

No! Shane and Chris barely speak now.
I don't want that rift to grow any wider.

To tell you the truth, I'm surprised
Shane doesn't already suspect. He's—

I DON'T GET TO HEAR

What she thinks Shane is because
Chris's arrival curtly cuts her off.

He breezes through the door, wearing
a clearly manufactured smile,

unaware that his figurative skeleton
has been outed, bones snapping, from

its closet. All it takes is the look we give
him to make his eyes start searching

for a clue. They find it on the coffee
table, in the form of a cell phone.

The grin falls away, and he starts to
sputter, but there is no lie that can

cover this, nor any explanation to
prevent the coming earthquake.

Should I stay and shore up my sister?
Should I go, allow a private collapse?

Chris ignores me as he half stumbles
toward Missy, right hand reaching,

cupped slightly, as if for something fragile.
She takes two small backward steps,

halts him with a quiet plea: *Why?*

A QUIET PLEA

May seem understated,
but when called into play
at the proper moment, it

can

serve as a power move—
like a pawn placing a king
in check. A wise player will

take

great care to interpret
the future, near and far,
before initiating action.

Where a straight-on
charge will force

a man

to plant his feet and raise
a strong defense,
a quiet plea could convince
him to lay his weapons

down.

QUIET

Shrouds the kitchen this morning,
everyone sleeping off my birthday
party, even though Andrea, Jace,
and I were the only ones drinking
anything stronger than lemonade.

Jace's parents only drink at home.
Pretty sure the only reason they bothered
to come was that Brianna asked
them to. I glance at the scrumptious
orchid, sitting beside the crumb-

covered cake plate. It is lovely.
But I have no idea how to keep it
alive. Which makes it the perfect
metaphor for my marriage. All
I could think about on my run

today was Bryan. Everything about
him is new. Exciting. Fearless.
Things I want to be too. And
I can be, with him. The only time
I'm scared anymore is when I try

to figure out the bottom line.
I love Jace. But I'm in love with
Bryan, who loves his wife but says
he's in love with me. "Love" is
safe. "In love" is reckless. Alive.

TONIGHT WILL BE RECKLESS

Bryan and I are going to the Topaz.
Who knew Reno had such a place—

a club for couples, with a few single
women allowed in the mix. *They lock*

the doors at ten, Bryan told me. *So*
we need to be there a little before.

At ten, there are no rules except
everyone must agree to participating

in the debauchery. "No means no."
But everyone is there to say yes,

unless there is no attraction to whoever
happens to be attracted to you.

If I said I wasn't nervous, I'd be lying.
But it's a good kind of nervous,

anticipation prickling tiny goose bumps
all over my body. I'm almost afraid

to drink this cup of coffee. Don't think
I can handle much more stimulation.

And I'm not even there yet. The weird
thing is, in the early days of my love

for Jace, I would never have considered
doing something like this with him. In

fact, had he wanted to, I would have
died from humiliation and jealousy.

Somehow, with Bryan, there is no
jealousy. Maybe it's because our love

already carries us beyond the bounds
of "normal." (Is jealousy normal?)

Maybe it's because I'm more mature
and better equipped to understand

the concept of taking pleasure in
my partner's pleasure, even if it's with

someone else. Maybe it's just because
I've turned into a regular pervert.

I really don't know why. I really don't
care why. It's enough that I feel

this way. Now I just have to make it
through the day—a regular Saturday,

with my husband and kids. I hear
stirring now. A drowsy buzz of voices,

headed this way. I stash all thoughts
of the Topaz. Consider breakfast.

IT'S A HOMESPUN AFFAIR

Pancakes with strawberries
and whipped cream, left over
from last night. (Only teenagers

would want whipped cream
on top of chocolate cake with
chocolate icing.) All sleepy-eyed,

Jace saunters in to help.
He sidles up from behind,
wraps his arms around me.

Forty looks great on you,
he says. *And I bet fifty*
will look every bit as good.

He kisses the back of my neck,
drawing squeals from Harley
and Bri, a long sigh from me.

"You're full of it, but thanks
anyway." I offer the spatula,
and he takes over the flipping.

Despite everything, a large
measure of love sifts down, blends
with a heaping bowlful of guilt.

Surrounded by my family,
soaking in pleasant banter,
I think about calling tonight off.

BUT AS MORNING GIVES WAY

To a crazy-hot August afternoon, tempers
flaring, along with the temperature, I am
happy that common sense did not prevail.

I need diversion. I need escape. I need to lie
to make my getaway. Somehow, the "night
out with my writer friends" gets easier

every time I use it. The plan is to leave my car
in the Walmart parking lot. Inside it is
the loose-fitting dress I wore to conceal

the critically short skirt and sheer blouse
I greet Bryan in. He takes one look, whistles
through his teeth. *I think I just changed*

my mind about sharing you. He kisses
me with such intensity I want to climb
into his lap, urge him inside me right here

on the front seat, like a couple of kids.
Instead, I move his hand to my exposed
thigh. It begins a slow upward crawl,

explores the edges of my stockings.
Garter belt? he exhales. *Oh, you are my*
kind of girl. What else are you hiding?

I WON'T KEEP

A whole lot hidden at the Topaz.
It's pretty much a dive, all done
down in red Naugahyde and
brown linoleum, with low, low
lighting to disguise cracks, chips,
and wrinkles. It smells old.
But the place is crowded—maybe
twenty-five couples mill around,
waiting for the ten o'clock lock.
Most are older than me, but some
are attractive enough, and all assess
us with blatant interest, including
the bartender. *Ooh. Someone new.*
He checks me out openly. *Nice.*
I'm Paul. What's your poison?
Bryan orders mojitos, and when
Paul sets them down, he says,
Flash 'em, this round's on me.
What the hell. That's what I'm
here for, right? My scooped-neck
blouse is stretchy lace. One quick
tug and the tits of a stranger
spill out. (Someone who calls her
breasts "tits"!) This is a whole
new Holly, one I wasn't really sure
existed until this moment. But she
does, and she's just getting started.
At ten on the nose, Paul goes to
the door. *Anyone want to leave?*
No one does, so he pushes
the lock and the party begins.

IT GOES IN MY JOURNAL

As "fiction" titled ***Bitter Orange***

At the Topaz, they lock the doors at precisely ten every Saturday night. Tonight the place is crowded with couples. Hungry. Starving. Thirsting, despite the flow of alcohol. At ten-oh-five, the quenching begins.

I am half of a couple. The other half is a relative stranger, though one I am oddly comfortable with. And because we have nothing vested in our relationship, there is no jealousy when a woman, younger than Iand quite beautiful in a leonine way, approaches us. "I'm Lorraine," she says. "Do you party?"

"That's why we're here." My partner pulls all his attention away from the peripheral action—already becoming quite hot—and directs it toward Lorraine.

Her own other half watches from a table near the back of the room. She nods toward him. "That's Micah. Go say hi. What are you drinking?"

A sudden shimmer of nerves makes me reconsider, but a big gulp of rum-flavored courage pushes me toward Micah, who is every bit as beautiful as Lorraine, in a completely masculine way.

A short round of introductions is all that's required.
By the time Lorraine joins us, drinks in hand, Micah
has already made his intentions quite clear.
"Let me make you more comfortable."

He pulls off my blouse with a practiced
hand, and before I can think about what
might come next, he has lifted my breasts
from the confines of my bra. "Lovely," he says.
"Don't you think so?" he asks Lorraine.

In answer, her lips, cool and silk-smooth,
wrap around my nipple. Oh, God. This girl
is not like the other. She is not gentle, her
actions almost like a man's. Lorraine
licks and pinches, right, left, and Micah
moves into director mode. "Sit up on the table,
facing me," he says. Then, to Lorraine, "I want
you in panties only." The two of us comply.

Micah eases a hand up under my skirt,
slides the thong of my own panties to one side,
and as his thumb begins a slow, slippery ride,
Lorraine stands over him, facing me. And now
I kiss a girl for the second time. She tastes of orange
peel—bitter, sharp. I bury my head between
the plentiful rounds of her breasts. Inhale.
Her skin is warm and softly scented with ginger.

And now, as if I've done this a hundred times
before, I move my mouth to taste her nipples.
They are larger than mine. Luscious.
My partner's hands pull me backward to lie
across the table. He kisses Lorraine as Micah's
tongue finds the sweet spot between my legs.

It all becomes a heady mix of men. Tongues.
Hands. Fingers. The unique brine of woman.
The heat of cock. Condoms. Don't forget
those. And, God, orgasm. Mine. Hers. Theirs.
I think other people are watching. Touching

themselves because this foursome is amazing.
Beautiful people doing incredibly sensual
things. Segue to dirty, nasty things. And . . .

And for a second—but only a second—
I flash on Jace, at home with the kids.
The disquieting thought makes me ask
myself: what kind of wife and mother
has group sex with strangers in public?

PUBLIC SEX

Is a curious thing.
Many who participate
aren't exactly porn-
star quality.

Not

every swinger is
one of the beautiful
people, and yet,
not only do they
bare it all

for

strangers, they do
it with panache.
Imagine you and
a fifty-something
beer belly, doing

the

dirty, live, in front
of an audience while
the one you love
performs with some-
one who bears a

faint

resemblance to
your great-aunt Jo.
That takes a sense
of humor. And it
takes an eclipse

of heart.

Marissa

ECLIPSED

An apt description of this Sunday—
shadowed by uncertainty. Curtained.

I don't even know how to feel.
I stopped being angry at Christian a long

time ago. Anger requires energy,
something I don't dare waste on

what cannot be altered. Five years
of deception—nothing can change

that. I'm hurt, I guess. But it's more
like a dull throb than a brilliant bolt

of pain. And somewhere, I knew.
Yet I chose to ignore every sign, too

sucked into my own little closet
of sorrow. Hey, how can a spouse's

affair compete with witnessing
your child's valiant battle to live,

knowing she's destined to lose
it? It's all a matter of degree, really.

I'm sure I will never forget this.
Could I forgive it? I don't know.

FORGIVENESS

Is the last thing on my mind, however.
Right now, I just want to get through
today. Christian handled Shelby's morning
CPT, took her out for a walk. He went

to the grocery store to buy stuff
"for a special dinner" with yet
another *I'm so sorry, Marissa.*
I'll never touch her again. Promise.

What he told me yesterday, after
Andrea made a necessary exit, was
that he'd already broken things off
with Skye. Months ago, in fact.

The pictures suggest otherwise,
as she was definitely with him on
his last trip to New Orleans. *I'll still*
have to travel with her sometimes,

was his explanation. *The job right*
now pretty much demands it. But
I swear we'll always have separate
rooms. Skye understands that.

If you want, I won't even sit next
to her on our flights. Please, Marissa,
you have to believe me. His voice
was building toward hysteria, and

I let him go on without comment.
What could I say, anyway? All the lies!
So many years! It wasn't just an affair.
It was a committed relationship, and

his commitment to her—his love for
her—drew him far, far away from me.
How many of those nights when he
straggled into the guest room very

late did he come in wearing her
plastered to his skin? Did he shower
her off? Did he fall asleep inhaling
a drift of her? Did he dream of her?

Of them? Resignation gives way
to the gnaw of anger now. It grows
like a plant filmed in time-lapse,
shoots its vines through my body.

They wrap around every nerve ending,
squeeze. "No!" The word escapes me
in a scream. "You fucking son of a whore.
How could you do this to me?"

To me. To his family. His home. To
the memory of what we were and never
can be again. An acid rain of tears falls,
bitter against my skin. I hate him.

THE SMACK OF FOOTFALLS

In the hall reins me in. It's Shane,
running to see what happened to

me. I dry my eyes, but residual anger
keeps them brimming. He measures

me with a single discerning glance.
What happened? What did he do?

I just shrug. Still don't want Shane
to know. What good would come of it?

"Nothing. I'm sorry. I didn't mean for
you to hear anything. We had a fight is all."

A fight about me. He states it matter-
of-factly. Of course he'd think that.

"No, no. Not about you at all. About . . ."
Shit. Now what do I say? "About a new

SMA treatment I saw. Your dad doesn't
think it would be worth a try. But I do."

That seems to satisfy him. *Mom,
you probably don't want to hear this,*

but I agree with Dad. He's right. I didn't
want to hear that. *I think you should let*

the disease run its course. Shelby deserves
a dignified death. More treatment won't

stop her from dying. But it will take away
her dignity. I don't want to watch that,

and neither does Dad. And I don't think
you should, either. He pauses, watches

a new thread of anger blossom.
"I can't believe you said that! Where

did you get such ideas?" Then it hits
me. "From researching HIV? Is that how

you feel about Alex, should he develop
AIDS? That he deserves a dignified death?"

Yes, Mom. That's exactly how I feel.
Once it becomes obvious he has no

choice but death, I pray it's dignified.
I hope I'll be there to help him through

it, but that will probably be many years
from now. I know the odds of us

staying together that long aren't good.
I mean, we're both young and stupid.

He smiles, and that small burst of light
somehow manages to make me smile too.

WE ARE STANDING HERE

Semi-smiling at each other when Christian
comes in, loaded down with groceries.
He starts to say something, notices

Shane's body language. Looks at me
helplessly, certain I've told. But
I shake my head. "We're talking about

death." Now his expression shifts
to one of bewilderment. "Dignified
death, actually. For people we love."

I . . . uh . . . oh. Christian turns away,
puts the bags on the counter, begins
to unload them. *I got steaks. Thought*

we could barbecue. He spins back
around, says to Shane, *I bought an*
extra one, in case you wanted to invite

Alex to join us. Whoa. Major gesture,
even if it is coming from a suspect
place. *I'm sorry we fought yesterday.*

Shane is stunned into momentary
speechlessness. He recovers quickly,
though. *Alex and I will still both be gay.*

Christian nods. *That's what I hear.*
Guess I'll have to get over it.
You're still my son, Shane. I love you.

PUNGENT WORDS

Sharp with
apology. A bitter-
sweet entreaty for
reconnection, at least
if he is to be believed.

Shane looks
at me with some-
thing more than dis-
belief in his eyes. Can
what I find there be fear?

Christian waits
patiently for some
response. He's never
been what you'd call good
at patience. This is a major test.

One of us
really has to
yield, but I don't
think it should be me.
I'm totally idling in neutral.

Finally, Shane
reacts, in his usual
smart-ass way. *Action*
speaks louder than words,
Dad. But steak is a good start.

Christian grins.
And rib-eye too.
Thought your mom
was looking a little anemic.
Wiseass. Like father, like son.

SHANE GOES TO CALL ALEX

And issue what will doubtless be
a very surprising invitation. When
it's clear that he's out of earshot,
Christian pauses his pantry stocking.

You didn't tell him, did you? Why not?

"What good would it do? Look, if
everything else still goes to shit,
what just happened now was almost
worth it. Thank you for reaching out."

He shrugs. *I meant it. I do love him.*

"I never doubted that, Christian. I just
wasn't sure you'd ever admit that love
for him again. I'm glad you took
another look in your heart."

I love you too. He starts toward me.

"Don't." The word stops him cold.
"Please don't touch me. It will just
make me think about you touching
her. Shane's right. Words are cheap."

But I thought I could move back into . . .

"No! Are you kidding me? God,
Christian. That night, after the fireworks?
That night made me hope we could
put our lives back in order. Find

something resembling love again.
And then, nothing. Not a single kiss.
Not one kind word. In fact, you went
straight back to her, didn't you?"

No . . . Yes. But that night made me rethink . . .

"Whatever, Christian. Look. I'm not
ready to talk about this right now.
I can't stop thinking about you and
her, and five fucking years of lies!"

He hangs his head. *What are you going to do?*

"I don't know," I answer honestly.
"This is just so unfair. It would have
been easier if you'd walked out on me.
Given me the chance to make a new life."

How do you know a new life would be better?

Valid question. One I already have
the answer to, after much deliberation.
"If I knew without a doubt it would, you
wouldn't be standing there right now."

A NEW LIFE

Why do people ponder beginning
anew, abandoning one half-baked pie
in favor of starting from scratch:

picking

weevils from stale flour,
forever missing a few;

sifting

through obstacles—lumps,
clots, and sea salt cement;

scraping

the Crisco can, praying shelf
life is longer than expected;

mixing

and kneading and shaping
and half baking it all again.

Oh, give me pastry, hot from the oven,
flaky brown, the kind you must nibble
lest you miss its melt upon your tongue:

fruit,

coaxed ripe by northern sun,
sliced to translucency,

sugared

just beyond tart, spiced
with cinnamon, grate of nutmeg, a

brandy

splash; everything wrapped
in toasted wheat, tossed with

honey

and butter, unsalted sweet,
still married to the cream.

Andrea

STILL MARRIED

The phrase applies to too many
people I know who shouldn't
still be married. Mom and Dad,

sorry to say. Holly and Jace. Missy
and the asshole. Thank God I had
enough sense to call it quits before

a bad thing turned horrible. I mean,
I know you have to factor in the kids.
With my parents, Miss and I would

have been relatively okay. We had no
real expectations. Yeah, I know it's
easy to say now. And I know the not-

exactly-a-revelation about my suspect
heritage somehow managed to be
a blow to the gut. But putting it in

perspective, what difference does it
make? When it comes to my dear
friend Holly, three young lives hang

in the balance. Sometimes I want
to shake her, as a solid reminder
that parenting is more important

than having some guy-not-her-
husband tell her how sexy she
is. Not to mention, taking serious

advantage of that. But as much as
I like Holly, she isn't my blood.
Whatever she does doesn't much

affect me, not even when I have
to listen to her brag. Or whine.
Marissa, however, is my sister.

Despite our detachment of late,
she will always mean the world
to me. It wasn't my mother who

taught me the facts of life—even
though evidence of the meaning
was often in easy view. Missy told me

about menstruation, what to do for
it. What it meant re pregnancy.
When I got pregnant anyway, she

was there in the delivery room,
coaching me through the pain. Kept
me sane, when no one else bothered.

MULLING OVER

What Chris did behind Missy's back
while she waded through the septic
tank makes me want to kick his ass.
Listen to me—the pacifist. (Wuss.)

I don't even like to raise my voice
or defend myself when necessary.
But once in a while, something really
pisses me off. Something like this.

God, here Miss is, full-time caregiver
to a dying child (though she won't
admit that Shelby is failing). A child
that belongs to both of them, and yet

Chris conveniently forgets that, while
running around the world with some
other woman, leaving his wife to do all
the dirty work—physical and emotional?

Does the man have no honor? No
feelings? No tiny shard of love left
for Missy? No compassion for her
view of death hovering in the near

distance? Is it in the testosterone?
Chris. Dad. Steve. Geoff. Robin. If I
consider the men I've had relationships
with, it would be easy enough to chalk

it up to a "guy thing." But then there's
Holly. I'm about ninety-nine percent
sure all that flirtation has led to
infidelity. Not that she's admitted

as much as a stray kiss to me.
But she's got something going on
with this Bryan. When she talks
about him and his writing, the tenor

of her voice changes. Goes totally
giddy. In fact, she sounds a lot
like Harley, gushing about Chad.
Has the world gone completely

mad? Whatever happened to
morality? To follow-through. To
"until the big D pries us apart."
On the other side of things, what

ever happened to indignation?
To screaming fits and buckets
of tears. To kicking a philandering
jackass straight to the curb.

Okay, I've got to stop obsessing.
It's not my call. Guess I'll pull
Harley away from her PlayStation,
take her to Tahoe for a bike ride.

BUT BEFORE I DO

I think I'll check my email.
There's one from Mom:

CALIFORNIA HAS BEEN FUN.
MORE ON THAT WHEN I SEE
YOU. BURNING MAN LOOMS
IN A COUPLE OF WEEKS. OUR
PLAN IS TO STOP BY ON MARISSA'S
BIRTHDAY. ANYTHING SPECIAL
IN THE WORKS? LOVE, M.

Someone should do something
special for Missy's birthday,
that's for sure. Maybe hire
an assassin? Okay, maybe not.
I answer:

NOTHING SPECIAL PLANNED
YET. LET ME THINK ABOUT IT.

And now, even though Miss
specifically told me not to,
I spill the whole lurid tale
of spousal deceit. When I finish,
I consider the delete button.
But I don't use it. Maybe Mom
can talk some sense into my sister.
Mother to daughter, from someone

who's tripped in those sandals.
I'll get an earful from Missy,
or maybe the silent treatment.
But at this point, I think she needs
solid, emotion-free advice.

I MEANDER OVER

To Facebook, where I find
two new friend requests.
The first is from Brianna:

HARLEY GAVE ME YOUR
FB ADDY. FRIEND ME, PLEASE.
DO YOU PLAY FARMVILLE?

A quick check of Harley's page
shows three friends: Mikayla,
Trace, and Brianna. I make four.
The second request is from Vern.

NEW TO THIS FACEBOOK
THING. I NEED ALL THE FRIENDS
I CAN GET. HELP ME OUT?

Looks like he's got plenty already,
many of whom work at the DMV.
Wonder if they Facebook there.
I go ahead and accept. Why not?

There is also one new message.
From Robin.

THOUGHT THIS WOULD BE
A GOOD WAY TO STAY
CONNECTED. LET'S BE FRIENDS.
WHY HAVEN'T I HEARD FROM YOU?

Piss-poor timing. I don't
send him a friend request,
but I do return a message:

DIDN'T YOUR GIRLFRIEND
TELL YOU I CALLED?

DEFINITELY TIME

To get out of here for a few hours
of personal mother-daughter bonding.

"Harley," I call. "Put on some shorts
and tennies. We're going for a ride."

The south shore Tahoe bike trails
are lovely this time of year—snaking

through thick tracts of old-growth
evergreens, not far off the water's

edge. Harley and I have ridden them
once or twice annually since she still

pedaled a bike with training wheels.
Even in the heat of summer, altitude

plus shade plus lake cooling mitigate heat,
make the sugar pine–infused cruise pleasant.

It's a short drive from the south end
of Carson, maybe a half hour. Harley

remains fairly quiet for the few miles up
the mountain, past Cave Rock and Glenbrook,

then through downtown South Shore, where
three blocks of casinos remind us we are still

in Nevada until an unnoticeable state
line crosses us into California. Snared

by my own musings, I don't think much
about the dearth of chattiness until we reach

the Y where Highway 50 goes east, while 89
turns west. As I choose the latter, it comes

to me. "You're awfully quiet." The remark
draws a huge sigh and I know whatever's

bothering her is big. *What if someone*
tells you a secret, and you promise not

to tell anyone else, but it's the kind of secret
somebody else really needs to know?

Is she psychic or something? "Well . . .
sometimes you do have to break a trust,

if not telling means a person's welfare
might be in jeopardy." Physical or mental.

Okay. That's all she says for the moment.
I expect more. But I give her the space

she needs to make that decision
without encouragement from me.

I SQUEEZE INTO

A crowded turnout. Other bikers
and hikers are already out on the trail.
We unload our bikes, check the tires
for air, start on our way, Harley still

silent. We pass Pope Beach. I can't
not think about that day here with
Robin, and I tumble into a regular funk,
so I pedal faster, hoping to outpace

the vacuum trying to suck me in.
Harley has no problem keeping up.
Her coltish legs are stronger than
mine. A mile or so on, out of breath,

I pull to the side of the bike path
where a little bridge crosses Taylor
Creek. Harley and I watch the water
for a few minutes. Finally, she decides

to spill. *I promised I wouldn't*
tell, but I have to, even if Bri
gets mad at me. She heard Mikayla
on the phone, talking to Dylan.

Mikayla's pregnant. She's trying
to figure out what to do. She doesn't
want her parents to know, but I
think they have to, don't you?

Not just big. A whopper.

SPILLING A SECRET

Whatever its size,
will have varying
consequences. It's not
possible to predict
what will happen

if you

open the gunnysack,
let the cat escape.
A liberated feline
might purr on your lap,
or it might scratch
your eyes out. You can't

tell

until you loosen the knot.
Do you chance losing
a friendship, if that
friend's well-being

will

only be preserved
by betraying sworn-to-
silence trust? Once
the seam is ripped, can

it be

mended again?
And if that proves
impossible, will you be

okay

when it all falls to pieces?

FALLING TO PIECES

That's how my life feels. Fractured.
Crushed. Disintegrating. And the weird
thing is, it's all because of that stupid

little word: love. I've fallen in love
with Bryan, and it's tinting everything
normal about me with shades of insanity.

I'd have to be crazy to walk away
from nineteen years of marriage. Crazy
to rattle the lives of my three children.

Crazy to break up the home I've so
carefully crafted. Find a way to support
myself, when Jace takes great care of me.

And even if I decided to do all that,
Bryan is married too. He's made it clear
he's staying with his wife, no matter what.

A very big part of the "what" is
he swears he's in love with me too.
He even wrote a poem for me. For me!

I've read it a dozen times, almost have
it memorized. I fold the paper, tuck it
into my journal. Dedicated to Holly:

DRY SPELL

You are like rain, forecasted
to quench a summer's thirsting,
thirst grown beyond easy need, to life or death.

I watch the clouds
approaching windward mountains, slate
bruising black beneath expectation.

The western window
darkens as, laden, the curtain falls,
descends to veil peaks and rifts, draws nearer.

Is it thunder that I hear?
Or is the sudden rumble but the flurry
of hurried birds, on wing against unceasing drought?

One warm, wet spatter
stings the dust, stamps its ragged mark,
imprints a welt of hope upon the arid parchment.

Promise sizzles in the air,
wrapped in threads of ozone, electric
with desire so bold it borders ecstasy.

Claim this vacant sky.
Cast your shadow, speak to me in thunder,
throb against thirsting skin and flesh grown fallow.

Oh, give me rain!
Gift me with downpour, fill this empty well,
the reservoir drained to grit by lingering dry spell.

THE LAST STANZA

Gives me chills. Being with Bryan
is like walking in a downpour, thunder
booming in the distance, the electric smell

of ozone hanging in the air. He captured
us perfectly. Thinking about him gets me
up in the morning. Walks me through

the day. Makes me smile, when nothing
else can. It's all wrong, and I know it. But
what else can I do but steal as much time

with him as possible? One very big
problem now is having sex with Jace.
I really don't want him to touch me.

And he's starting to notice. I've been
trying to sneak into bed after he's asleep.
That's easy enough on weeknights, when

he has to be up early the next day.
But on Fridays and Saturdays he stays
up later. The last time I claimed a migraine

he said, *Another headache? Funny,*
you never used to be prone to them.
Better get in and see your doctor

before I have to whack off so hard
my pecker gets blisters. He smiled,
but I don't think he was being funny.

WONDER WHAT HE'D THINK

About the Holly who
flashed her boobs
for a free drink before
offering herself up like
a sacrificial piece of ass
at a club called the Topaz.
I worried about that girl
for years in the back of
my mind, though I didn't
know why until the night
I first saw her in action.
Okay, I realize she's always
been stashed inside of me,
and if she'd had an earlier
opportunity to reveal
herself, I would have
found that Holly sooner.
Marriage is a cover.
A safe place to stash
those unseemly desires
society doesn't sanction.
Asylum. Not *for* the insane.
The kind that actually makes
you go just a little crazy.
I went a little crazy
that night. And it felt
great. And now I'm afraid
I'll want to do it again.
Remembering it almost
makes me horny enough
to go find my husband.

ALMOST, BUT NOT QUITE

I start to send Bryan a text. Reconsider.
His wife is on vacation this week,
so they're spending it together in
San Francisco. Beautiful there, late
August. Wish I were with him, riding

cable cars and maybe taking in a Giants
game at AT&T Park. And I hope
that's all they do. Can't stand the thought
of the two of them sharing a bed
at the Fairmont. That should be me!

Does Bryan ever get jealous, thinking
about Jace and me together? Does
he simply expect that's what I'd do?
This territory is all so new. How can
I be jealous of him with his wife,

when seeing him actually having
sex with Lorraine didn't bother
me at all? Oh, I know. It's that damn
little word again, only in a whole
other context. Does he love his wife?

God, it's just all so confusing, and I'm
totally straight. Maybe that's what I need.
A late-morning Bloody Mary, to help
put it all in perspective. Perfect. Why
not turn into an alcoholic too?

I'VE JUST ABOUT SOLD MYSELF

On doing exactly that, when the phone
rings. Home phone, not cell. Can't be

Bryan, not that I'm obsessing about him
or anything. Nope. Andrea. "Hey, girl."

Long pause. Deep sigh. Then,
Holly, I probably have no business

telling you this, and in fact, I've
debated whether or not to keep

quiet for a few days now. Harley
told me something that Brianna

confided in her. Something you
really need to know. I only hope

my waiting so long didn't allow
Mikayla to make a bad decision.

"Mikayla?" What is she talking
about? Another long pause, and

finally she says, *Mikayla's pregnant.*
Brianna overheard her discussing

the problem with Dylan on the phone.
She's considering her options.

IMPOSSIBLE!

That's my first thought. Mikki has
been grounded all summer. But, no.
Not quite all summer. And then

there were those nights she went
out her bedroom window. Those
early mornings we caught her

sneaking in. I realize Andrea is
waiting for my response. "I . . . uh . . .
Are you . . . ?" But no, she can't be

sure. "Thanks for letting me know.
I should go. Thanks again." Oh my
God. Why didn't I . . . ? Wait. Before

I freak out completely, I'd better
go find out if this news is accurate.
It might not be. (But then Bri

wouldn't have said anything to
Harley if she wasn't sure.) But maybe
she heard wrong. (Come on, Holly.)

Now I really want that drink.
Except I don't think my lurching
stomach could keep one down.

I start toward Mikayla's room,
but passing the hall bathroom,
I hear the unmistakable sound

of someone throwing up, just
on the other side of the door.
I knock. "Mikki? Are you okay?"

A fresh round of retching, and
then a tiny-voiced answer. *Do*
I sound okay? No, Mom, I'm not.

Snappy, but morning sickness
can make a girl bitchy. I try
the door. Locked. "Can I come in?"

Just a minute. Movement.
Water in the sink. Finally,
the door opens and Mikki stands

back. Her sleep-mussed hair
is plastered around a very pale
face. Why tiptoe? "So, it's true."

What's true? Defiant. But the look
on my face must tell her I know.
Who . . . who told you? She crumbles,

and when I open my arms,
she collapses into them. "Doesn't
matter. What's important is that

you don't make any hasty
decisions. How far along are
you? Do you have any idea?"

LISTEN TO ME

Half mom, half clinician.
Half emotional, half logical.
Half very pissed. Half very scared
for my daughter. But no more scared

than she has to be. She trembles
as she nods against my chest. *I've missed*
two periods. At first I thought no way.
I can't be. But I took a test. Two blue lines.

She starts to cry. *Dylan says he'll pay*
for an abortion. But I don't know if
I can do that. But I don't know what
else to do, e-e-either. She stutters

to a stop. "Mikayla, I know the idea
of an abortion is distasteful. But
you're only seventeen. Having a baby
would . . . impact your life."

She rips herself out of my arms.
No shit! Jesus, Mom. I'm pregnant,
not stupid. I've thought and thought
about this. Abortion is more than

distasteful. It's kind of murder. This
is up to me, not you. And anyway,
when did you decide to play mother
again? Leveled. With nothing but the truth.

NOTHING BUT THE TRUTH

Simple enough to claim
that's what you want,
when you're dissecting

lies.

The truth, in its entirety.
Not abridged. Not groomed.
Not embroidered.
But complete candor

can be

like a mountain trail.
Steep. Rutted. A precarious
slide, reaching a too-often
unhappy conclusion.

Easier,

sometimes, to gulp
down giant spoonfuls
of uncertainty than it is

to swallow

throat-clogging capsules
of what really is.

Marissa

THE TRUTH

Hasn't exactly set me free.
I'm more tied up in knots
than I've been since I found
out about Shelby's illness.

Christian has done his level
best to try and win me over.
He's still camping out in
the guest room. My choice.

But nine days and counting,
he's shared the dinner table
every night with Shane and
me. And sometimes with Alex,

whom he manages to converse
with in a civilized fashion. As if
that weren't enough, he's also
making a concerted effort to

slow down his drinking. Not
stop, not completely. But as far
as I know, he doesn't touch
a drop until after dinner, and

then, it's a nightcap or three.
He's clear. Articulate. From
time to time, even funny.
Almost the Christian I fell in . . . for.

I CAN'T BRING MYSELF

To use the *L* word. Don't want
to combine that emotion and Christian
in the same jumble of thoughts.

Don't want to remember when
it wove us together, or how we once
lay in each other's arms, saturated

with it. Can't bring myself to consider
how he so cavalierly gave it away
to someone new. Someone beautiful

and young. Someone not me. I'm not
sure if there is even the smallest seed
of it left. Some spore that, driven by

fire or rain, might find just enough life
force inside to sprout and grow anew.
The morning after our fireworks night,

I thought there might be. Or did I?
Wasn't any small spark of hope, really,
extinguished by a downpour of doubt?

In the short term, what does any of it
matter? I still have to care for Shelby.
Still have to worry about Shane.

For the foreseeable future, my life
is not going to change a whole lot.
In the long run, who knows?

EVERYONE HAS AN OPINION

About what I should do. And they all
seem to want to make Christian pay in

some fashion. Andrea made her view
clear immediately, and she hasn't changed

her mind. *Take him straight to divorce*
court. Nail him for child support

and alimony, which a judge would
award you instantaneously. That man

wouldn't seem nearly as attractive
without a big, fat bank account.

I should have known she'd tell Mom,
though I asked her not to. Not a big

deal. Mom would have found out
sooner or later anyway. By the time

she called, she had already thought
through what she wanted to say.

I can't tell you what to do, or even
offer advice. But I want you to know

a couple of things. The first is, this
idea of your father and I traveling

together in a little trailer had nothing
to do with money. Believe it or not,

we managed to invest enough along
the way to assure a comfortable

retirement. This was a last-ditch effort
to keep our marriage intact, despite

too many years tiptoeing around extra-
marital relationships. Mostly your dad's.

But I am not guilt-free. Sometimes you
cheat for revenge. Sometimes it's all about

boredom. But often people stray because
something is lacking or someone is hurting

and can't find solace in their partner.
I'll tell you this. Had I known, at your age,

the depth of one or two of your father's
peccadilloes, I would have hauled off out

of there. By the time I found out, I was
too old to move on. Scared of searching for

new love, with boobs flopping to my belly
button and skin like sun-broiled leather.

SPONTANEOUSLY

My right hand strayed
to the corners of my eyes,
where daily, it seems,
the shallow lines trench
a little deeper. A question,
both small and large, surfaced.
"Was staying together worth it?"

In some ways, yes. I'm not
alone, and your father and
I understand each other. We
don't fight much anymore,
but then, we're pretty much
argued out. Life has taken on
a simple rhythm. I'm content.

Content. Not happy. Major
difference, when you stop
to think about it, and I did.
Then again, I haven't been
happy or content in a long
time. One more question.
"But do you love Dad now?"

That one took longer for her
to answer. She almost labored
to find the words she wanted.
Damaged love is like injured
skin, I guess. Sometimes a
wound will heal completely.
Other times, it leaves a scar.

IT WAS AN EVASION

And I didn't pursue it further.
What she said was enough,
the meaning of her words clear.
But she wasn't quite finished.

Here's the thing, Marissa.
I don't think you're in a good
position to shake things up
anymore than they're already

shaken. Your plate is more than
full, just taking care of Shelby.
Chris is paying the bills right
now, and that's important. But

keep your guard up. I'd hate
to see your hurt compounded.
And keep your options open.
Don't stay until it's too late to leave.

That message too was spring-
water clear. She left it at that,
let me know she and Dad will
be here for my birthday. Two

days from now, I will turn forty-
four. Another year dissolved
into a stream of duty and doubt.
Another year passed away.

THE LAST PERSON

To weigh in on things was Drew,
who happened to stop by a couple
of days after everything blew.
He knew something was wrong.
I mean, we've been friends forever.

At that point, everything had agitated
in my head long enough to build
a full kettle of steam. I was more
than ready to vent. Shane wasn't home.
Shelby was full-on into *Dora the Explorer.*

So I let go. Told the story. Halfway
through, I cried. By the end, my voice
was just shy of a wail. I think I scared
Drew a little. But he took it all in.
And when I finished, he had this to say.

I always thought he was a bastard.
You deserve better, M'issa, but I've
told you that before. I hope you
know I'm always here for you . . .
His hand lifted, came to rest against

my cheek. *My door is always open.*
And here's the deal. Chris has enough
resources to hire an outside caregiver.
If nothing else, I'd make him do that
for you. You deserve a little freedom.

He cupped my chin in the palm
of his hand, lifted it until I had
to look into his eyes. At that moment,
I was vulnerable. Fragile. Had he
straight kissed me, my defenses

might have crumbled. Surrendered
to the overwhelming need to be
cherished. Instead, it was Drew
who retreated. He did kiss me.
But gently, and on the forehead,

his lips a pout of fog, cool
on my skin. *I'd take you out
of here right now if you would
come. I know you can't. Not yet.
I love you, M'issa. Now. Always.*

He might have kissed me then,
the way we used to in our youth,
but the mood was interrupted
by the sound of a key in the lock.
We edged apart, just as Christian

came through the door, home
early. *Hey, whose car . . . ?* It was
then he saw Drew, sitting close to
me. His eyes grew dark. But he said,
Oh, hello. Good to see you again.

AS MUCH AS HE HATED

Drew being there, what else could
he say? And what could he do but
pretend to be totally okay with it?

I liked that. Liked that slender rush
of power. Pretty much since our
wedding day, Christian has made it clear

that he was in charge, leaving me
on the verge of impotent. Lacking
control. But that is no longer the case.

And yes, I like how that feels. I brew
this morning's coffee dark and strong,
the way I learned to love it. Christian prefers

a lighter roast. But he does not complain
when he joins me in the kitchen now.
Instead, he pours a cup silently, doctors

it to acceptable. He turns. *I'm hoping*
to convince you to take a short trip to
Monterey this weekend. For your birthday.

I looked into hiring someone for Shelby.
She has great references, and your mom
agreed to oversee. Think about it.

It will take some thought. A few
days at the ocean sounds amazing.
But Monterey is where we honeymooned.

A HONEYMOON

Used to be all about discovery.
Sampling the artichoke, peel by peel,
on the way to the heart, and once past
the thistle, oh what delightful plunder.
Now, however, a honeymoon

isn't

so much a pleasant education
as it is an extravagant vacation.
Who these days gets married
without taking a test drive?
An electric connection is not

a promise

of compatible preferences,
nor equal appetites. Dipping
a body part into unevaluated
fluid to analyze temperature
seems like a wise approach.

It's a

long way from wedding night
till death-do-us-part, and if
the grass appears ever so much
greener, right over there, forever
becomes a matter of

let's wait
and see.

Andrea

WAIT AND SEE

That's Marissa's plan for her marriage,
such as it is. I've given her my view,
more than once. But it's her decision,

so I'll back off, though it's unpleasant
to watch her husband's phony
cheerfulness and over-the-top attention.

I have no clue how she can stand it,
or how she could have agreed to go
to Monterey with him this weekend.

Make or break, was Mom's opinion.
Personally, I think it will all fall down,
but Marissa wants to try, so okay.

Monterey is supposed to be her big
birthday celebration, but all things
considered, we thought she deserved

a small party at home, with the kids
and our parents. Chris invited the new
caregiver too, so Shelby, Shane, and Mom

could get to know her in an informal
setting. I figured he'd hire some cool
drink of water in a tall, shapely glass,

but Pamela is more like hot cocoa in a mug.
Warm, and sweet enough, but plenty of
nutritional value. She knows her stuff and

handles Shelby with respect for her feelings
as well as her needs. I like her. Wish someone would have thought to hire her on

sooner, instead of allowing Missy to lose
herself inside her focus on her child.
Then again, my sister is obsessive about

her duty. Last night, she had to force
herself to let Pamela take over Shelby's
CPT, thread her into a lovely party dress,

and put her in the stander. When Shelby
coughed, Chris would have to stop Miss
from interfering with Pamela moving

to help. It will be a learning process,
as will Chris's ability to become anything
resembling a "normal" husband, if that's

really what he has in mind. Hard to
believe is all, and none of his obvious
butt kissing appears organic to me.

But it *is* Missy's life. And even if all this
only comes down to more help for Shelby
and her, I'll keep my lips zipped. For now.

IN THAT DEPARTMENT

My mother and I have come to uneasy
agreement. It's more important for

Mom, who will be living in Missy's
house for a little while, even beyond

the coming Monterey trip. *After much
internal debate, I told your father*

*that I'm tired of the nomadic life.
I want to find a little place here,*

*close to my girls and their children.
I'm even finished with Burning Man.*

When faced with the ultimatum
of agreeing or moving on without her,

he decided it might be okay to reroot
in northern Nevada. Burning Man,

however, was not on the table for him.
He plans to spend Labor Day Weekend

on the playa, Mom or no Mom. *It's
tradition, man. Three days on my own*

*won't kill me, not that I'll exactly be
alone out there. If I have to settle into*

suburbia again, I think I deserve
a little wanton partying first.

Once, that might have boiled into
a down-and-out. Mom has definitely

mellowed. *This way I'll be here*
for your birthday too, she told me.

Burning Man often conflicts.
Not that it really bothers me.

I hardly ever do anything special
for my birthday anyway, except

maybe take Harley to the fair. This
year, she plans to go with Steve.

Or, more likely, with Chad. Despite
the hurt of him putting the moves on Bri,

Harley's still all moony over the creep.
I can tell every time she comes back

from Steve's, though she doesn't talk
about it much to me. At least the thing

with Mikayla opened up the channel
to discuss pregnancy prevention.

I WASN'T GENTLE

She already got all the basics in sex ed
at school. It's those gritty, little details—
like a guy promising you won't get
pregnant because (choose one or more):

> One: you told him you're a virgin,
> and it's physiologically impossible
> for it to happen the very first time.
>
> Two: he's Catholic, and after much
> practice he has become an expert
> at the withdrawal method.
>
> Three: he must be sterile because
> he's never, ever, as far as he knows,
> gotten anyone pregnant before.

Beyond the humorous rhetoric, I told
her how the body responds to stimuli.
Digital. Oral. Even something as simple
as a kiss, once heat curdles it from sweet

into lustful. And because the moment
was right, and I felt like I should, I gave
her the lowdown on Steve and me—
why we got married in the first place.

Her: *You mean, you never loved Dad?*
Me: "I thought I did, at the time."
Her: *Why did you divorce him, then?*
Me: "Because I loved you more."

TRUTH IS A SHARP SPEAR

I hope, on the heels of the news
about Mikayla, it will pierce all
sense of "It can't happen to me."

Especially since she's camping
with her dad, Cassie, and Chad
for a couple of days. School starts

soon. It's an end-of-summer thing.
Which means I have the evening
to myself. I pop a Lean Cuisine

into the microwave, pour a glass
of wine, and take it into the living
room to find some crass reality TV

program. As I pick up the remote,
the doorbell rings. Weird. No one
ever comes over. But maybe it's Mom.

Nope. The peephole outlines a shaken
Jace. I swing the door wide. "Jace?
Are you okay?" Everything about him

confirms his *No. Not really. May*
I come in? His face is pale, but his
cheeks are flushed windburn red.

"Uh, sure." I stand back to let him by.
Notice his odor—sweat, the obnoxious
kind that comes from anger or worry.

This must be about Mikayla. I trail
Jace to the living room. "Do you want
a drink? I just poured myself some wine."

He glances at the glass on the coffee
table. *Sure. Why not?* He sits on the sofa,
waits in silence until I return from

the kitchen, matching wineglass in one
hand, bottle of merlot in the other. Pretty
sure we're looking at a second round.

I pour his glass full, watch without
comment as he fortifies himself with
a couple of swallows before finally asking,

What do you know about Bryan?
Most unexpected. Jace studies my face,
trying to interpret whatever expression

the pointed question might encourage.
"Bryan? You mean the one from Holly's
writers' group? Not much. He's a teacher . . ."

No! I mean what do you know about
him and Holly? What has she told you?
Please, Andrea, tell me the truth.

I pull my chair a little closer, look
him straight in the eye. "Jace, I have
no idea what you're talking about."

I don't think I've ever so closely noticed
the color of his eyes before—the dark
of coffee, speckled gold. A sudden swell

of anger deepens the brown; the flecks
disappear. *All those nights she said*
she was with you. Did she lie to me?

My first reaction is total denial.
But then I remember a time or two
when she asked me to cover for her.

I can't do that now. "I'm not sure.
Look, Jace. Where is this coming
from?" He reaches for a small journal,

sitting beside him on the couch.
I was looking for her address book
and found this. He hands me the leather-

bound notebook. *She says it's fiction,*
and some of it looks like it could be.
But a few entries mention him by name.

I start flipping through as he finishes
his first glass of wine, pours another.
I take the first sip of mine now.

There's poetry in there too. Stuff
he wrote for her. Read it. All of it.
I . . . I just can't believe she would . . .

THE REST

Falls into his glass, muffling the sharp voice
of his pain. He drinks while I read. Partway
through, I start to drink in earnest too. I see
more than Bryan here, but her obvious love
for him far outweighs her licentiousness.

I've waited all day, just to hear him say hello,
the voices of my family white noise behind
escalating need. Bryan, where are you?

The sexy stuff isn't all fiction, in my opinion.
I don't need to tell Jace that. He knows it.
When Holly mentions girls'-nights-out excuses,
a hot wave prickles my skin. How dare she?
And why write it down, or save his poems?

We shed our clothes like snakeskin, inch by
shuddering inch, take pleasure in the slow
abandon of denim, satin, and tenuous morality.

Two wine bottles sit, empty, on the table.
But they are no more empty than the wet night
of Jace's eyes. I move beside him, slip my hand
over his, to calm the tremors. "God, I'm so sorry."
His head tilts into my shoulder and a tiny drum

roll begins in my chest. The rot scent of merlot
cloaks his sweat, the blend masculine, primitive.
We don't speak. Something very wrong and very
right is at work here. Some convergence we can't
fight. So we don't. And suddenly, we're kissing.

I WISH THE CONFRONTATION

Would have been nasty. Vicious,
even. So much easier to defend
yourself when the other person
attacks with vehemence. But when
Jace came into the bedroom, holding

the journal, he wasn't so much calm
as confused. Like he just couldn't
believe the words he found inscribed
on those pages could possibly
have been connected to me, let alone

written by me somehow. *Hey, I . . .*
uh . . . was looking for your address
book and . . . uh, found this.
He lifted the book, pinched
between his thumb and forefinger.

I tried to keep my expression
indifferent. "Oh, that. I told you
I was thinking about writing erotica,
right? I've got a pretty great imagination,
don't you think? I only hope it pays."

There was a slow creep of crimson
up his neck, onto his cheeks. *Are you*
saying that's all made up? Yes or no,
you wouldn't really try to publish it,
would you? Have you no self-respect?

"I'll use a pen name," I joked. But
he didn't smile. "Honey, that stuff
is fiction. And that kind of writing
really does pay okay. Betty says
you can make a decent living at it."

First of all . . . A swell of anger
began a visible throb at his temples.
. . . *I don't give a spit about what
Betty has to say. And it's not like
you have to go out and make a living*

*for yourself. I've worked my ass off,
at a career I don't especially love,
to make sure you and the kids are
well provided for. But my biggest
question is, what's up with this Bryan?*

Hearing his name come from
Jace's mouth was surreal. The two
don't belong together. "Bryan is in
my writers' group. He's working
on a young adult fantasy . . ."

Then it struck me—the stream
of consciousness musings about
him, sprinkled in the notebook.
I made myself look totally humbled.
"Okay, listen. The truth is, Bryan

is kind of cute, for a guy his age. So
I used him as sort of a model for one
of the characters in a story I'm writing
about middle-aged couples and how
they spice up their marriages."

Is it better or worse when lies come
that easily? "Jace, you don't have to
worry about Bryan, okay? I love you."
But the last sentence seemed tacked
on, like it didn't belong there, either.

Jace opened the journal's back cover.
Tucked between the last few page
spreads were Bryan's poems, written
for me. *And what about these?*
His hand shook as he pointed to

Dry Spell. Again, the lie slid, toad-
slick, from my mouth. "Bryan
writes poetry and suggested I study
it to learn poetic devices and imagery.
He gave me a few to look at."

It all sounded plausible to me,
but Jace was unconvinced. *Holly,*
you have been slipping further and
further away from me. I hope this
isn't why. But I'm really scared it is.

I HAD NOTHING TO SAY

In response, but I didn't need to have,
at least not then. He turned and left

the room, taking the journal with
him. I followed him into the hall,

but he never looked back as he exited
the house. That was last night. I have

no idea where he might have gone.
Zero clue when he'll decide to come

home, or where his head will be at
when he gets here. I tried calling

his cell. No answer. Phoned his office
this morning, but the receptionist

said he wouldn't be in. I suppose
he might have gone to his parents',

but no way I'm trying there. God
help me if they ever find out, however

things shake loose. Jace's mom would
take great pleasure in ripping me apart.

I wonder if she'd enjoy rubbing her son's
nose in *Don't-say-I-didn't-warn-you.*

BY NOON

Still no word from Jace.
  I'm approaching batshit crazy.
  He wouldn't have gone out,

gotten wasted, and hit a pole
  or been arrested for DUI, would
  he? So not Jace. But the times

are more than usual. Should I
  call the hospital? The cops?
  They'd call me, wouldn't they?

I need to do something. Talk
  to someone. Bryan. I pick up
  the phone. Think better of it.

He said he'd call me when he
  could. Andrea. Not sure what
  to say. But anything is better

than the silence. I dial her
  work number, but it goes to
  her mailbox. She must be at lunch,

so I call her cell instead. On
  the fourth ring, she answers. Slow-
  voiced. Sleepy? "Hey. Are you at home?"

  Crazy long pause. *Y-yes. Hang*
    on, okay? Comes the crisp rustle
    of sheets and a low male murmur.

PERFECT

Andrea has three dates a year
that involve sleepovers, and here
I interrupt her with my problems?

She must have dropped the phone.
I can barely hear her tell whoever's
in her bed, *Shh. It's my friend, Holly.*

"Oh, wow. I'm sorry. Didn't know
you had company. Call me later
if you can. I need to talk to you."

Commotion in the kitchen reminds me
I am not the only one here, nor the only
one with problems. I hear Bri yell,

Just because you're pregnant
doesn't mean you get to be a bitch.
Good thing Jace isn't here after all.

But now Trace has been dragged out
of the dark. He stands at the doorway,
drop-jawed, eyes glittering surprise.

On top of it all, the telephone rings. Jace?
The machine answers before I can reach it.
In a long moment after the beep, a tense voice

crackles, *I'm trying to reach Holly Carlisle.*
This is . . . Sarah Hill. Pick up! I can't. Shock
stuns me still. Then she adds, *Her mother.*

IN THOSE MOMENTS

those precarious spikes
of time when anger eclipses
sanity like a militant satellite, white-
hot inside your head, gravitational
weight compounding exponentially
toward black hole, critical mass
near, and you realize survival
lies in a detonation of words,

would a whisper do?

On those days
when sorrow manifests itself
as a sentient beast, hungered
by a season of sleep, creeping
up from behind, no time to run,
no place to take cover, and seizing
you by the throat, sinks its claws
into your chest to open you wide,

would a tear suffice?

In those hours
when need unfolds you from deep
creases of sleep, leaves you
shivering beneath sheets of darkness,
body and brain merged into a river
of primal rage, rushing
headlong toward cataract,
a torrent that only an all-night,
sweat-slicked fuck can assuage,

would a kiss satisfy?

Marissa

A SEXLESS TRIP

That's what I agreed to, and Christian
has been accommodating. Monterey
is beautiful. Our hotel overlooks
the ever-moving Pacific. The susurrus
of evening waves is a lullaby, and yet

tidal crash wakes me in the morning,
when the heavens are cushioned gray.
The fog burns off around midday,
revealing a startling cornflower sky.
The ocean has a split personality.

I'm wondering if Christian does too.
As we wander Cannery Row, browsing
curio shops and art galleries, he is
attentive. Smiling. But is it sincere?
I can't help but think back to our

honeymoon. Walking so close we
resembled Siamese twins. Kissing
and touching, in quite inappropriate
public locations—restaurants, side-
walks, the beach, the aquarium.

I can never think of penguins without
remembering Christian, face against
the glass enclosure, as a little emperor
flirted with him from the far side.
We haven't laughed so hard since.

At least, not together. And I'm
sure I haven't laughed that hard
on my own. The only thing
I'm not sure of is if Christian ever
laughed that hard with . . . see,

here I go, and I really have to stop.
It's counterproductive to any
forward movement at all. I'd be
lying if I said I wasn't enjoying
the trip. It's been years since I've

been more than twenty miles
from home. Years since I traveled
over the Sierra and down the coast
by car. Years since I've spent so
much time in such close proximity

to my husband. Uncertain, his hand
asks for mine. Tentatively, I give it.
There is memory lodged in the cradle
of his palm, the texture of his skin,
the way his fingers wedge mine.

There is comfort there too, and in
the way his stride adjusts to mine,
in how people flow around us. In
feeling like half of two, instead of one.
These things remain. What's missing

are words.

WE GRAPPLE FOR THEM

And in that struggle, I see hints
of the other side of Christian:

Frustration, too evident in
the cement clench of his jaw.

Distance, the ethereal detached
from the flesh and bone.

Impatience, in the soft thrum
of his heel as we sit in silence.

In two nights and three days,
we have talked about where
to eat. What to do. The weather.
We did spend a few words worrying

about Shane, but Christian won't let
me obsess about Shelby. He insists
she's in good hands, and I believe
that. But she has been the biggest

part of me for five years. And still,
we do not approach what we must:

Explanation. I really need to
understand every "why."

Forgiveness. Is it possible?
And am I willing to offer it?

Tomorrow. Do we dare look
that far? Do we make plans?

THIS EVENING

We are sitting at the far end of our
hotel's long, narrow lounge, sipping
wine and watching the tide's relentless

rise. The cabernet is pricey. Bold.
Considering my relative abstinence
the last few years, a few sips have

given rise to a soft buzz. Enough
to make me say, "Thank you for
the weekend, Christian. It's been . . ."

> *Why do you still call me Christian*
> *when everyone else calls me Chris?*
> The question is so out of left field,

it takes a moment or two to collect
my thoughts. "I don't know. I guess
I like it better. That's who you were

when we met." A little more wine,
for courage. "Why? Does it bother you?"
He's never said a word about it till now.

> *It's just . . . it reminds me of Mom.*
> He never talks about her, either.
> *Dad wanted to name me Benjamin.*

"Really?" Another story I've not heard.
"He was more into the Old Testament?"
Oh, yeah. Hellfire and brimstone.

Christian (not Chris) smiles. *You know*
it. He was all about that going-to-hell
stuff. At least, until he started to qualify.

Funny how it's easier to point fingers
at your neighbors than toward yourself.
But then he sobers. *I still miss her.*

I study his face through wine-heavy eyes.
He looks like his mother, only she never
allowed a single stray strand of gray.

Christian's blondish hair is woven
with silver threads. "I know. But she's
watching over you right now."

No. The hushed tone of his voice can't
deny his conviction. It's total. *If she were*
still alive, she'd have nothing to do

with me after what I've done. She wouldn't
feel differently in heaven, if there is one.
Adultery was numero uno on her sin list.

He's so serious, I can hardly believe
it. "Aw. Come on. Surely murder
would have been a notch or two higher."

I didn't flinch when he said the word
I can barely consider. He cringes now.
There weren't any murderers in her family.

I'D THINK IT WAS THE WINE

Talking, but Christian's tolerance level
is much higher than mine, and cabernet

is no match for his usual Johnny Walker.
His eyes are clear, his enunciation crisp.

"Your mother loved you very much,
Christian. Whatever you have done,

I know she has forgiven you. And"—
not sure he cares, but—"God has too."

> His head starts rocking side to side.
> *No, no, no. There is no forgiveness*
>
> *for sin like mine. The Old Testament*
> *trumped the New on this. God is all*
>
> *judgment. Look how he's punished*
> *me! First my mother. Then Shelby.*

"Stop it. You don't really believe that.
What happened to your mother was

an accident. And Shelby was a genetic
roll of the dice. Nothing more."

> *Genetics* is *God. And God gets*
> *pissed when you misspend love.*

SUDDENLY WE'VE SEGUED

From adultery to love. Not that I ever
believed five years together could
have been only about sex. Sometimes
it's a real bitch to be proven right.

"So, you were in love with her, then."

> He turns his attention away from me,
> back toward the rise-and-breathe
> of the incoming sea. *Yes. Very much so,*
> *at least at first. She was just so . . . new.*

"Compared to what? Old me? Used me?"

> The words are frothed with anger,
> but he doesn't sidestep. *I have no*
> *excuse, Marissa. I was smitten, that's*
> *all. Smitten and stupid. I didn't realize . . .*

"What about now? Do you still love her?"

> He swivels toward me again, looks
> straight into my eyes. *I'd be lying*
> *if I said no. But I'm telling the truth*
> *when I say I love you so much more.*
>
> *Whatever I feel for Skye will fade away*
> *in time. I believe that, the same way*
> *I believe you and I were meant to be*
> *together. But if you say no, I understand.*

INELEGANT TRUTHS

Scattered in front of me
like used paper wrappers
and bits of tinfoil. Litter.
I wanted his honesty.
That's what I thought.
Outside, the Pacific sighs.
I knew he was in love
with her. Wishing it
wasn't so couldn't make
it a lie. He has chosen
not to lie to me now.
How can I be angry, when
nothing has changed at
all except his willingness
to expose his troubled soul?
Inside, a younger couple
saunters, tandem, to the bar.
He isn't worth a second glance,
but she sizzles in a skirt
that barely curtains her
pubic region. Any man
would look, and Christian's
chromosomes line up
that way. He doesn't even try
to disguise the rotation
of his eyes. It bothers me.
But why? Would I feel better
if he pretended not to do it?
If I decide to stay, will I ever
be able to trust him again?

AND WILL I EVER WANT HIM

To touch me again, in the way every
husband should touch his wife, and
every wife should long for? Part of me

wants to try. To see if I can have sex
with Christian without thinking about
his hands, traveling collarbone to hips

down Skye's (narrower, longer) torso,
pausing to caress her (larger, higher)
breasts. Lowering his mouth to her

(tauter? pinker?) nipples, circling
them with the tip of his tongue before
moving on. And licking her (flatter, browner)

belly as she arches her (straighter) back,
opens her (sleeker) legs, inviting his
face to plunge between them, inhale

her peculiar pheromone perfume. To
sample her unique favor, savor its taste
in the wet of her orgasm without first

seeking his own. And when at last
he lunges into her, hearing her moan,
no scream, until she comes and he

comes and they come together.
Can Christian and I ever have sex
without doing a threesome with her?

THREESOMES

Are often awkward—
the indelicate weave
of body parts tangles
in too many ways.

Six legs

with knees, ankles,
and thirty toes, easily
accomplish trauma
when thrashing about. Likewise

six arms—

a half dozen shoulders
and elbows, plus three-times-
ten digits. And then there's
the confusion of

three faces

and six eyes, trying to
decide what to look at;
three mouths, uncertain
of what needs to be kissed;

three tongues

with a plethora of places
to lick and spaces to explore.
Someone better take charge
because a threesome

lacking clear direction is chaos.

Andrea

AN ABRUPT DIRECTION SHIFT

Can roil your life into chaos,
make you rethink boundaries.
Possibilities. Definitions. Here's

one I've been thinking a hell
of a lot about. *Friend.* The dictionary
defines *friend* as a person who is

"emotionally close; somebody who
trusts and is fond of another."
Up until a few days ago, my internal

thesaurus would have listed Holly
as a synonym for friend. But I don't
see how we can ever be friends again.

I'm sleeping with her husband.
And worse, I'm crazy about him.
I'm pretty sure that disqualifies me

as her friend. Wait. What am I
saying? I'm one hundred percent
sure that disqualifies me as "me."

Okay, I've always had a little thing
for Jace. A trifling worm of affection.
But I never expected it to become bait.

JACE TOOK THE HOOK

Ran hard and fast with it, and
I'm not sure who it surprised more.
That night when he came over
with Holly's journal, and we found
ourselves kissing on the couch,

our first reaction was to jerk apart,
weak apologies stumbling from both
our mouths simultaneously. "Oh,
wow, I'm s-sorry, Jace. That was . . .
unexpected." Almost word for

word, second for second, he said,
Oh my God. I'm sorry, Andrea.
That was . . . surprising . . . And
because of our random duet, we
started to laugh. Inappropriately,

I guess, but then, everything about
this mess is inappropriate. And it all
started with Holly, which compounds
the myriad problems. And that night
we were both drunk enough for it

to seem really very funny, despite
the fact that the kiss was deadly
serious. We left the enigma dangling
between us. *I don't suppose you*
have anymore wine? I think I need it.

He obviously didn't, and neither
did I, although had he gone away
then, I probably would have drunk
it solo. "I keep the cellar well stocked,
in case of emergency." We were bulldozing

straight toward a major disaster,
but at that point, neither of us cared.
I went to the kitchen, brought back
another bottle. Didn't give it two
seconds' worry, thinking about sitting

back down beside Jace, who claimed
the corkscrew, opened the wine,
and poured our glasses deep. I waited
for him to talk. Finally, *I've been feeling*
her pull away, but Holly is like a colt . . .

er . . . filly. Headstrong. I was afraid
of reining her in. Afraid she'd bolt,
or kick me in the teeth. Looks like
she did both. Not to mention . . .
I can't believe she'd do these things.

I wasn't sure if he wanted me to agree
or try to explain or say anything at all.
I was acutely aware of the warmth
of his thigh against mine, of the softness
of his skin when our hands bumped

from time to time, while reaching
for our glasses, which somehow kept
emptying. It was a small effort to say,
"Holly really hasn't confessed anything
to me, Jace. But she has changed.

She's restless, which is probably not
uncommon for women her age,
especially those who have been in
committed relationships for many years.
But Holly's restlessness is profound."

I hoped he understood my message.
I thought it would be insensitive
to come right out and say I thought
most of the journal was autobiographical.
And I realized at that point my motives

might be questionable. We were
on the same page. *I knew something
was coming, just not how big it was.
I didn't try to head it off and now
have to wonder why I didn't.* His hand

found mine again, and that made his
last sentence even more ambiguous.
Morality tilting one way, logic the other,
I only knew one thing. "I can't let you drive
home. You can sleep in Harley's room."

DESPITE EVERYTHING

His response—his very first thought—
was, *What about Holly? Should*
I call and let her know I'm here?

"It's after midnight, Jace. I don't think so.
One night of worry won't kill her.
Maybe it will make her think."

He snorted. *Like she's worried about*
me anyway, right? Concern for her
family hasn't exactly slowed her down.

Fuck it. Let's get drunk. He divvied
up the last of the wine, signaled a toast.
To the future. Whatever it looks like.

"Uh, Jace? I think we're pretty
close to drunk already. But I'll call
your toast and raise you one.

Here's to friends who bring other
friends into your life." Our glasses
tipped together, made a rich crystal

clink. We sipped in silence, musing in
private corridors. Eventually, the clock
chimed one. I looked at Jace, who

returned a heavy smile. *I really,*
really hope you have a spare toothbrush.
My mouth tastes like a winery smells.

"I keep a few around. For Harley's
friends, who rarely smell like merlot.
Come on. Let's go find one."

I led him to the guest bathroom,
showed him the spare toothbrushes.
"Harley's bedroom is straight across

the hall. Sheets are clean. I changed
them this morning. Take an ibuprofen
and chug a big ol' glass of water. Best

hangover preventative I know of.
My bedroom's down there. If you
need anything, just let me know."

> *Okay if I take a shower? I smell . . .*
> he sniffed—lightly. *Not too good.*
> *Wow. How did you put up with that?*

I laughed. "It wasn't easy. Help
yourself to the shower. Harley's gel
is bubblegum. If you want straight soap,

try the bar on the sink." I didn't really
want to leave, wanted to see him naked.
Realized how smashed I was. "Night."

I closed the door behind me. Left
his nakedness to my imagination.
The sound of the shower made me shiver.

I SINCERELY DID NOT EXPECT

Another thing to come of that night.
What I anticipated, come morning,

was a hangover of gargantuan proportion,
and a thank-you note on the coffee table.

As per my bedtime routine (even when
drunk on my butt), I used the Waterpik,

brushed the residual goo away. Rinsed with
plaque-killing mouthwash. Washed my face

with age-fighting cleanser, toner. Slathered
on the priciest night cream I can afford.

The "fine lines" (aka wrinkles) aren't fooled
by my ridiculous attempts to keep them

at bay, but at least I can say I tried if I ever
find someone to not-quite-impress but me.

In the winter, I wear flannel to bed,
but in summer I slip between the sheets

with nothing to mitigate the cool
envelope of cotton against my skin.

Not quite an hour later, that's how
Jace found me. Enveloped. Awake. Naked.

I SWEAR, AGAIN

I did not believe he would come.
Hoped, yes. Meditated, yes, pressing
mental invitation out my door, down
the hall to the room, not my daughter's

that particular night, but offered
to a stranger-friend in desperate need
of consolation. Yet who was more
in need? What happened after my door

whispered open could not answer
that question. I closed my eyes, feigned
sleep. He tiptoed bedside, assessed
the rise and fall of my chest. When

he asked, *May I please sleep here*
tonight? the request belonged to a child.
I rolled toward him, lifted the edge
of the top sheet, and when he inched

in, he smelled of straight soap,
fruity shampoo, and mint, atop a haze
of merlot. He was naked too. But not
in a hurry. There was no demand

within his request to share my bed.
There was only a dusk-soft plea, one
I met with a necessary question.
"You won't be sorry tomorrow, will you?"

Wine or guilt, our lovemaking
that night was slow. Clumsy exploration,
as if neither of us had ever done it
before. We laughed about it, though.

And when we woke the next morning,
plaited together, we tried again. Much
better. We both called in sick, fell
back into bed. The third time was close

to perfect. When we finished, sex scent
hung thick as incense in the air. Jace
held me, ear against his chest. I listened
to the *whump-whump*. "Are you sorry?"

> *No.* His fingers combed through
> my sweat-damp hair. *I just don't*
> *know yet what this means. What*
> *about you? Are you sorry?*

"Not yet. Some things take time
to process. I suspect this is one."
Just then, Holly called. The necessary
interruption snapped us into the moment.

I watched Jace go into the bathroom,
new stories etched in the leather of
his skin. That's how I've remembered
him, over and over, for the last three days.

STORIES IN LEATHER

Once you celebrated

skin, bared

it on altars of sand,
anointed it with scented oils,
invited Apollo's kiss.
It wasn't like it had to be

suede—seamless,

buttery—and the muscles
underneath weren't always granite
contours. But you didn't care
who looked when you peeled
off faded jeans,

flaunted youth,

dove into sun-dimpled surf,
emerged, shedding sequins
of ocean. Oh, the cool
of cotton beneath your back,
desire a hot seep, lured
to the rain between

parted legs.

Nakedness comes harder
now, decades from Pacific cliffs—
eroding landscapes

crushing passion

into fossil,
skin a word-scarred journal,
creased around the eyes.

Holly

A JOURNAL

Is a dangerous thing to keep.
When you're young, you have to
hide it from your parents, at least
if it has anything interesting inside.

First crush.
First kiss.
First feel-up.
First fuck.

My high school journal recorded
all these, plus the details. I stashed
it between my mattress and box
spring. One day Mom decided

to flip the mattress with a change
of sheets. That's right, she found all
my secrets, in one little book.
She went ballistic. Mama never

relied on grounding. She was more
of a belt person. You would think
wearing welt tattoos for a week plus
might have made me more careful.

Reckless.
Irresponsible.
Egocentric.
Narcissistic.

Jace has accused me of being
all those things, and you know,
he's right. I could throw a few
applicable terms in his direction.

Emotionally absent.
Short-tempered.
Unadventurous.
One-trick pony.

But what would be the point?
We're pretty much stuck in limbo.
He knows the stuff in this very adult
journal is mostly true. He's hurt,

of course. I could try to tell him
he's partially responsible. But it
doesn't matter at all. The end result
is still the same. I'm miserable here.

Jace, though miserable too, seems
oddly at ease the past couple of days.
Maybe he went out and got a revenge
piece of ass. Wait. No, this is Jace.

Dedicated.
Faithful.
The epitome
of loyalty.

HE NEVER TOLD ME

Where he spent the other night, and
I had zero right to ask. He came home,

went about his business, and that was
that. Except the wedge was wider.

Which means he probably *was* at
his parents' house. But you know, now

that I don't have to worry about keeping
Jace happy, I sure don't have to worry

about pleasing his parents, do I? Bet
they'd be pissed to know he and I are

still sharing a bedroom. Cohabiting,
totally to keep the kids in the dark.

School starts today. Mikayla launches
her senior year, eight weeks pregnant,

give or take. She's determined to stay
in school as long as she can. Deliver

a healthy baby. The rest is still up in
the air. And her father still doesn't know.

We bribed Trace to keep his mouth shut
with the promise of driver's training,

so he can get his license as soon as
possible. He'll be sixteen in January.

All he wants, he said, is a regular way
to escape the insanity that is his family.

Oh, Trace. You've only chipped the ice-
berg. Brianna begins her freshman year,

all breathless expectation. Mikayla
bought her sister's silence with clothes.

Mik's wardrobe is to die for, and they
wear the same size. (At least for now.)

Bri will be the best dressed in her frosh
class, hands down. I watch my kids now,

at the far side of their childhood,
hustling around the kitchen, making

lunches and approximating breakfast.
At least they didn't have to catch

that damn six-thirty a.m. school bus.
Mikayla will drive them. Next thing

you know, they won't need Jace or me
at all. Freedom, as Papa used to say, is

a spit and holler away. There's a slingshot ride straight back to Elko.

I'VE BEEN THERE

A lot these past few days, in daydreams
and in a nightmare or two. Returned to
its house-heavy hillsides and flat tracts
of playa and steep canyon climbs up
into the Ruby Mountains. Relived great

days, cheering at football games, and bad
days, upchucking algebra. Recalled
the faces of good friends and boyfriends
and sneaking off campus for a smoke
and making out in a backseat or two.

And snaking through all of that, Mama
and Papa and church and praying
I wouldn't really, as Mama always said,
go straight down to the devil when
you die, because God doesn't love

whores and liars. Which I mostly was,
in her eyes, because *the apple don't*
fall far from the tree. Only through
discipline and God's loving-kindness
will you end up different than your mother.

My birth mother. Sarah Hill, no
longer a figment of my imagination.
A flesh-and-blood birth mother, whose
voice—gossamer thin as dragonfly
wings—I have committed to memory.

THE TIMING OF HER CALL

Couldn't have been much worse.
My entire existence is in upheaval.
Emotionally, I'm a wreck. And right
smack in the middle of it all, here

comes the call I've been hoping for
since I was old enough to understand
what adoption was. It seriously took
me an hour to process the idea that she

might be inviting me into her life.
I picked up the phone to call her back
three or four times. Finally, Mikayla
dialed the number for me. When

Sarah answered, I could barely choke
out, "Hi. Uh . . . this is Holly?" It came
out a question. "Uh . . . you called
earlier?" Another question. Sheesh.

> *Holly. Yes. Well, this is awkward,*
> *I know. But I was so happy to hear*
> *from your daughter. Mikayla told*
> *me you've been looking for me.*
>
> *I never left Nevada, just in case.*
> *I hoped . . . prayed . . .* Her voice
> cracked. One big, long fissure.
> And then we were both sobbing.

TURNS OUT

She lives just outside of Vegas.
Has been married twice but
not to my birth father, who is,
in fact, Paul Driscoll, who did,
in fact, have sex with someone
other than his wife, *several*
times, according to Sarah,
and one of those times
resulted in me. Soon after
Sarah delivered me, she moved
to Tonopah with her parents,
one of whom still lives there.
My grandfather died several
years ago, but my grandmother,
Sally, is seventy-six and *looking to*
live forever, Sarah said.
I also have a half sister,
Tia, whom I will meet
in exactly five days, when
I fly down to Vegas with Mik.
After all her persistence
on this, not to mention
the results, I figure she
deserves to come with me.
And maybe, hearing Sarah's
story firsthand will make
Mikki think long and
hard about having her
baby, and the probable
advantages of adoption.

ULTERIOR MOTIVES

Can come back to bite a person,
but I think a hunk of reality
is in order for my daughter.

Anyway, I don't want to go alone.
I need someone to hold my hand.
I wish it could be Bryan, but that

would be completely inappropriate.
I thought about asking Andrea,
making it a girls-only birthday bash

Vegas weekend. She turns thirty-
seven on Friday. But that didn't seem
right, either. Sahara would totally

make it that kind of a trip, so no.
And of course, Jace is a definite
uh-uh. Even before the implosion,

he was not supportive of my search.
Though we're barely speaking
at this point, I had to let him know

> where Mikayla and I will be off to.
> His response was not unexpected.
> *Whatever, Holly. Add a little more*
>
> *shit to your plate. On the other hand,*
> *maybe filling in the blanks will make*
> *you feel complete. Sorry I couldn't.*

A VERY BIG PART OF ME

Is sorry he couldn't too. Today
is my family's thirteenth "first day

of school." I remember Mikayla's
first day of kindergarten, how anxious

she was to leave our little fold, unlike
Trace, who flat refused to let go

of Jace's leg. Is Jace thinking about
that now, as he starts arranging

the few minutes left before the kids
have to go? *Okay, lunches in back-*

packs. Everyone have their supplies?
Do you remember where to meet

after school? Mikayla, is your car
gassed up? Here's some money.

Be sure to fill up on the way home.
Trace, could you please comb

your hair? Bri, you look beautiful.
You aren't nervous, are you?

If I close my eyes and just listen,
I can almost fall back into "normal."

FALLING BACK

Is a multidefinition phrase.
There's the clock, rewound
an hour to encourage early rising
in the shadowed months,
though the low slant of light

doesn't

make crawling away from
the warm hearth of dreams
easier. In a way, this achieves
forward movement.
Falling back can also

mean

hurried retreat—a reverse
scattering, in earnest hope
of escaping injury, death, or
capture. The term might
also apply to a procrastinator,

starting

off well after the gun, unhurried
and unworried about finishing
first—lateral passage;
or to some courageous soul,
willing to cede all control

over

personal safety and collapse
backward into the arms
of strangers in a slow-motion,
up-and-down leap of faith.

Marissa

FAITH

Whatever small measure of faith
I once owned was lost years ago,
buried beneath a monstrous heap
of self-pity. I can't believe it took

finding out about my husband's
long-term love affair to yank me
out from under the morass. Time
to disengage inertia, create forward

movement. I'm just not exactly
sure how to start, or what I want
to move toward. Entrepreneurship,
I think. Can't imagine going to work

for someone else, punching a time
clock, being told what to do. Not
now that I have fewer shackles.
Or at least they're a lot looser.

Christian hired Pamela to come in
twice a week. Two consecutive days
out of every seven, allowing me
a measure of freedom I'd forgotten

even existed. Christian also took
Shane to get his driver's license,
and once he passed the test, bought
him a decent used car. Scary,

to think about Shane driving.
I made a deal with him—we'll
pay for his insurance as long
as he promises not to drive under

the influence. Ever. His response
was typical Shane. *Jeez, Mom,
do you think I'm a total stoner?
Call me Mister Lightweight.*

Wonder what he considers
a heavyweight. Anyway, he gave
me his word. At this point, I trust
him more than I do his father.

Regardless, I will not ask Christian
to leave, at least not right now.
The weekend was not the romantic
getaway he'd hoped for, but neither

was it a complete failure. We talked,
an accomplishment in itself, though
difficult. It was like someone pulled
back a big rock to let the truth,

all ugly and fanged, slither out
from underneath it. It coiled there
between us, hissing and rattling,
until it finally exhausted itself.

WHEN CHRISTIAN GOT HOME

He hit the ground running, of course.
He's halfway to St. Louis by now.
And yes, Skye is with him. The thing

is, even if I asked Christian to transfer
her to one of their other offices, he'd
end up in that city eventually. Do I

want her fired? Not really. Work
may have hooked them up in the first
place, but at this point, if they want to

be together, they will be. If I ever
discover that has happened, there
will not be another chance. Christian

requested the damning cell phone back,
and I gave it to him, but not before
emailing a copy of those photo files

to myself, for two reasons. One, in
case I need them to back up a demand
for alimony. And two, I'm kind of

thinking if Pamela proves dependable,
I'd like to go to some of those very
same places. Greece? Yeah, it's been

on my list for years. And Costa Rica.
And New Zealand. World travel is on
my to-do list. With or without Christian.

BUT IT'S BACK TO ROUTINE

For me at the moment. Afternoon
CPT coming right up for Shelby.

Before I can exit the kitchen,
Mom comes in, carrying an armful

of packages. *Look what I got for*
your sister's birthday. She opens

a Macy's bag, extracts an oversized red
leather purse. Sooo not Andrea. Must

have been on sale. "Really nice, Mom.
Did you talk to Andrea about dinner?"

I tried. She seemed awfully tentative
about her plans for Friday night.

Something going on with her, I think.
But whatever it is, she's not talking.

"New man, maybe. She tends to stay
pretty close-lipped about them

anyway. Burned once too often." I tell
Mom the short version of the Robin

story, omitting the sex-on-the-beach
scene. I mean, Andrea *is* her daughter.

IT IS KIND OF NICE

Having her stay here for a while.
After living in such a tiny space
for so long, she definitely knows
how not to be intrusive, while

still being available. She hasn't
pushed me to discuss Christian
or our weekend or any decision
I might have come to. But she's

here for me, if I want to talk.
I'm not much more forthcoming
than my sister is. We are our
mother's daughters, after all.

Maybe one day, when our kids
are having partner problems,
Andrea and I will open the flood-
gates, spill stories in an effort

to give our children our best shot
of advice. Meanwhile, however,
"It's time for Shelby's CPT. Why
don't you give Andrea another call?

If we're doing dinner and a movie,
I need to make sure Pamela is available."
The movie was Harley's idea. *Chick
flick bonding,* she called it. I can't

believe she started high school.
When was the last time I even saw
her? Two years ago? Three? She is
on my mind all the way to Shelby's

room. "Dark in here, Shelbs. Close
your eyes for a minute so Mommy
can open the blinds." I closed them
to keep the early afternoon sun at bay.

This time of year, it angles in harshly
until around three p.m. "There. That's
better. Now I can see my girl." I turn
from the window, toward the bed.

And I don't like what I see at all.
Shelby could camouflage with
the sheets, her skin is so pale. I yank
back the covers. The rise-fall

of her chest is shallow, though she
doesn't sound anymore congested
than usual. "How ya feeling, little
fortune cookie?" Shelby manages

a tiny smile and a weak *Goo . . .* ,
but when I roll her whisper-frail
body, it offers no resistance. Routine
finished, I go straight for the phone.

WHAT I WANT TO HEAR

From Dr. Malik is a dismissal
of my concerns. But as Shelby's regular
doctor, he knows her almost as well

as I do. *Take her to emergency at*
St. Mary's. I'll meet you there in forty
minutes. Better to err on the safe side.

Apprehension begins a noticeable
gnaw in my stomach. I enlist Mom
to help me swaddle Shelby in a light

cotton blanket, carry her straight to
the van, and strap her in. "Will you
come with me? Please?" I try hard

to keep my voice from betraying any
hint of fear, for Shelby's sake. But Mom
knows I'm scared. *Of course, honey.*

In less than fifteen minutes, we pull
into the ER parking lot. Mom goes for
help, returns almost immediately with

a young orderly, tugging a gurney. *I'm*
Gordon. Dr. Malik let us know you were
coming. Let's get Miss Shelby inside.

Gordon lifts her gently, as he might
an antique porcelain doll. His voice
remains calm, his manner relaxed.

AS SUMMER DIES

June promises wither, fuel
October passion,
a sensuous mingling
inconceivable

in spring—tangles of auburn,
sienna, and honey gold.
Fall's arrival surprises
the valley, and it reverberates
with hurried
preparation.

Cacophonous instruments—
chain saws, chippers, shredders,
and mowers—play
a dirge for September, ready
her remains
for the funerary fire.

A strike of the match,
and the pyre bursts color,
auburn, sienna, and honey
gold, threaded blue beneath
a sheer shroud

of morning. Autumn hovers,
incense, masks the scent
of early winter. Settles in
like sea-heavy fog,
blankets the corpse
of summer.

Andrea

OFFICIALLY, SUMMER

Still has three weeks to go. But our
usual stifling Labor Day is a temperate
seventy-five this year. Autumn, come
to call early. What that means as far
as winter is anyone's guess.

And officially, I am thirty-seven today.
But when maintaining a death vigil,
birthdays don't seem very important
except as reference points. I have
already celebrated many more

birthdays than Shelby ever will.
The strangest thing is, though we
always knew this time would come,
no one expected it. When Mom
called to let me know, I felt like

a freight train had just jumped
track and landed in my living
room, engine still screaming and
belching diesel. The doctor gave
Shelby maybe a week, sent her home

to hospice care. Her little heart
is tired, her hummingbird body
flimsy as cellophane, her colorless
skin almost as transparent.
Yet she wears a perpetual smile,

as if she looks forward to leaving
us. The hospice worker is a stout
woman named Stella. She comes
once a day, but there isn't much
need. Mom and I are here to help

Marissa with whatever she needs.
She only leaves Shelby's bedside
to use the bathroom, or when Chris
manages to talk her into stretching
her legs. He flew straight home from

wherever he was when he got
the news and seems as devoted
as Marissa is to Shelby's comfort.
It's touching, really, especially
when he sings to her, and that

is often. At the moment, he is
crooning a bastardized version
of the Beatles' *Michelle: My Shel,*
my belle, these are words that
go together well. My-y Shel.

Marissa sits stiffly, eyes closed.
I might think she's asleep, except
her head bobs in time to Chris's
gentle beat. Mom is in the kitchen,
fixing chili for whoever might feel

the need for sustenance. The smell
of frying onions wafts throughout
the house, fragrant. But it can't
mask the blend of odors here
in Shelby's room—perspiration,

oxygen, and discarded Pull-Ups.
Shane has claimed emptying
the trash as his contribution to
making Shelby as comfortable
as possible. He'll be home from

school soon. Marissa insisted he
go every day. *You can't get behind
the very first week. Junior year
is important.* And so he goes, but
he comes straight home. I wish

Dad were here for him to talk
to, but the old man is off on
his pilgrimage, with no means
of communication. I've encouraged
Shane to open up, but he dams

his grief inside. In that he too
closely resembles his parents.
When the coming storm rages
and the levees go, the damage
will be incomprehensible.

SITTING HERE

With nothing to do but think and wait
is pointless. I slip quietly from the room,
wander to the kitchen. Mom has her back

to me, and when she turns, her face is tear-
streaked. No need to ask if she's okay. None
of us are. "If you've got things covered,

I think I'll run home for a few. Check on
Harley. Grab a shower. I smell like . . ." Carrion
is what comes to mind, but I say, "B.O."

We could all use a shower, couldn't we?
Go on home. If anything happens . . .
She shakes her head, turns back to stir

the pot simmering low on the stove.
Food and death. Somehow, the two have
become interwoven in the human psyche.

We eat, to celebrate our living. We eat,
to feed our memories. We eat, to keep
from talking when words are meaningless.

When I open the door, a river of sunlight
floods over the threshold, lifts the gray
shrouding the curtained room. Nearby,

a dog barks at a passing car, frightens
a covey of quail into startled flight.
Today, the ordinary seems extraordinary.

FRIDAY EVENING

On a holiday weekend, traffic is ugly.
It takes almost an hour to get home,

and when I finally do, the house is empty.
Hollowed of energy. Holly picked

Harley up from the bus stop. I asked
her not to mention Shelby's condition

yet. That news should come from me.
Death is largely an unknown quantity

for Harley. I'm not sure whether
to prepare her for it or wait until

its meaning becomes concrete.
I check messages. One from Holly,

letting me know Harley is safely
in her care, with a sidebar from

my daughter. *Happy birthday, Mom.*
Don't forget about the rib cook-off!

A local Labor Day Weekend to-do.
I take Harley every year. But this year?

I just don't know for sure. The machine
beeps. One last message. From Jace.

Very sorry about your niece. Let me
know if you need someone to talk to.

His voice is a campfire in the wilds.
Of course I need someone to talk to,

and of course I want it to be him. Here.
With me. Holding me. Kissing me. Lov—

Stop. Can't think that way. No one has
talked love. It would be enough to talk

life. But to talk at all is problematic.
I can't exactly call their house and ask

to speak to Jace. Affairs are complicated,
and a fling with your best friend's spouse

is way beyond complex. It's bewildering.
Right now, a shower beckons. I run the water

hot. I need to steam off more than sweat.
I wash my hair twice. Use a sea sponge

to scrub away dead skin cells. When I finish,
I tingle clean. Smell like apricots and ginger.

And for a moment, I forget where I just
came from, thinking instead about where

I might be going to. I wrap myself in a big
old fluffy towel. Happy birthday to me.

I AM STANDING NAKED

In front of my closet, trying to decide
what to wear, when the phone rings.
The disembodied voice of the caller
ID lady approximates: *Jace Carli-izle*.

You're home. His voice is warm
with sympathy and I thaw, just a little.
*Everyone went to the cook-off in Sparks.
Would you like me to come over?*

"Oh, yes. Please." He's on his way.
I look down at my unclothed body,
suddenly just a little embarrassed
by it. Why didn't I stay on Harley's diet?

God, now I sound like Holly. And why
did I have to think about her? What
should I wear? Shorts? Nope. Those
would show my legs. Jeans? Not casual

enough. Lingerie? Yeah, right. That's
me—major vamp. Maybe I could strip,
give him a little lap dance. Damn it.
Holly, again. Could I be more pathetic?

I want to slap myself. Jace is coming
over. That's what I want. Everything's
okay. I slip into an age-soft pair of capris,
a clean tee shirt. I think what I really need

is to allow myself the relief of a good
cry. But then my eyes would get all
red and swollen. My nose would run.
I'd look like hell, and tears won't change

a thing. I am dry-eyed when the doorbell rings, but when I open it and Jace
steps inside, arms opened in invitation,
I accept and fall apart completely.

He holds me while tears swell into sobs.
I cry until I go weak, spent emotion
soaking the front of Jace's soft cotton
shirt. "I'm sorry." Lame. Really lame.

Hey, now. Nothing to apologize
for. Come on. Still propping me up,
he guides me into the kitchen, sits me
at the table. *Have you eaten today?*

I shrug. "Some cereal for breakfast."
He nods, as if to say, *I figured as much,*
starts rummaging through the refrigerator.
"I'm really not all that hungry, though."

Good thing. Not much in here. How
about I order in some pizza? Starving
yourself won't help. He doesn't wait for
an answer. Looks like it's Domino's.

SUDDENLY THAT SOUNDS REALLY GOOD

Pizza. Something normal. And—why
not?—a beer. Pizza and beer. Perfect.

I get up, go to the fridge, grab a couple
of Corona Lights, hand one to Jace.

We talk about Shelby. Marissa. Chris.
We drink beer. The pizza arrives.

I pick off the pepperoni. We talk about
rib cook-offs. Birthdays. Funerals.

Finally—I can't help it—I ask, "How are
things with you and Holly?" I want him

to say awful, and he sort of does. *We*
hardly talk at all, and when we do,

we fight. I know it's hurting the kids,
but I don't know how to avoid that.

We find something else to talk about.
Finish the pizza. Drink more beer. I start

to feel almost normal. A mellow buzz
begins to soften the razor-edged pain.

Jace looks at me, a question in his eyes.
I nod. What I need now is comfort sex.

COMFORT SEX

Sometimes you just want
a loud, long, licentious fuck.
Anything goes. No sound allowed
but the soft-speak of sheets
and unbidden vocalizations.
But that kind of sex

is

often best enjoyed with no
expectation of a repeat
performance. A five-star dessert,
compared to sugar-free Jell-O—
the everyday low-cal, low-carb
treat that, with rare exception, will

not

rank near the top of anyone's
"most desired" list. Segue to "most
requested," you might find the daily
lay, no real effort required except
the post-activity cleanup. But every
now and then, sex becomes

about

remembering you're wanted.
Knowing you're alive. Folding
yourself into someone else's skin
and suckling their life force
to rekindle your own. Resurrection
within the fusion of

orgasm.

Holly

FUSING LIVES

Old, newer, and just-discovered,
is like mixing a variety of not-quite-
finished-off cereals, shaking the blend,
and seeing what ends up on top.

Raisins? Nuts? Little oat clusters?
Mouse turds, maybe? What if you
decide you want what's on the bottom
after all? How do you discard the rest?

I'm not sure what to toss or how to do it.
I only know I can't go back to the way
it was when this summer started—
hungry. Always hungry for . . . what?

Not love. I had that, times three kids
and Jace. Is four times mediocre
equal to or greater than one time
spectacular, minus a monumental dose

of his commitment to someone else?
Sex, yes, my mouth did water
for something beyond the day-to-day
let's-get-this-over-with variety,

but even now that I've experienced it,
I'm not satiated, and I don't know that
more or kinkier or any other type of
different will make me feel any less empty.

Last night, I took the kids to the rib
cook-off, and when they wandered off
on their own, I strutted my stuff down
the street, and yes, I turned some heads.

And while that didn't exactly feel bad,
what I really wanted was to be with
Bryan, who happened to be there
with his wife. I couldn't even say hello.

Our eyes met as we passed each other,
and his hand dropped away from
her waist, and seeing that made me
flush heat, like a hit of vitamin B_{12}.

We haven't connected, except by texting,
since before he and she went off to San
Francisco. School started, for one thing.
Please tell me I wasn't just a summer fling.

Do teachers have those too? He smiled
at me, but his eyes dropped away too
quickly. And when I turned—subtly—
hoping he'd spare another glance my way,

instead I saw his hand lift again to her
hip, ride its gentle sway. I no longer
connect to Jace like that, and a little voice
insists I should consider it a warning.

THAT SAME VOICE

Keeps nagging at me not to get
my hopes up about meeting Sarah
Hill. Mikayla and I are off to Vegas

today. It's only an hour flight,
and we plan to return first thing
in the morning, so all we take are

small carry-ons with a change
of clothes, toothbrushes, lotions, and
makeup, the last two neatly packaged

in the requisite plastic bags for
easy TSA viewing. Tickets, printed
out. ID, within reach. Good to go.

Jace drops us curbside. Comes
around to give us goodbye kisses.
Take care of your mom, he tells

Mikayla. Then, to me, *Keep your
head, and don't expect too much.*
No wonder I have that nagging

little voice. "No worries. I've got
things pretty much in perspective."
And why not? I've had four decades

to put them there. "We'll call tonight.
I gave Andrea your cell number, in
case she needs you to pick up Harley.

They're at the rib cook-off. Lucky
Harley. Two days in a row. She'll be
sweating grease and barbecue sauce."

He smiles. *Sounds delightful.*
Okay. That airport cop is giving
me the evil eye. Better go. Love you.

"Love you too." There is no
valid emotion behind the words,
nor within the quick kiss I give

him. It's all for show, but how
could the kids *not* notice the rift
between us? It wedges wider

every day. "Okay, Mik, we're off."
Midday Saturday, the airport
isn't especially busy and security

takes no time at all. "We've
got an hour before our flight.
Want some lunch?" Mostly

because I could use a drink,
and beyond security, the sports bar
is the best place for sandwiches.

Mikki looks at me like I've lost
my mind. *Uh . . . no. I'm barf-*
free right now, but if I eat . . .

I STILL WANT A DRINK

Liquid courage, I've heard it called,
and I'm in dire need of a shot—or two—

of nerve. I deposit Mikayla in a seat near
our gate. "Back in a few. If you change

your mind, I'll be at the bar." The scathing
look she gives now reminds me of Jace.

Think that's a good idea? You don't want
to be drunk when you meet her, do you?

"First of all . . ." It comes out louder than
I intended. I lower my voice, and my temper.

"I don't plan to get drunk. And I don't
think you have the right to tell me how

to live my life, or how I want to meet
my mother. I'm a grown-up, Mikayla."

Her eyes drill into mine. *Maybe you*
are. But sometimes lately, I wonder.

To engage or not to engage—the age-old
question. I choose the latter, offer a smile.

"Sometimes I wonder too. Anyway,
being a grown-up isn't all that much fun.

You might consider that before you
decide to become one at seventeen."

I leave her to consider, go to the bar,
and since time is relatively short, order

two Bloody Marys. Can't get drunk off
those. Two much vegetable content.

I down one, nibble the green olive,
think about my daughter's observations.

What, exactly, has she seen to make
her question my maturity level? I'm sure

she has heard Jace and me argue, but
we try to keep the ugly words behind

a closed door. Is she privy to details?
I finish the second drink, arrive back

at the gate minutes before they call
our flight. The nervous edge has been

blurred, but my speech is sharp when
I tell Mikki, "Anytime you want to talk,

I'm here for you, okay?" Which turns
out to be funny, because we don't say

one word to each other all the way to
Vegas. I use the silent hour to nap.

ON THE FAR END

We catch a cab to our hotel. I chose
one on the strip because Mik has never
been here before and I wanted to immerse
her in the luscious sleaze factor. Plus,

> they're cheap this time of year. Even
> during the day, the garishness is obvious.
> I watch her eyes go wide at the flesh
> advertisements. *God, Mom. Disgusting.*

"Vegas was built on disgusting, m'dear.
But it's kind of fun too, don't you think?"
The cabbie turns into the Venetian, with
its tall pillars and marble walks and canals

carved from sand. So much beauty, not quite
disguising the ugly underbelly of this city.
We check into our suite—they're all suites
at the Venetian—and neither of us quite

> believes the impossibility of the room.
> *God, Mom . . .* (her favorite phrase)
> *A sunken living room, and did you see*
> *the bathroom? Can we stay an extra day?*

"Not this trip. But maybe we can come
back sometime soon." I want to add,
"But not with a baby." Instead, I say,
"Go relax. I'll let Sarah know we're here."

SARAH AND TIA

My mother and half sister arrive
within the hour. I answer their knock,
trembling trepidation. First impression:

Sarah Hill is definitely my mother. For
while I might have inherited a feature
or two from Paul Driscoll, overall I am she,

from my body type to the arch of my eyebrows. Second impression: she is every
bit as nervous as I am. Tia, on the other

hand, wears a halo of suspicion around
a face that bears a slight resemblance
to my own. "Come in. Please." My sister

walks by wordlessly, but my mother
pauses. Gently places a hand against
my cheek. *I was afraid this day might*

never come. I'm happy we can know
each other. Her touch is foreign,
her skin calloused and low-desert dry.

I flinch, look for deception in her eyes.
Perhaps I inherited "liar" from her too.
But I see only curiosity, and a hint

of some indefinable need. "Come on. Your
granddaughter can't wait to meet you.
And we have some catching up to do."

WE TALK LONG INTO THE EVENING

Sharing as much information as we
can squeeze into our time together.
Sarah's a preschool teacher who

hates network television;
has three Maltese poodles;
is dating a "hot electrician";
writes poetry and short stories!

Tia is a social worker who

loves sports—televised and live;
goes to church every Sunday;
is married to a prison guard;
is working on a novel!

When I tell them I'm a writer too,
there is much discussion. And then
Mikayla asks a question that stops

all conversation. *Wasn't it hard*
to give a baby up for adoption?

Sarah is direct. *Not at first. No one*
encouraged me to keep her, and I
just couldn't see doing it on my own.

Mikayla isn't finished. *You said*
not at first. What about later?

Later I regretted my decision.
She turns to me. *I'm sorry I wasn't*
stronger. Her words are an echo.

Close. Distant. Hollow.

WORDS ARE AN ECHO

A random repetition.

Laughter. Rhetoric.

A clash of cymbals
in empty sky, tambourines
against cloud pillows.
Words are an echo,
and when the wind tires,
they will crash,

empty syllables,

on sharp-toothed cliffs below.
Words are a breeze, weightless
as a hint of jasmine
whispered to the night.

Formless. Purposeless.

Trivial, except for the shiver
they leave in their wake.
Words are a breeze, and when
August descends, brazen,
they will

surrender

to summer's lust.
Words are a shadow, elusive,
a scatter of promises
miring truth in abstraction.

Illusion. Theory.

The vastness contained in four
inches between two people
on one couch.
Words are a shadow,

a source of light,

shuttered.

Marissa

THE HOUSE IS SHUTTERED

And not just the windows.
Everyone here has shuttered
our fear and sad uncertainty

behind a curtain of smiles.
We smile at each other. At
Shelby, whose light withdraws

ever deeper into the husk
of her humanity. I can't stop
her retreat. No one can. Death

hovers at the foot of her bed.
Waiting. Inviting. And I know
it is only her overriding love

for us that keeps her here.
If I were brave, I'd tell her
to let go. Instead, I read her

stories. And Christian sings
her songs. And Mom repeats
nursery rhymes. Volleys

of words so she knows
she is not alone as her heart
hiccups toward its last beat.

FRIENDS KEEP STOPPING BY

I wanted them to know so
they would have the chance
to tell Shelby they love her too.
So she might understand, in some
small way, her impact on this world.

Claire came with her baby.
Once, the sight of that bubbly,
perfect child might have sent
waves of envy washing over
me. Instead, she was a bolt
of life against the dark backdrop
of descending night. Appreciated.

Doug Schneider brought Joey,
who doesn't understand that
Shelby will never again take
swim therapy with him. He told
her all about his new doctor
and his new school and I swear
his words broke through
her semi-conscious shell and
she smiled. At least a little smile.

Christian didn't so much as blink
when Drew dropped in, stuffed
Barney in hand. He cradled the gift
in the crook of Shelby's arm, shooed
me from the room, tuned in to the real
Barney, and told me to take a bath.
I settled for a quick shower.

Perhaps the biggest surprise,
visitorwise, was Andrea's ex,
Steve. His fiancée, Cassandra,
was on his arm, and though
to look at her is to think "pole
dancer," she marched right into
Shelby's room and didn't flinch
at the sight of her. In fact,
she told her all about her day,
shopping for an engagement ring,
which she proudly showed her.

Steve, on the other hand, stayed
well back from the bed, as if
worried death might be contagious.
But he did come, and before
he left, he told Shelby, *Be strong.*
I hear it's pretty great where
you're going. Catch you on
the other side. There were tears
in his eyes. And in mine too.

Andrea wasn't here when Steve
showed up, a lucky coincidence.
She has spent more time here
than necessary, not that I don't
appreciate it. Within our mostly
silent waiting, we have somehow
grown closer, words unnecessary
to the synergetic exchange of love.

AS FOR MY SON

I want him to go to school.
Hang out with his friends.
Spend time with Alex, who
has been my ally in that.

I half expected Christian
to argue, but he seems to
understand the need for Shane
to escape fate's steady approach.

Death is not a dinner table
topic. Shane has only talked
about it with me once. *Are they
sure? What if they're wrong?*

When I told him every sign
pointed to the proximity of
her demise, his resilient veneer
shattered, and he was a small

child again. *No! It's not fair!
Why did God let her live
at all, if he was only going
to give her this little time?*

"I can't speak for God," I said.
"But I have thought long and
hard about this. Shelby has given
us a glimpse of human perfection,

because inside that flawed
body is a spirit untouched
by greed or artifice or hatred.
Shelby is the essence of love.

And so maybe the reason for
her short time here is to show
us how we might love better."
I didn't realize then that Christian

had been at the door listening.
Later he found me out on the deck,
watching the city light, window by
window, burst by colorful burst.

He circled his arm around my
shoulder, and I didn't push it
away. *I heard what you told Shane.*
It resonated because I have asked

myself the same question before
and never found that answer.
Thank you for giving it to me.
I spent the last hour watching

Shelby sleep, thinking about
the too-few hours I gave her, and
what she managed to give back
to me. If I'd have thought . . .

Had I known . . . Oh, God, Marissa,
I am so sorry about everything . . .
Every motherfucking thing. His chest
heaved then, and I turned into him

and the next thing I knew, we
were kissing. Tenderly at first
and then with passion born of
the need to feel something not sad.

Something representative of living.
Some little semblance of love left
breathing in the ruins. And in that
kiss, I found exactly that. What I

thought was a corpse, lifting
a fog against the mirror placed
above its lips. I don't know if
it has a future, but for now I need

to nurture any remaining thread
of life, however frail. As angels call
Shelby ever closer home, I sleep
only when will fails me, and only

by her side. Too soon, I'll return
to my bed, and when I do, I'll invite
my husband back beneath the quilts.
At least, long enough for answers.

IT IS JUST PAST DAWN

When she opens her eyes
to see the sunrise, framed

by frothy pink curtains,
opened to let the new day in.

Fittingly, it is purple—violet
and crimson, against the creep

of storm clouds. She has slept
more than not, so her barely

audible *Pri-ee* surprises me—
a small surprise of great magnitude.

"Yes, Shelster. Very pretty."
Christian is right here next

to me, so when Shelby says,
See, and tries to lift her hand,

he looks where her eyes
are pointed. Shakes his head,

as if to rid it of cobwebs. Tenses
suddenly. Hisses, *Can you see her?*

I glance around the room.
There is no one but the three

of us. "See who, Christian?"
He shakes his head again. Blinks.

Nothing. No one. I thought . . .
It looked like . . . Mom. But . . .

He stands suddenly, takes
hold of Shelby's hand. She gifts

him with her loveliest smile,
draws one long, shallow breath.

On the exhale, she is gone.
"No." But I don't have to check

her pulse to know her heart
has finally given up. And yet

I repeat, "No." Christian
gathers me in before I can fall.

Together, we weep for our
angel, freed to soar at last.

The noise of our tears brings
others—Mom. Andrea. Shane.

But only the one who holds me
can claim an equal share of grief.

I AM SOON GRATEFUL

For the others, who handle
the many, varied details
of death. The big decisions
were made days ago. But until
the funeral director comes
to collect Shelby's remains,

I won't let go of her hand.
It's warm, still. And as it cools,
I want to keep it nestled in
the warmth of my own.
I'm vaguely aware of people
talking. Maybe even to me.

What does it matter? No
amount of talk can bring her
back. Am I selfish? I must be.
Shelby can run now. She can
fly. And if Christian is right,
and his mother came to get

her, she is with those who
love her. I didn't see anyone.
But in his certainty, a small
amount of comfort. Except
her hand has grown cool, despite
the warmth of mine. How can

her summer departure be
so steeped in cold?

chipping away; become a steady drip,
wearing away; become a rivulet, eroding

away the walls she has constructed
to hold back the sorrow? I've seen no

sign, except the single burst of grief
when Shelby passed away five days ago.

Labor Day, the very day Dad helped torch
the giant Burning Man out on the Black Rock

playa. Appropriate, somehow. Especially
with Missy going on about a bonfire to keep

her Shelby warm. She even asked about
cremation. But Chris wouldn't hear of it.

He has been her rock. And he has made
the difficult decisions. Today, while we

remember Shelby through our eulogies,
and witness the lowering, her bedroom

will be cleared of every stick of furniture.
Bedding and curtains will be discarded.

Her clothing will be folded and boxed,
along with Barney and Dora, and placed

on her closet shelves. Next week, walls
will be painted, carpeting replaced.

EVERY TRACE

Of Shelby, removed or put away.
At first, Chris wanted all her clothes,
toys, and CDs carted off. It was
Dad who talked him out of it.

Women grieve differently than
men. They need tactile reminders
to hold their memories. One day
she'll want to touch a piece of Shelby.

Dad, the philosopher—a rare view.
If I picture him, I mostly see an aging
longhair, tripping around the woods
or sitting at the table, drinking strong

coffee. I also remember him flirting
with women not my mother. Feeling
them up, in fact, and arguing with Mom
about what that meant. Yelling. Storming.

But just this summer, as if through
whole new lenses, I have watched
him welcome his gay grandson's
boyfriend into our usually closed fold;

play with his dying granddaughter,
drawing her attempt at laughter;
and when she finally left this world,
cushion the blow for us who remain.

Right now he is greeting people
coming through the door. Missy
sits at the front of the church,
cardboard. Chris is beside her,

as he has been almost every minute
since we found them, plastered
together and weeping for their still-
warm child. But is it love or death

that keeps him there? Will time
gnaw away what seems to be total
devotion? Or is it, in fact, all for
show? I don't know, and it's not

up to me to decide. I do know I've
changed my mind. I hope things
work out between them. I hope
forgiveness is achievable, and that

it can help rebuild their marriage
and create a future together. On
the other side of Chris, Shane sits,
holding hands with Alex. Not long

ago, that wouldn't have happened.
Chris has experienced some
fundamental change, one I never
believed possible. I was wrong.

A HUGE ADMISSION

Because if I was wrong about
that, I have to ask myself what
else I might be mistaken about.

My daughter is at my right. Shelby
was gone before I said a word,
and Harley reacted with unexpected

anger. *Why didn't you tell me?*
I had the right to know. I had
the right to say goodbye. God, Mom.

I'm not a baby. I understand
that people die. Why do adults
try to hide the ugly stuff from

their kids? People die. People
fall out of love and get divorced.
Or they fall out of love and stay

together when it's obvious they
shouldn't, like Bri's mom and dad.
All they do is fight. It's stupid.

I'm sure my mouth fell open,
and I'm positive Harley noticed.
"How do you know they fight?"

I've got ears, Mom, and so does
Bri. Her dad thinks her mom is
sleeping around. And guess what

else. He still doesn't know
Mikayla is pregnant. Don't you
think someone should tell him

before baggy shirts can't hide
it anymore? Especially since
she's going to keep the baby.

It was all news to me. Of course,
I've been swallowed up by funeral
planning, not to mention wake

preparations. It will be at my house,
which does not wear death like
a shroud. As the music begins to play—

Let the Sun Shine In, sung by Shelby's
favorite Imagination Movers—Harley
turns, gives a small wave to Brianna,

who leads the Carlisle family to seats
near the back. Holly and Jace aren't
fighting at this particular moment,

but the distance between them
is noticeable, and for an instant,
that makes me sad. Sadder.

And for the rest of the service,
through a swirl of prayers, homilies,
and eulogies, I consider why.

UP UNTIL NOW

I have managed to stash guilt
somewhere behind the notion
that Holly asked for whatever
she got and Jace deserved better.

While that is probably still true,
I need to ask myself a few hard
questions, like what happened
to my personal sense of morality?

Do I consider Holly my friend?
Do I want to play even a small
role in the corrosion of her
marriage? What would my child

think of me, if she ever found
out? Would Jace reconcile
with Holly if it was possible?
Is it possible? Even if it isn't,

how long do I want to keep
sneaking around? Isn't part
of loving someone wanting
the entire universe to know?

I feel a little sick, like I've been
spinning in circles and come
to a sudden stop, everything
shifting from dizzy into focus.

I AM STILL WOOZY

When the service ends. After brief
condolences, we form a procession
to follow the hearse to the cemetery.
I send Harley with Mom, Marissa,

and Chris, ask Dad if I can ride with
him. I suppose it is rather an odd
request, because as soon as we're
under way, he asks, *What is it?*

"Do you love Mom? I mean, really
love her, after all this time and all
you've been through? Don't say yes
unless you mean it." I kind of expect

an immediate yes, but that's not
what I get. *To answer that question
correctly, I need it in context. So
where exactly is it coming from?*

How to approach this, without
just coming clean? "First, were you
ever completely, totally, had-to-have-
her, insanely in love with Mom?"

When he says yes, absolutely, I ask,
"Then why the other women?
And if you were in love with any
of them, why did you stay with Mom?"

THAT STOPS HIM

He considers how to answer, and
just about the time we reach the gates

of the cemetery, he says, *I was young*
and selfish when I went running around

on your mother. I told her she was
welcome to run too. She did, but it

was contrary to her nature. And yes,
I fell in love with a couple of women

along the way, but that kind of love—
the kind rooted in sex—burns out

fairly quickly. I stayed with Leah mostly
because of you and your sister, but

what I discovered by staying was love
born of friendship. She may not feel

the same way, and if that is so, I'm truly
sorry. Yes, Andrea, I love your mom.

Relationships are complicated. As I
follow several to Shelby's grave, I realize

there's one huge question I've avoided
asking Jace: "Do you *still* love her?"

HUGE QUESTIONS

Are most easily avoided
by detouring widely
into vast fields of

minutiae.

When someone looks
at you, silent in demand
for answers, diversion
may best be found in

trivia.

Should that person give
voice to pesky queries,
try to slow the advance
with a barrage of

details.

When all else fails
and the ax initiates
sure descent, baffle
the interrogator with

bullshit

and run like hell.

Holly

MUSINGS ON AN AUTUMN RUN

The sun has grown lazy in its climb,
lounging late behind eastern hills,
finally opening its drowsy solar eyes
to merely blink at hazy whitecaps
afloat in pastel skies.

Breathe in. And run.

This breeze is warm for October,
beyond the border of equinox. Hints
of autumn are everywhere—splashes
of sunflowers and spilling leaves.
Apples. Pumpkins. Chrysanthemums.

Breathe in. Breathe out. And run.

The quail have had a good year.
A montage of trident-shaped footprints
reveals a covey, busily foraging.
They consider my approach, launch
late in noisy unison, a geyser
of silver feathers.

Breathe in. Out. Run from. Run to.

Hoping, like the hesitant quail,
I can find my wings when I must.
Wondering when I'll decide I must.

FOR NOW

I will stay with Jace.
I know it won't be forever.
There is not even the slenderest
ray of love's light left between us.

He asked for six months to try
to change my mind and I agreed.
But it wasn't his plea that made
me decide to stay. It was logic.

I don't have a job. Can't pay
rent or buy food. Can't take care
of my kids on my own. And one
of them is pregnant. Jace totally

freaked when he found out,
mostly because everyone knew
except him. He's trying to convince
Mikki to consider adoption.

I don't think that will happen,
not after my mother's words
of wisdom. Personally, I question
Sarah's sincerity. Easy enough to say

you regret something when that
something is standing in front
of you. I'm glad I met her, but any
real bond will take time to build.

SPEAKING OF TIME

I have formed an eight-month game
plan. That will take me to the first week

of June. The kids will be out of school.
Mikayla will have had the baby. It will

be easier for me to make a major move.
The most critical element is stashing money.

Jace doesn't know it, but I have sold
a couple of trashy novellas, plus *Essential*

Oils. Straight to ebooks, fifty percent royalty
rate. People are buying them, and the company

is hungry for more. Hopefully, I'll soon
have a decent income on the horizon.

I'm writing every chance I get, everything
on my computer and password-protected.

Live and learn. I did tell Andrea about
selling them. Her reaction was totally weird.

Is that really *how you want to make*
a living? She was pissed. *What about*

your kids? What about Jace? How do
they feel about it? Or don't they know?

When I told her that they, in fact,
don't know, and I absolutely do not

want them to find out, she acted
completely put out, then had the nerve

to ask, *How much of those stories*
is true? It was almost as if she'd read

them. But I never showed them to her
or ever confessed anything she didn't see

with her own two eyes. "Not much," I lied.
And then I turned the tables. "So, who

was that guy you were in bed with when
I called you that day? New boyfriend?"

She turned fifteen deepening shades
of red. Hemmed and hawed and finally

sputtered, *Just an old friend. Sympathy*
sex. And it was only a couple of times.

We left it there, scratching in silence.
Something has worked its way between

Andrea and me, but I'm not sure exactly
what, or if it will work its way out again.

I HOPE IT DOES

Friendship is a bad thing to lose,
especially in the shadow of a failing
marriage. It's good to have someone

to talk to. Someone you can trust
to throw you a life preserver when
the breakwater finally fails. Who

knows? Maybe one day Tia and
I can be real sisters. Our first meeting
left me doubtful. She seemed to think

I want something from our mother.
I hope I made it clear that I am not
out for whatever meager inheritance

there might be. Sarah's not exactly
living large. Come to think of it, I hope
she's not looking for handouts from me.

Hard to trust strangers. Hey, it's hard
to trust people you know and love,
especially when you can't trust yourself.

For now, I'll still see Bryan when I can.
Maybe the kinky side of me will trump
sticking it out with his boring wife.

Yeah, I'm a dreamer. And if that
particular dream doesn't work out,
I guess I'll just have to dream bigger.

DREAM BIGGER

You think. Stop letting
small-minded people
dictate your future

when all

they really want is for
you to accomplish
the work of two, for minimum
wage. Reach higher, or

else

plan for retirement
in a cardboard box, praying
global warming is more
than a catchphrase.
And if that

fails

to be the case,
hope freezing to death
is really as simple
as falling asleep,
to the lullaby of teeth chatter.

Dream bigger

before you can't remember
how to dream at all.

Marissa

I DON'T DARE DREAM

And the funny thing is,
my subconscious apparently
knows that. I haven't dreamed,

at least not dreams I can
remember, in the month since
Shelby found her wings. I can't

bear to use terms like "passed"
or "went to sleep forever" or—
the worst—"died." Funny, but those

hard-core Christians want faith
to be the key to the kingdom. What
if death is, in fact, the key to faith?

If there is a God, would he care
which way it went, if it meant
finding him in the long run?

I haven't exactly found him,
but I'm willing to open myself
to the possibility. And Christian

has accepted him again. Which
means not a whole lot to me,
except for the hope in his eyes.

BECAUSE, WITHOUT HOPE

What are we, but on a fast
track to despair? Okay, a cynic—or
maybe someone smarter than me—
might see this as naivety.

But you know, I've lived
naïve. Lived informed. Lived
bombarded by more than most
ordinary people will ever

experience in the entire
span of their lives. I'm only halfway to my own final parting.
Maybe not even that, if

I'm lucky. I kind of figure
I've used up my share of bad luck.
It's past time to immerse myself
in living again, and by that,

I mean taking chances.
Risking a little to gain a lot, fully
aware that the word "promise"
defies definition. Outcomes

cannot be predicted.
There are too many variables.
Sometimes you have to close your
eyes to forecast the weather.

ONE THING I CAN'T PREDICT

Is what will happen with Christian
and me. We are in counseling, and
through the discussion, some things
have come floating to the surface.

Truths not easy to hear or to process.
Our therapist asks hard questions,
does not accept cliché answers. Those,
Vera says, are like placebos for cancer.

Vera: *How was your marriage before*
Marissa got pregnant with Shelby?

Me: "It was good. Solid. We had Shane.
We had friends. We did things together."

Christian: *Marissa, you practically forgot*
I was there after Shane came along.
You were a great mom, but I was so happy
when he started school because I thought

then you could spend a little attention
on me. But then you wanted a girl and
directed all your energy there. We had
friends, yes, and when they came over,

that's all you talked about. Shane—
his grades, his school plays, the funny
things he said. And trying to get pregnant.
And then you got pregnant, and it was

all about that. Hoping you wouldn't
lose her. How you painted the nursery.
You never had any idea about the new
technologies I was developing. Me.

At work, they were calling me a genius.
But talking about ITV bored you to tears,
so I quit asking you to listen. Skye listened.
And she made me feel like a fucking genius.

Me: "So, it was *my* fault you had an affair—
one that lasted five years and, oh yeah,
included falling for a woman who you
happened to be around a whole lot more

than me because you spent all your time
at work?" But with a thud, what he said
sunk in. "You're right. When you finally
came home, I didn't want to talk about ITV.

Did it ever occur to you that, even pre-
Skye, I was jealous of your work?"

Slipping toward cliché. Vera braked
us. *So why did you choose to stay?*

Me: "Shelby." Christian: *Shelby.*

She wasn't what pushed him away.
She was what brought him home.

HOME IS DIFFERENT NOW

The main thing is the smell—furniture
polish and tile cleaner and the vanilla
of candles. No more medicine. Alcohol.
Residual diaper odor. At first, I was angry

that Shelby's room had been stripped
of her. When we got home from the wake
and found every trace of her gone,
I started screaming. I was like a teakettle,

emotion trapped inside and left to boil
until nothing could hold back the steam.
No one tried to stop me, and when I was
all screamed out, I understood my baby

was gone. Her room is empty for now.
No furniture on top of the plush new
carpeting. Nothing hanging on the fresh
paint. Mauve. A muted Barney tribute.

The painters discovered two boxes
in the closet and brought them to me.
Inside were Shelby's clothes and toys,
not that she had many of either. Those

she did have were well loved, especially
a stuffed purple dinosaur. I kept that,
took the rest to the Salvation Army.
One keepsake to soothe the haunting.

HAUNTING

Did you ever take flight,

hushed

beneath a shower of moonlight,
clothed only in cool velvet
darkness,

running,

absorbing the black like a lover,
in and out and in again?
And did you collapse
into the lap of the earth,

soft

in skirts of summer
grass,

rustling

as you pressed into her
and asked for answers?
Could you hear her reply,
or did you think her whisper

merely

a sigh or a heave of September
wind,

chuffing,

and did you later understand, beg
her to tell you again? Did she comfort
you with a mist of jasmine and a subtle
shift on her axis, offering a glimpse
of eternity,

haunting,

a solar ghost condemned to night
much darker than your own?

CONDEMNED

To a life without men. Maybe that
really is my fate. I don't know. One
thing I'm sure of, though, is I can't see

Jace anymore. I told him at the wake.
Holly didn't come, but he did, and
when everyone was busy drinking

and eating, we ducked outside. I got
straight to the point. "You're still in
love with Holly." It wasn't a question.

Jace was standing very close to me,
and I fought the familiar tug. He
didn't exactly admit it. *How I feel*

about her doesn't matter. Holly
wants to move out. If it wasn't for
the kids, she'd already be gone.

I took two steps to the side. "Jace,
I am so grateful for the time I've had
with you. But the only way you and I

could ever be right together is if Holly
is totally out of the picture. She's my friend,
and she's your wife. And I can't be with

someone who's in love with someone
else. If you still love her, you have to
convince her to give it another try."

He talked her into six months.
Who knows what her decision will
be? I only know it was the right thing

for me. In the days since, I have heard
from would-be and former lovers,
none of whom were right for me.

Vern called to offer condolences,
which only reminded us both of
Valerie, my friend and his wife.

Cheating on one friend was more
than enough. I could never make
it two. And I told him that's what

it would feel like. Geoff asked me
to the Renaissance Fair. I joked my
way out of that one. "I'm sorry, but

I have nightmares about men in
codpieces. Something rooted in my
childhood serfdom, I guess."

He laughed, said okay, and there
was acknowledgment in his answer.
I don't think he'll call again.

I DID NOT EXPECT

Robin's call. In fact, it came from so
far out of the blue at the dinner table

    that when caller ID announced it,
    I dropped my fork. *Pick up!* urged Harley.

She asked about Robin exactly once
after he went to Vegas. I thought she was

happy he'd exited our lives. Turned out
she was worried about me. I never told

her about the other woman, or my one
Facebook exchange with Robin. With

her sitting there, I kind of had to answer.
"Uh, oh, hello. So nice to hear from you."

    My tone was snarky. His was conciliatory.
    Andrea, I'm so sorry. Liz is an old flame

    who happened through town and asked
    for a place to stay. I couldn't say no, right?

I agreed he couldn't but didn't really
want to discuss it further with Harley

tuning in to every word. I borrowed
an Aussie phrase. "No worries, mate.

Listen. Harley and I are finishing
dinner. How about I get hold of you

on Facebook?" I did, and we now
correspond fairly regularly. I haven't

closed that door completely. Fact is,
I do really like him. And Liz, he swears,

has gone on her way. I believe him.
But Vegas is three hundred and fifty

miles from here. Barring one of us
moving—highly unlikely—I'm not

sure how our relationship can thrive.
But at least we're friends. I think

male friends are a very good thing
for a woman to have. I'm glad Drew

is there for Marissa and maintaining
a much bigger presence in her life.

Chris doesn't dare say a goddamn thing.
Drew is her safety net. And she needs one.

HER HEALING IS SLOW

Like the tarrying end of Indian summer.
A careless eye might see only the bronze
and scarlet splendor, clinging to the treetops.

But keen observers view the scaffold
branches beneath tenuous leaves. Only
the strong survive winter. I will be here

for Marissa, and for Holly if our friendship
can endure. Harley and Bri are tighter
than ever, so I hope it's possible.

As for me, there is a new prospect,
at once tempting and daunting.
I bumped into Anthony Malik—

Shelby's doctor—standing in line
at Whole Foods. I'd been to his office
with Missy a couple of times and he

asked how she was doing. Something
kind of clicked between us. We've been
to dinner a couple of times. No sex (yet),

no strings, no promises. No Harley
introductions. But I like how I feel
when I'm with him. That's enough

for now. I can make it on my own.
But wish to love again. One man. One
me. Parallel lines. And no more triangles.

PARALLEL LINES

It has been noted that
a line is a collection of points
along a straight path
that continues

forever

in opposite directions.
Two lines that go
on and on indefinitely

and never

intersect are parallel.
Lines that intersect,
forming ninety-degree angles,

are

called perpendicular.
Perpendicular lines cross
each other, as

parallel

lines never can. Today,
I'm thinking about how easy
it is to be perpendicular.
And about how, while parallel

lines

may not intersect,
parallel lives often do.